DAISY ENROLLED

The
Cement Duck

ALMA KENNEDY BOWEN

Alma K. Bowen

iUniverse, Inc.
New York Bloomington

The Cement Duck

iUniverse books may be ordered through booksellers or by contacting:

iUniverse
1663 Liberty Drive
Bloomington, IN 47403
www.iuniverse.com
1-800-Authors (1-800-288-4677)

ISBN: 978-0-595-53290-2 (pbk)
ISBN: 978-1-4401-0470-1 (cloth)
ISBN: 978-0-595-63345-6 (ebk)

Library of Congress Control Number: 2009923908

Printed in the United States of America

iUniverse rev. date: 2/25/2009

For Lessie and Lucy
who listened so patiently

Preface and Acknowledgments

The Cement Duck is a work of fiction about Serena Sheppard, a wife, mother, and bank teller in northeast Georgia, who wants to keep her family together. It is about the habits and actions of local people when the Georgia mountains were still somewhat isolated. It revolves around the actual facts of a giant bank scam that happened there in 1971.

The money that was taken was more than 300 times the annual salary of local working people who drew the best salaries. The amount was so large that the *Wall Street Journal* reported it, saying it happened in a "back country bank." The *WSJ* later published a long two-part series beginning on its front page about how the theft occurred, but at that time the investigation was still under way. The articles could not name the man who walked in and opened accounts at the bank and also could not name local people who were believed to be involved.

The FBI investigation was thorough, examining all aspects of the incident, and *The Cement Duck* uses details from the investigation. The idea for the swindle originated after a woman at a construction company in a northern state decided to get married and resigned from her job. The growing of marijuana in the Chattahoochee National Forest played a significant role. The chief schemer died in a shoot-out. The conclusion of the investigation, as related in *The Cement Duck,* is based on what actually happened.

The names of both the northern city and the Georgia town where the bank was located, as well as names of all the characters directly involved in the swindle, have been changed. The characters of Serena, Trey, and other bank personnel portrayed in *The Cement Duck* are fictional and not based on any living persons.

The information about the legendary skyjacker D. B. Cooper is familiar to any person living at that time who kept abreast of national news. I have included something about the Goat Man, and every reader who lived in Georgia in the '60s will remember him. He was real.

The yards on Highway 197 actually existed and so did a costumed cement duck.

I grew up in Habersham County and worked in the newsroom of the *Times* of Gainesville when the theft occurred. I later traveled all over the United States and other countries both for pleasure and for business. The more I traveled, the more I came to love and appreciate the mountains of north Georgia.

I could not write this book about mountain people without describing the mountains, and all the stories told by the fictional local residents are based on actual happenings.

I cannot name all the people who helped me write, but I must thank my granddaughter, Heather Bowen; my daughter-in-law, Christy Bowen; my friends Johnny and Peggy Vardeman, Harriette Taylor, Wayne McDaniel, and Dr. Lorraine Watkins.

I offer a long overdue thank-you to Lessie Smithgall and the late Lucy Palmour, who both listened so patiently years ago and offered encouragement about my wish to write a book about the giant swindle.

Chapter 1

Serena Sheppard passed the cement duck again as she drove south on State Highway 197 on her way to work.

In northeast Georgia in 1971, life-size, gray cement ducks and rabbits were popular lawn ornaments. They were placed here and there on the grass or in flower beds and were usually unnoticed by passing drivers.

But this cement duck was different. About eighteen inches high, it had been placed very near the highway and was regularly outfitted with different clothing and character props. Today, it was wearing dark sunglasses shaped like stars. The points of the stars were exaggerated, making them look like small explosions.

Serena had no idea who lived in the house and outfitted the duck, but she found it amusing and entertaining. No living member of the bird or fowl family had a place in her life because she was terrified of anything with feathers. It was a fear that left her deeply embarrassed when something such as a wren or swallow flew unexpectedly close. She never failed to scream and run, then apologized to anyone who heard her. Not once had she tried to explain or point out the small scars on her cheek and arm.

She knew her fear was unreasonable, wanted to find a way to laugh at it, and thought that maybe a featherless duck with personality could help. She pretended the duck was there especially for her. She looked at it every time she passed, using its appearance to predict how her day was going to evolve.

Her predictions were almost always correct because she always knew what to expect. She loved her job as head teller at Cameron National Bank, and the nearest thing to a surprise at work was if a friend did something special, maybe for her birthday.

Smiling to herself, she thought that maybe the duck's tiny exploding sunglasses indicated something different and exciting was going to happen that day at the bank. She knew such a prediction was wrong. Nothing exciting ever happened. After all, she was responsible for other people's money. It was necessary that her work be serious, repetitive, and standard.

Arriving at her parking space at the usual time, she had forgotten the duck, and she walked toward the bank expecting a routine day. She was going to be doing the same thing today she did every day—talking to customers, counting their money, and making sure their bank deposit slips were correct.

Rounding the building and seeing the dignified Cameron National Bank with its glass front behind white columns, she was surprised to see that the lights were already on. She could see men standing around inside, all of them wearing dark business suits.

She saw the bank president's car parked in front of the bank, along with four other cars that she didn't recognize. Tags on the cars said Fulton County, which meant they were from Atlanta. Two of the cars also had the word "Avis" on the back, indicating that the drivers had probably flown to Atlanta, then rented a car to drive to Cameron. *Why would we have such visitors this early in the morning? What's going on?* Serena wondered.

She went inside through the back entrance and placed her handbag underneath her teller window, as she always did. A couple of strange men were looking at papers spread out on the secretary's desk, but neither one acknowledged her presence. Other men were in the president's office.

Serena went to the small back room to make coffee. While the hot brown liquid was slowly dripping from the fresh coffee grounds, she nervously stepped into the ladies' room. Without thinking about what she was doing, she glanced in the mirror at her hair and lipstick.

Returning to the back room, she wet a couple of paper towels and cleaned the top of the counter and the little table. As each minute passed, she thought, *What on earth is going on?*

She walked back to her teller window, where she picked up an old brochure about proper banking practices. Returning to the table in the back room, she sat down, looked at the brochure without seeing it, and drank her coffee. Still, no one had spoken.

It was only a couple of minutes before Joyce Williams, the other full-time teller, joined her. "Who are all these people?" Joyce whispered before pouring a cup of coffee.

"I've never seen any of them before," said Serena.

Phil Anderson, the bank's loan officer, walked in to hear their words and said, "I wonder if Mr. Norris is selling the bank."

Neither Serena, nor Joyce, nor Phil could know that the strangers were FBI special agents and federal bank examiners. They were beginning a detailed examination of every record in the bank in an effort to find out what had happened to more than one million dollars.

Serena, Joyce, and Phil could not know that they were facing a shocking, traumatic period in their lives. Later, the investigators themselves would be astonished when they learned that the money had disappeared simply because a woman 700 hundred miles away, a woman who had never heard of the town of Cameron, had fallen in love and resigned from her job as a bookkeeper.

Chapter 2

It had begun in Philadelphia four months earlier. On July 10, 1971, Evelyn Farrell tried to keep a solemn expression as she wrote her resignation from Merrill Construction Company. It was difficult not to smile constantly because she was astonished that her entire life was changing in a way she had once dreamed about.

Merrill Construction Company offered construction services all over the East Coast. Hotels, hospitals, shopping centers, and dams that formed new lakes all carried the Merrill brand. As a young girl, Evelyn couldn't believe her luck when she was hired by the company. She had graduated from high school with honors, and teachers had not hesitated to recommend her for a secretarial position at Merrill.

Now she was going to be married. Years earlier, she had decided that she had missed all opportunities to share her life with a man. Now she was preparing to resign and work out her notice while anticipating a small wedding ceremony. If she had been told that her departure would start an underground chain reaction greatly changing the lives of people in a Georgia mountain town, she would have laughed in disbelief.

She stopped writing her resignation and took a small mirror from her desk. She looked at her face in awe-struck wonder. How could it be possible that she still looked like the same person when she felt so different? She still had the same round cheeks, the same "fat eyes." Evelyn quickly touched up her lipstick and looked at the eyes that her precocious young niece once described as "fat" because they were large and slightly bulging. The child apparently hadn't noticed the warm, brown irises and long, thick lashes.

Evelyn had never had a positive thought about her personal features. She was the only one of three sisters to look like their father. She had been an overweight child with orange-colored hair and a multitude of orange freckles. Her sisters were slim, beautiful, and black-headed. During their youth, they refused some of the many boys asking for dates, but Evelyn was almost never asked.

When she reached her thirties, the chubby teenager with orange hair had become pleasingly round, with barely visible freckles, beautiful burnished gold curls, and a quick wit.

By the time she was thirty-six, Evelyn had worked her way up to become assistant head bookkeeper at the construction company. She enjoyed a large circle of friends and was active in both her community and her church. Disappointments and hurts during her teenage years caused her to pretend no interest in men, and she frequently referred to herself as "an old maid." She responded coolly to any member of the opposite sex who showed the slightest interest in her.

The cherry trees were in full bloom in Philadelphia when Buster Wilkie became a part of Evelyn's life. He was the forty-year-old superintendent at Merrill's—a rugged, tough-acting individual. Evelyn and Buster had known each other for more than two years, but their conversations had never strayed from the subject of work. Their jobs put them together once a week when Buster brought job reports into Evelyn's office.

One Friday, the day before the baseball season opened, Evelyn took the reports Buster handed her and enthusiastically mentioned her support of the Phillies. Her words caught Buster's attention, and he asked her to go to the first game with him. The Phillies won, and Evelyn and Buster shared their knowledge about the team, talking and laughing together as they left the stadium. At Evelyn's apartment, Buster simply stopped the car and let her get out without prolonging the outing. She didn't invite him in.

They didn't see each other again until the next Friday, but, when he walked into her office, they really looked at each other for the first time. She tried not to notice the attractiveness of his straight, dark-brown hair and wondered why she had never noticed the gold flecks in his blue eyes.

Buster looked at Evelyn's hair, pulled tight to the back of her head, and wondered how she would look if he could take out the pins. He had always been impressed with her knowledge of the Merrill operation and her efficiency in the office. Now he saw her as a soft, attractive woman.

Buster had married when he was twenty-two years old. His wife had never wanted children, and he had given almost all his attention to his work. He was twenty-eight years old when she left him, and he had vowed never to remarry. He had dated now and then for twelve years, but never became serious.

That day, he asked Evelyn to go to another game with him, and soon they were dating on a regular basis.

They had been dating for only five months when Buster got an offer from Howard Construction Company, with headquarters in Pensacola, Florida. Not only would this require him to move from Philadelphia, which averaged twenty inches of snow a year, to a state that boasted of its continuous sunshine, but he would make considerably more money. Six months earlier Buster would have accepted the offer without hesitation. Now he found that he did not want to move away from Philadelphia because it would mean leaving Evelyn. He forgot that he had vowed never to remarry and bought a diamond engagement ring.

As soon as he saw her, he said, "Evelyn, I've got a good job offer that will require me to move to Florida."

Evelyn did not respond and only looked at him as she felt her chest squeeze around her heart. Her only thought was, *No, he can't move away.*

As she stared silently at him, he reached into his pocket, handed her the ring box, and said, "I want you to go with me. Will you marry me?"

Evelyn couldn't speak and only dropped her head forward.

"Does that mean you're saying yes?" he asked.

She spoke then, her *yes* barely audible.

Evelyn gave Merrill two week's notice, and Buster gave three week's notice. Both thought Merrill needed at least three weeks to find an engineer for the construction superintendent's job. While Buster was working out the third week's notice, Evelyn would have time to prepare for her small wedding ceremony and pack for the move. Buster and Evelyn both thought his job duties would be the hardest to fill. Neither had any idea that Evelyn's resignation from her job as assistant head bookkeeper would cause the most damage.

Their relationship was innocent and trusting. Neither had planned it. They went about their days in a fog of happiness, never knowing that they would be the reason for a mysterious crime of major magnitude in the state of Georgia.

Chapter 3

James Maxwell was astounded when Evelyn gave him her notice of resignation. "Why? Why are you leaving us?" was his response.

"I'm going to marry Buster on July 25, and I want you to be at our wedding. He's got a job offer he can't turn down from a company in Florida. The Walt Disney people are getting ready to open a new Disney World. We're moving there."

Maxwell was totally surprised that Evelyn was going to marry. She had never mentioned that she was dating Buster. More than that, he couldn't believe she wanted to leave the Merrill office. He was thinking about what he could do to keep her on the job. "I'll talk to Sam and get him to keep Buster here. I don't want you to leave," he said.

Evelyn was not surprised at Maxwell's answer. She knew she performed most of the management duties for Merrill's business office without the salary of a manager's position, but she was proud of her ability and had always known it would not benefit her to complain about the extra responsibilities.

Maxwell, a short, plump individual with pale skin and thin hair, went immediately to the office of William Jenkins, the Merrill treasurer. There he asked Jenkins to go to Sam Merrill, president of the company, seeking a salary increase for Buster Wilkie to match the salary offered by the Florida company.

It was two hours before Jenkins returned to Maxwell's office saying that Merrill had refused the increase. "Merrill's exact words were: 'I will never buy off an employee who has accepted a higher offer,'" Jenkins said.

Maxwell managed to brush off Jenkins's information without saying much, but he was fast finding himself in a quandary, and he deeply resented the people who had put him there. He knew Merrill could well afford a higher salary for the superintendent. It would have been so easy, but refusal of the request was putting Maxwell in the position of revealing how little he really knew about the day-to-day management of the office.

As chief accountant, James Maxwell had long ago abdicated most of his duties. He spent the majority of his days in his office with the door closed. He read magazines, planned exotic vacations that he always took alone, and, during political campaigns, he talked on the phone for hours at a time. He always made contributions to his favorite candidates and wanted to have as much information as he could before he gave his money.

Maxwell did not have a family or any known relatives and had no close friends. He especially enjoyed the company of young boys, but had almost never allowed himself to sample this activity. He deeply feared his preference, knowing that society condemned same-sex relationships and especially would not approve of a forty-year-old man spending time with a young boy, only thirteen or fourteen years old.

He had managed to get this far in life without sinking into personal pleasures that would have made his long-dead parents turn over in their graves. His parents had enjoyed simple, conservative lifestyles. They had never even spoken the words "homosexual" or "pedophile" and would have abhorred such persons. They had adored Maxwell, their only child, and always wanted him to get married and present them with grandchildren.

Three weeks after Evelyn's wedding and departure, a despondent Maxwell left the office and made his usual stop at Palmero's bar, where he spent his late hours almost every evening. On this evening, he was approached by Sandy McMahon, a well-dressed man in his thirties, whom he had met previously during his one visit to the Playboy Club. In their first conversation, McMahon had told Maxwell that he was a physician.

They began talking again at Palmero's and, after a few drinks, Maxwell talked about how he was miserable at his work because his employer had allowed his assistant to leave. McMahon was a good listener and encouraged Maxwell to talk. "You'll feel better just because you talked about it," he said.

McMahon began meeting Maxwell every evening, and soon Maxwell revealed to him how his boss had given him a dressing-down because of an audit of his department. The audit was highly critical in general and said Maxwell had not implemented safety precautions recommended in previous audits.

McMahon ordered more Scotch and mineral water drinks for them both before asking what the auditors had said, and Maxwell didn't hesitate to explain in detail. The criticisms were: (1) the excess supply of blank checks was kept in a safe, but the safe was left unlocked most of the time; (2) a schedule of the bank where checks were to be written was posted on the bulletin board in the break room so clerks would know which checks to use; (3) all the checks written by the firm were signed by a facsimile signature machine which was left unlocked at all times; and (4) the lockbox, which received the checks after they were signed so employees could match the checks with invoices, was not a lockbox at all because its top had been removed.

McMahon listened intently to Maxwell, sometimes shaking his head with apparent sympathy. He was actually recognizing a golden opportunity and was rapidly making mental notes.

Later, McMahon felt the time was right, and he told Maxwell that he really wasn't a doctor, after all. He attempted to rationalize his dishonesty by saying, "I always wanted to be a doctor, and I guess the reason I pretend to be one helps me keep faith in myself."

McMahon had always listened sympathetically as Maxwell talked about his dissatisfaction with his job, and that's all Maxwell wanted. The fact that his new friend had been dishonest about his profession didn't matter at all.

Little by little, McMahon revealed the skills that were providing him a good livelihood. He was a professional con man, an expert at arranging swindles that were extremely profitable to all concerned.

"You know those safety precautions at Merrill's that the audit criticized? Have they been corrected?" McMahon asked Maxwell. Maxwell muttered something about planning to correct some of the problems as soon as he had time.

"Well, this situation is a dream come true. Things can happen here that could give you and me both a truckload of money, and there's no risk. You will probably lose your job, but, from what you've said, you're not that well paid and ready to quit anyway."

Maxwell didn't have to think twice before he answered. He had no happiness in life, and any kind of change had to be better. "Tell me what to do," he said.

"I'll make all the arrangements and let you know what to do. It'll be best if I keep the details on the project to myself and tell you only what you need to know. That way, none of the others will know you are involved. All you'll have to do is get me a few of those blank checks with the facsimile signature. We'll just have to find a bank that will cooperate and allow us to cash the checks."

Maxwell enthusiastically nodded his head several times in agreement, and the deal was done.

During all the meetings between Maxwell and McMahon, two people had been watching. One was McMahon's bodyguard and constant companion, a muscular man named Jan Godlewski. The other was Trey Bowman, an FBI special agent. Bowman had known about McMahon's shady activities for eight years. He believed the con man should be permanently locked away, if only he could gather enough evidence to keep him there.

McMahon, a personable, handsome man, was free now because the judge had liked his good behavior while behind bars. His last prison term was for swindling three women. He had romanced all three women at the same time, promising to marry them, although he was already married. He had talked each of the women into loaning him several thousand dollars to pay his debts. After he failed to repay a loan from one of the women, she had secretly gone into his wallet and found notes with the phone numbers of the other two. She contacted them and talked them into joining her in reporting McMahon as a thief.

Bowman didn't believe McMahon could go straight for any extended period of time. He knew McMahon now was separated from his beautiful wife, a honey-blonde pediatrician named Rebecca, and he was already living with another beautiful woman, an airline attendant named Kimberly Lloyd. McMahon lived an expensive lifestyle without earning a paycheck, and Bowman believed he was continuing to get money through some kind of deception.

Chapter 4

On a Monday morning, September 7, a few weeks before Serena Sheppard arrived at work to find Cameron National Bank full of strange men, another stranger had arrived on the scene. While casually checking the night deposits, Serena looked out through the glass doors as a shiny new Cadillac pulled up outside. Such an automobile was rarely seen in Cameron, and a man she had never seen before got out of the car and walked in.

He was an eye-catching individual with longish, dark-brown hair and a perfect Fu Manchu mustache over his upper lip and down the sides of his mouth to his jawline. He wore a dark suit with pointed Italian shoes, a white shirt, and a colorful tie.

The stranger introduced himself as Jarvis Salisbury and asked to speak to the bank's president. Serena, who was listening intently to the man's Yankee accent, asked the secretary nearby to take him to the office of Paul Norris. The secretary rose from her desk and escorted the visitor a few steps to the president's office. After she introduced the two men to each other, the stranger reached over Norris's desk to shake hands before he stepped back and closed the office door behind him.

About an hour later, Serena stepped into the back room to have another cup of coffee and half a doughnut. She needed something to help her make it until her one o'clock lunch break. Phil was in the back room storage area getting a pack of loan forms.

"Did you see that man who came to see Mr. Norris?" Serena asked.

"The Yankee with the fake sideburns?" Phil asked.

"I didn't see any fake sideburns. He looked like someone important. I wonder what his business is."

"Who knows? You're right. He didn't look like our usual customer," Phil said.

Serena took another sip of coffee before she said, "Exactly what do you think makes an 'unusual' customer for us?"

"The man this morning definitely spoke perfect English in a clipped manner. Nowadays a Yankee accent is not as noticeable around here as it would have been years ago, but his accent still makes him stand out," Phil said.

"And he walked fast, like he had something very important to do, something that had to be done quickly. He also looked extremely confident, like he is used to giving orders and being obeyed," Serena said.

"Maybe he's strange to us only because we usually know everyone who comes in," Phil said.

Back at her teller window, Serena smiled as Jack Hudson, one of her regular customers, came in to make a deposit. Hudson, a black man, did not grow chickens himself, but he was well known as a good friend of the town's poultry producer. He ran errands for the producer's family, as well as for the processing plant's office personnel, and he kept the beautifully landscaped yard around the producer's home in perfect condition. He always wore a matching khaki shirt and pants, somewhat like a uniform.

Hudson had two boys in the local high school, and his main goal in life was to see that his two sons got a college education "so they can get a good job."

"Put this money in my savin' account, please," he told Serena, giving her a large jar of coins that included a lot of pennies.

"How is the world treating you this morning, Mr. Hudson?" Serena asked as she began to count the coins.

"I'm doin' well," he answered, "an' I wish I could say the same for my neighbor, Frank Banks."

Hudson liked to talk, and Serena began sorting dimes into dollar groups before she asked, "What happened to Mr. Banks?"

"Well, Frank's wife died 'bout three months ago," Hudson said in a low voice. "About a month ago, his daughter was searchin' through her mother's personal thangs an' found a paid-up life insurance policy for a thousand dollars. Frank's losin' his eyesight, and he thought Lily, his wife, had sent him a gift from heaven. I don't need to tell ya, Frank was a very happy man. His daughter filed for payment of the policy, an' a check was personally delivered by the insurance man a week later.

"Frank cashed the check an' put the money in his pocket. It made 'im feel safe an' secure to be able to get his hands quick on all that extra money. He knowed he cud take a nice trip if he wanted to, and he'd always wanted to go ta New York 'cause he has kinfolk there.

"He was lookin' at brochures that a friend picked up at a travel agency when another man come to his door. This man said he'd been contacted by Frank's wife 'fore she died. She'd asked 'im to come an' check tha roof o' their house for leaks."

Serena listened silently as she sorted pennies into groups of ten.

"This man told Frank that his house needed a new roof, an' a bad leak 'as developin' 'round the chimney. It'd do great damage to tha house if it wudden fixed before the next rain. He told Frank he only did roof work on the weekends, but he'd fix it so well that it wud last the next thirty years.

"Frank tol' 'im to do the work, and tha man answered that he'd have to be paid in advance. He said the price was a thousand and nine dollars, and Frank decided he cudden make the trip to New York after all. He gave 'im every cent he had in 'is pocket."

Serena said, "I'm glad Frank had the money. I know he wants to keep his home in good condition."

"But tha's not tha end o' tha story," Hudson said. "When the man left, Frank's other neighbor went to 'is house and said 'Was that yer insurance agent I seen leavin' yore house?' This time, tha insurance man wudden wearin' a suit an' tie ta come ta Frank's home. He was wearin' overalls and sunglasses. Frank said he thought tha man's voice sounded familiar."

"Do you mean the insurance agent came back and took Frank's money? Did Frank call the police?" Serena asked.

"You know it won't do no good for Frank ta call the police. It'll be Frank's word against the word of tha insurance agent. Frank ain't got no receipt and no material evidence a'tall to prove what the insurance agent did."

"Are you sure it was the agent?" Serena said.

"He knowed Frank had tha money, and tha fake roofer told Frank his house'd be fixed tha next weekend. It's been a month, and no one 'as come ta work on tha roof yet."

"Oh, Mr. Hudson, I'm so sorry. I wish I knew some way that Frank could get his money back," Serena said. She had finished counting the coins and gave him a copy of his deposit slip for thirty-seven dollars.

"Ms. Sheppard, ma'am, I don't know why I al'ays want to tell you 'bout the things that are troublin' me, but I consider ya my friend. I also know ya never repeat what I tell ya."

"I just wish I could do more than listen," Serena answered.

"I appreciate ya listenin'," Hudson said. "I've taken up too much of ya time. Have a good day, ma'am."

As Hudson walked across the lobby and out the front door, Serena wondered how any person would prey on an almost blind man, taking all his money that way. But she knew Hudson was right. The police had to have evidence before a crime could be proven. Hudson had not said the words, but it would be a black man contradicting the words of a white man, and Serena couldn't think of any way the black man could win.

She looked toward Mr. Norris's door, and it was still shut. The stranger was still there. *My goodness. He's been in there an awfully long time*, she thought.

Chapter 5

The bank president's face brightened when the nicely dressed stranger was personally escorted into his office. The man's confident walk said he wasn't a salesman, so Paul Norris knew immediately that this day was going to be different.

Salisbury introduced himself and said he wanted to talk to Norris about a major business plan. Norris asked him to be seated. Salisbury said he represented Merrill Construction Company, a large Philadelphia business planning a major development in the Cameron area. "My company is seeking a bank to handle large amounts of money, but the project is something that has to be kept totally secret for an indefinite length of time."

Norris assured Salisbury he always kept all business totally confidential.

"My company has learned that the state of Georgia is planning to extend Georgia 365, which now ends in Gainesville. As you know, it's a four-lane that already connects with I-85 in Suwanee, and the extension will come through here, through the outer city limits of Cameron," Salisbury said.

Gainesville, a much larger town about forty miles south of Cameron, was known throughout the state for its wealthy citizens and their political power. Gainesville officials had been able to get the Georgia Department of Transportation to build about twenty-eight miles of four-lane highway to Suwanee, connecting their town to Interstate-85.

The new I-85 flowed through Georgia to connect with other interstate highways in Alabama and Virginia.

Salisbury casually mentioned Merrill Construction Company in Philadelphia again and said his company was looking for a good opportunity in the southeastern United States to build a large regional shopping mall.

He put his briefcase on the desk and pulled out copies of road maps from the Georgia Department of Transportation. Unfolding a large map on Norris's desk, Salisbury pointed to the exact area where the four-lane highway was coming by Cameron. Prominent in the map's spider web of roads was a red inked line leaving Gainesville and passing through Cameron beside the old US 23 highway.

"I've been told to purchase substantial acreage in the Cameron area for the shopping mall, plus surrounding acreage for offices and residences. All my company needs is total cooperation from a local bank."

As if an added incentive was needed, Salisbury told Norris that the bank that handled the project would get a prime site in front of the mall for either a new headquarters or a branch office.

"This is not going to be just a row of small stores. It will be a variety of retail stores all under one roof. We will have a group of small eateries inside that will offer different kinds of food. Shoppers will be able to order their choice of food, take it to a table to eat, and visit with each other without leaving the mall," Salisbury said.

Norris had taken his wife to Lenox Square, a large shopping mall that had opened twelve years earlier in the prestigious Buckhead area of Atlanta. It had two fine department stores she loved, Rich's and Davison's. He had also visited a newer, much smaller, mall in Gainesville, built around a bowling alley. The Gainesville mall included the department stores of Belk's and Penny's plus Rose's, a discount chain store, and a number of locally owned specialty shops. Although the Gainesville mall was small, he had looked at the cars in the parking lot to determine where the shoppers made their homes. Each car tag had the name of the owner's home county, and they were from a large surrounding area, including his county of Habersham. He had also seen regular Cameron Bank customers coming out of the mall with packages. He knew that the mall's small size didn't keep it from being a profitable venture.

"What size mall are you talking about?" he asked Salisbury.

"We're planning 500,000 square feet gross usable space with at least two anchor stores to draw customers. Of course, we'll also need a good amount of acreage for parking.

"We prefer a Rich's Department Store as one of the anchors, but we're negotiating with the Gallant-Belk department store chain and Sears, Roebuck and Co. Rich's is well known and highly respected, but Belk's and Sears both have good business records, and, better than that, they have a proven understanding of this regional market. The Sears store can also offer catalog shopping along with its on-site retail merchandise.

"We want to draw customers from throughout northeast Georgia, and I think the people here in Cameron will be glad to have their own shopping center," Salisbury said.

Paul Norris had been in the banking business for thirty-three years. He knew how to control his emotions. He kept his deadpan expression, but his mind raced.

For years, he had been reading stories in the Atlanta newspaper about the proposed interstate connection. Expressways were touted as beneficial to any area they traveled, and Norris had concluded earlier, with disappointment, that the connector would benefit only Gainesville.

Interstate 85 was originally supposed to come close to Cameron but, during the highway's planning stages, Georgia governor Ernest Vandiver had managed to get it moved east to flow by his hometown of Lavonia. The interstate highway had opened almost six years earlier and crossed into South Carolina at the new Lake Hartwell, a man-made body of water that had completed filling in 1962 and was operated by the US Corps of Engineers. The finished Interstate 85 was nowhere near Cameron.

Now this stranger was assuring Norris that Cameron—his town—was going to be the major benefactor of the I-85 connector. Salisbury revealed a lot of knowledge about the highway and spoke with authority. Everything he said made perfect sense. There was no doubt that the mall would draw shoppers from many miles around. In addition to all the retail shops and the two anchor stores, the mall would also include popular restaurant chains.

Gainesville had invested much of its industrial market in the business of growing chickens, and now environmentalists were making waves about the waste from the poultry processing plants. Maybe a new regional shopping mall would make Cameron into a new Gainesville, without some of the problems of the old Gainesville.

There in Norris's office that morning, the two men worked out some of the details of their business agreement. Salisbury would open two accounts, one as Jarvis Salisbury and one as Salisbury Construction Company.

Merrill Construction Company was an old, established business that did work throughout the eastern United States, Salisbury said. A telephone call could be made to the banks where Merrill Construction did business, First Pennsylvania Bank or Fidelity National Bank, to verify that checks deposited in the accounts were good. No withdrawals would be made until there was time for the checks to be honored and paid through the Federal Reserve Bank from the bank on which they were drawn.

All withdrawals must be made in cash, Salisbury said, because he intended to purchase various tracts in cash to prevent anyone from knowing the identity of the purchaser. This way, the property prices would not skyrocket during the purchase period. When all desired property had been purchased, all the deeds would be recorded at once.

Once again, Salisbury had outlined a reasonable concept.

That day, Norris himself opened accounts for Salisbury, who used checks drawn on Merrill Construction Company. Each account had a deposit of $125,000, almost forty times the average yearly income of local residents.

When Salisbury walked out of Norris's office, he went to Serena's window and said, "This is a nice little town. I'm going to enjoy doing business here."

"What can I do for you?" Serena said.

"Thank you. It's nice to hear those words from a beautiful woman, but I'll be doing all my business with Mr. Norris," Salisbury said.

"Just let me know if I or anyone else can assist you," Serena said.

She didn't know why she felt like moving away from this man. She was finding it hard to keep a pleasant expression on her face and wondered if Joyce was feeling the same way. But Joyce was busy with another customer.

"I'll be seeing you in a couple of days," Salisbury said, walking toward the front door.

Serena could only feel relief when he was gone. She was still thinking about Hudson's neighbor losing his money, and she didn't want to waste time wondering about this stranger.

Chapter 6

On Sunday morning, Paul Norris was sitting in his usual pew at the First Baptist Church with his wife Carolyn. The preacher was getting very angry, as he often did when he talked about making illegal liquor, an underground industry that was well known in the mountains.

The fermenting of grain mash to make whiskey began taking place around Cameron after the first Scots-Irish settlers came into the mountains more than one hundred years earlier. During the Civil War, the US Congress decided that whiskey could be taxed, as one way of balancing the budget. Back under Washington control after the war, the Georgia mountaineers found that their only source of income was being taxed. They stubbornly refused to pay the levies and refused to stop making whiskey.

Since that time, the Alcohol and Tobacco Tax Division of the US Department of Revenue had been destroying illegal distilleries, arresting any person on the site and charging him with a felony. Meanwhile, mountain people joked about "the revenooers."

Paul Norris knew some of the families around Cameron who had been making whiskey for generations, and he couldn't suppress a certain grudging respect for them. These families were always referred to as bootleggers, and, occasionally, one or two token members were rounded up by the revenuers and sent off to prison for three or four years.

After one of these raids by the revenue agents, the remainder of the whiskey-making trade would stay quiet for a couple of months before cranking up again. After a mountain family became known for its intoxicating beverage, it was almost impossible to stop making it. Not only was the demand good, but it was their only source of income.

Some of the same people who publicly condemned whiskey would come knocking on the door at night and pay high prices for the bootlegged drink. For them, the words "White Lightning" had a little more class than "Moonshine," the word favored by the revenuers because the whiskey was almost always made under the cover of darkness in skillfully hidden stills.

The preacher was walking back and forth behind the pulpit working up to a high-pitched voice, sweating brow, and waving arms.

The parable of the prodigal son was the text of his sermon, and he told of the younger of two sons, who asked for early distribution of his family's estate. He couldn't wait to get his share of the money, so the father divided what he had between the boy and his brother. "The youngest son squandered his share in evil living," the preacher said.

"The people who make White Lightning cause today's young people to squander their lives, too," he said. "If this young man had lived today, he would have been drinking White Lightning. He would have been spending his time with gamblers and prostitutes. He would be wallowing in the lowest levels of life, but he eventually came to the end of his rope and had to change his attitude. After he spent all he had, a famine hit the land, and the only job he could get was feeding pigs. He himself had nothing to eat, so he went back to his father and asked to be one of his hired hands. His father forgave him and welcomed him back into the family with a feast.

"If you have someone in your family living this kind of life, you know they are on the way to hell and everlasting damnation, but they can change. All they have to do is ask God for help," the preacher said. "They will be forgiven of their sins and welcomed back into the Christian family."

Norris didn't know a single person who lived the kind of life the preacher was describing, and he began to think about his own life.

He had felt good when he woke that morning. He felt expansive, unrestrained, as he greeted his friends at church. Jarvis Salisbury's visit had totally changed the banker's outlook on life. The little town of Cameron was on the move, and Paul Norris was in the driver's seat.

Sitting in the pew, he thought of his own deceased father, Louie

Norris, who had died a sad and broken man. Now Paul had the opportunity to reclaim his father's dream.

Soon after the turn of the century, Paul's father had come from Tennessee to teach in a small boarding school at Cameron. There he had met the woman named Marylynn who accepted his marriage proposal and became Paul's mother.

In Cameron in those years a man had two choices in supporting his family. Louie Norris could scratch out a meager livelihood through farming. He could raise sheep or cattle, grow grapes, corn, cane, or apples. The second choice was making illegal whiskey and hauling it to Gainesville or Atlanta to sell.

The long hours of hard work required in farming would have been acceptable, but Cameron had only a few acres of good bottomland suitable for crops. Each of these acres was already used and unavailable. Apple and peach orchards were well established on any other suitable land.

The whiskey business was not to be considered. The elder Norris knew no one in his family who had broken the law, and he didn't want to be the first.

Although no good land was available, the Norrises decided they could support themselves on their own land. Paul heard many stories of how hard his parents had worked. During the first year of their marriage, the elder Norris farmed on rocky, hilly land, and each day he and Marylynn worked from before dawn till after sundown.

During the second spring, Louie Norris had friends to visit from Tennessee who said they wanted to finance him in the banking business. Life was hard for Louie and Marylynn, and both were anxious to make a change. They still hoped they would have children, and this move would open the career door for a future son. With the help of his friends, Louie opened Cameron's first bank using surplus funds of a few families to make loans to others. Precautions were taken to make sure the few families with surplus funds could always withdraw their money if need be.

Sixty-day loans were made to store owners, who used the loan to pay for goods, then sold the goods to pay the bank. Twelve-month loans were made to farmers, who paid the loan when the crops were sold.

The venture went well for more than a decade, and the Norris family's future was bright. But like so many others, Louie Norris was not ready for the Wall Street stock market crash in 1929. It happened a year after Paul was born, and the Cameron bank began to struggle.

Like so many other bankers, Louie Norris had invested some of the depositors' money in the stock market, and when word spread that the bank was holding worthless stock certificates, the major depositors rushed to withdraw their savings. Paul's father had intended to borrow money to keep his bank afloat, but everything happened too fast. The little Cameron bank was among those in Georgia that failed after the crash, and a lot of local families were left feeling bitter toward the Norris family. Paul's father became a traveling salesman for livestock feed.

Later, a neighbor invited him into his barn loft to look at baby kittens. Louie had planned to select one for Paul, but he fell from the loft into the building's hard red clay hallway and broke his back. He was bedridden for two years but eventually learned to limp along using crutches. Finally, the feed company rehired him for a desk job. While he was unable to work, Marylynn managed the household by carefully budgeting a small inheritance from her parents.

Paul Norris worked his way through the University of Georgia. After he came home with a degree in business and found work with Cameron National Bank, he began purchasing the bank's stock and rather quickly made his way up to become president. He rarely put his deepest business wish into words, not even in his private thinking, but Paul wanted to redeem the Norris family name in the banking world.

His parents had been dead a long time, and many of the individuals who lost money through the Norris family bank in the Great Depression were also dead. But Paul knew what a burden that bank failure had been for his father, and he always tried to operate Cameron National Bank in a manner that would redeem his father's name. Paul wanted each banking transaction to reflect the institution's purpose—to help local people achieve a better life.

This morning, Paul Norris felt as if his deepest dream was about to come true. A Norris was finally going to put Cameron on the map and put money in the pockets of local people. Maybe his father's legacy could be redeemed if his son could open the door for great wealth in Cameron and the surrounding region.

The preacher finally ended his sermon and brought Norris out of his thoughts by asking the congregation to turn to page forty-eight in their hymnals and sing "Standing on the Promises." Paul almost smiled at the name when the hymn was announced, because he was standing on the promises of one Jarvis Salisbury.

All the verses were sung very slowly as the preacher repeatedly asked members of the congregation to come forward and confess their sins or ask for prayer for a loved one. When no one responded, the preacher asked that the song be repeated; two people responded, and he announced the last stanza.

The last note of the song was still in the air when Paul leaned over and whispered into Carolyn's ear, "Let's take a drive in the mountains this afternoon."

Chapter 7

Carolyn Norris was walking toward friends. She was completely surprised and quickly looked back at her husband before talking to other members of the congregation. She and Paul hadn't taken a Sunday afternoon drive through the mountains in about fifteen years.

They left the church as quickly as possible without causing friends to question them. After they got into their black Buick LeSabre, Carolyn talked about the friends they had seen at church while Paul drove north. "Did you hear that Rose Bullard's daughter is divorcing her husband? Can you believe that? They've been married twelve years," Carolyn said, but Paul only nodded his head in exaggerated side motions indicating dismay.

"Rose's grandchildren are doing well in school now, but I don't know how they will do when their parents divorce."

Paul was quiet.

"I told Edith Stillwell that she looked great in that red hat, but I wish hats would come back in style. I used to love hats."

Paul had driven about fifteen miles when he finally spoke to say that he wanted to eat lunch at the Smith House in Dahlonega. He found the last parking space in the small parking lot, and inside they learned they would have to wait ten minutes before being seated at a table because the heavy tourist season was already beginning. The dining establishment was known for miles around for its family-style meals. Bowls of creamed corn, green beans, candied sweet potatoes, fried okra, creamed Irish potatoes, and platters of fried ham and chicken were placed in the center of one of the big dining tables with big platters of hot yeast rolls and cornbread, peach cobbler, and pitchers of sweet and unsweetened tea.

Paul and Carolyn were escorted into the Smith House dining room and seated at a table filled with strangers. Most of the diners said they would drink sweet tea, and waitresses poured tea from the pitchers into glasses of ice cubes and set them beside the plates. A few other diners asked for hot coffee.

The talk was amiable, focusing on neutral subjects such as food and weather. Two of the diners were fascinated with Dahlonega's history as the location of the country's first major gold rush. While driving on the back roads, they had seen a man squatted in a stream, and he appeared to be panning for gold. They wanted to know if it was true that gold still could be found in the area, and another person said he knew a man who carried a vial of gold dust around in his pocket. Still another person said the questioners could get better information at the town's gold museum, which had been established in the old courthouse.

Neither Paul nor Carolyn responded to any of the comments. Paul had completely lost his appetite, and, even though the food was tasty, Carolyn didn't want to consume so many calories. They were the first to leave the table, pay their bill, and go back to the car.

Carolyn could tell that Paul was very tense. He obviously had something on his mind and would eventually tell her what it was. While she was waiting, she was thoroughly enjoying the views as Paul drove farther north. It was a clear, sunny day in September, and no mist hovered over the mountains obstructing the view.

Carolyn had once made a trip out to the Western states and had been surprised to see that other mountains were much bigger, but not nearly as blue, as the mountains in Georgia. The mountains north of Cameron were said to be among the oldest mountains in the world, and they were almost gentle in appearance. The mountains Carolyn saw in the Western states ended in peaks that could only be described as challenging and forbidding, whereas the rounded tops of the mountains in northeast Georgia were welcoming and romantic.

Each spring, twists of white clouds wrapped like silk scarves around the purple mountains, and, upon coming closer to the slopes, visitors found them dotted with varying shades of pink, which was either mountain laurel, rhododendron, or wild azaleas, which were called honeysuckles by local residents. Spring also found spots of ground covered in blue bird's-foot violets.

The mist was heavy during the summer months, but nothing could ever completely obscure the beauty of the old blue hills. During September and October, the mist cleared, leaving the air crystal clear for the autumn tourists.

Today, the sky was blue with a few small, white, fluffy clouds, and the temperature in the mountains was warm at seventy-four degrees Fahrenheit. The trees were just beginning to change colors, making it entertaining to search out the early reds and yellows.

Splashing creeks and rivers caressed the mountains here and there. Occasional waterfalls created white silken ribbons on distant hillsides like decorations in a woman's hair. Carolyn thought about Amicalola Falls, which tumbled more than 700 feet over rock ledges. Despite warnings, a young tourist had fallen over the falls and died in the early summer. As a child, Carolyn had climbed up the center of another falls called Minnehaha where water fell down a one-hundred-foot rock staircase.

A few decades back, Georgia Railway and Electric Company, which became Georgia Power, built dams on some of the streams to produce electricity, and the federal government built dams to control flooding. The wonderful benefits of these stream barriers meant nothing to the people who were forced to give up their homes. One little town called Burton had 200 people, and they sold their homes and businesses to the power company with regret. The new Lake Burton, which covered all evidence of the town, was one of several lakes these dams created in the mountains.

Paul Norris stopped his car beside Lake Winfield Scott, a man-made body of water on a mountaintop. The lake was one of the last projects of the federal government's Civilian Conservation Corps, a massive effort in the 1930s and early '40s to provide jobs during the Great Depression. Winfield Scott, the man for whom the lake was named, was the US Army general in charge of removing Cherokee Indians from the area in 1838, almost one hundred years before the CCC began its restoration work.

Lumber companies had taken the trees from the Georgia mountains and left the land to erode. After the trees and the lumber companies were gone, the people had desperately searched for jobs without success. The CCC provided jobs and set up camps in the mountains, where young men repaired damaged land and built the dams to prevent floods. The buildings and retainer walls at Lake Winfield Scott were only one of the lasting examples of the skills of the CCC's stone masons.

The lake was almost lost in the Chattahoochee National Forest, and the water was too cold for most swimmers, even during the warmest summer months. Because it was so isolated, visitors were always few.

Today, a boy and an older woman, probably his grandmother, were walking the path around the lake carrying two homemade cane poles and a string of fish. The biggest fish on the string, at least a three-pounder, looked like a big-mouth bass, and the three or four smaller fish were rainbow trout. Carolyn imagined that they were going to fry their catch for their family's evening meal.

Norris didn't offer to get out of the car, but stared straight ahead for a few seconds before turning toward Carolyn without taking his hands from the steering wheel.

"I want to tell you something, and you can't say a word to anyone, not even our son, or anyone in your family," he said, referring to Carolyn's brothers and sisters. The Norrises' son also lived in Cameron and was employed with the feed company where his grandfather once worked.

Carolyn said, "Okay."

"I need more than just an *Okay*. Say 'I will not tell any living person what you share with me today.'"

Carolyn stared at him for about five seconds. She had never seen him like this before, and she anxiously held her breath before she repeated the words.

Norris began to talk. Then he released the wheel and turned toward Carolyn as the words rushed out. He told her about the stranger coming into the bank and about the grand opportunities the stranger had explained.

"I had a little trouble at first really believing it," Norris said, "even though I knew that what he said made sense. But I've been thinking a lot about it, and I know this is the chance I've always been looking for. I had to tell someone about it, and I know you will keep it to yourself."

"What if someone finds out? I'm not going to tell, but something as big as this is hard to keep secret," Carolyn said.

"You have to make certain no one finds out," Paul said, speaking slowly and emphasizing each word. "You and I are not even going to mention the subject again until the time is right."

To make his words more forceful, he said, "We'll say no more." He turned back toward the steering wheel and reached down and started the engine.

As they drove back down the mountain, neither spoke. Norris envisioned the new wealth coming into Cameron and imagined how the citizens would finally be grateful to him.

Carolyn became deeply worried about what success in such large measure would do to her husband. *Life is already good, and this will bring great change. What will this do to our lives?* she wondered.

She did not even look toward the mountains as the car headed back to Cameron.

One week later, Salisbury telephoned Norris from Philadelphia. He told him that he would come to the bank in two days. He needed to make withdrawals of approximately $225,000, and he wanted it in small bills. He added that he would make more deposits.

Two days later, Salisbury came into the bank again. As before, he was dressed to perfection. No hair was out of place, his suit and tie looked new, and he could have seen a reflection of his face in the shine on his Italian shoes.

After stopping by Serena's window to comment on the beautiful weather, he stepped into Norris's office. He withdrew $225,000 in cash and deposited Merrill checks totaling $250,000. The small bills he requested had required a special trip to Cameron National Bank by an armored truck from Atlanta, but Norris still did not have enough cash. He had to come to Joyce's window and take her two unbroken packs of twenties.

A few minutes later, both Serena and Joyce saw Salisbury come out of Norris's office with a large brown paper bag in his arms. The bag looked like one from a grocery store, and it was full of something. Was it money?

"I wonder what kind of business that man's conducting. We've never before had a customer like him," Serena said.

"He looked strange with his arms around that big paper bag," Joyce said.

After that, Salisbury quickly made three more visits for similar withdrawals and deposits. During each of these visits, he went by Serena and complimented her, once telling her that her dress color was ideal for "such perfect skin," and the next time telling her she was so beautiful that she should be in the movies. She only laughed at him and tried not to cringe visibly.

At each visit, he advised Norris that real estate purchases were proceeding as planned. "Details for the mall are being completed as we speak," he said on more than one occasion.

Chapter 8

In Philadelphia, on the eighteenth of October, William Jenkins, treasurer of Merrill Construction Company, received a telephone call from the cashier of Fidelity National Bank. The cashier advised Jenkins that Merrill's account was overdrawn by more than $100,000.

Merrill's had done business with Fidelity National Bank since the bank opened its doors in 1931. The company had never before had an overdrawn account, and the cashier assumed it was a bookkeeping problem. He didn't express concern and simply asked Jenkins to look into the situation. Jenkins protested that the company had more than $500,000 on deposit, a balance always kept in the account. He said he would determine the nature of the problem and call back.

Jenkins was a man who could make decisions, and he acted quickly. He immediately called James Maxwell, his head bookkeeper, and asked him to come to his office. Maxwell braced himself as he walked through the halls to Jenkins's office. McMahon had told him the evening before that this call would be coming any day. Opening the door quietly, he found Jenkins sitting very still behind his desk and staring straight toward him. Maxwell stepped into the office and sat down facing Jenkins.

"We have a problem with our checking account at Fidelity National. Have you reconciled the September bank statement?"

"What's the matter?" Maxwell answered. He thought he knew what Jenkins would say, but he had to ask.

Jenkins said, "Just answer my question."

"I haven't had time to work on the September statement yet because you know I don't have an assistant anymore," Maxwell said.

"Get the statement for me," Jenkins said.

Maxwell left the office again and was gone about half an hour. On his return he said, "You know that little fire we had the other night? I didn't think anything was lost or missing, but now I can't find the bank statement. That whole file is missing."

Only a few days earlier a small fire, believed to have been caused by hot cigarette ashes in a trash can, burned one set of drapes and a cardboard box of papers sitting on top of a filing cabinet. No one was called in to examine the incident, because nothing of real value was lost. The windows were cleaned, the charred box and papers were cleared away, and routine business had continued.

Jenkins called the cashier at Fidelity National and asked that the statement and all the checks for September and the first weeks of October be duplicated. More than 600 checks had gone through the account during this period, and it took more than a week to send a duplicated statement to Jenkins.

When it was finally delivered, Jenkins again called Maxwell into his office. He said he wanted help in examining the bank statement. Jenkins spread the pages of the statement on his desk, and he and Maxwell looked at the entry of each check.

Jenkins was the first to speak up. He had noticed that the dates on several of the checks placed them out of numerical sequence. Each of these checks was made payable either to Jarvis Salisbury or to Salisbury Construction Company. "Who is this Jarvis Salisbury?" Jenkins asked before requesting that Maxwell bring in the Merrill company records. Again they began to look at each of the transactions, and there was no record of anything with the name of Salisbury.

"Bring me our check supply," Jenkins said. He was so intent on his search, he didn't notice that Maxwell had almost nothing to say.

On examination of the unused checks, Jenkins saw that twelve checks were missing. Another examination of the statement showed that the ten checks written to Salisbury totaled well over one million dollars—to be exact, $1,131,600. The checks had been deposited in Cameron National Bank in Cameron, Georgia.

Merrill Construction Company did not have a job currently

underway in Georgia or anywhere in the Southern states. There was no reason the company could be doing business in that area.

Jenkins immediately asked his secretary to get the Cameron bank on the telephone. Speaking to the head cashier, Serena Sheppard, he asked whether Jarvis Salisbury had accounts at the bank. Serena said Salisbury had two accounts there, and, at Jenkins's request, she told him that the current balance in both accounts totaled $2,600.

Jenkins asked to speak to the president of Cameron National Bank, and, as she transferred the call, Serena told Paul Norris that she had given the caller information about the balance in both accounts.

"This is Paul Norris."

"What is your position at Cameron National Bank?" Jenkins said.

"I'm the president," Norris said.

"I'm calling about two accounts that your bank has, one in the name of Jarvis Salisbury and one in the name of Salisbury Construction Company. When were these accounts opened?" Jenkins asked Norris.

"I believe you already know the balance in these two accounts, and that is the only information I can give you," Norris said, following standard banking procedure.

"Well, let me tell you. We think that those checks may have been stolen from Merrill Construction Company and forged," Jenkins said.

"Now, let me tell you, sir," Norris replied. "Our bank has followed all proper procedure on those two accounts. You can check with Fidelity National Bank. They have paid the checks."

"I'll get back with you," Jenkins said crisply and hung up.

Jenkins rested his forehead in his right hand with his elbow on the desk. He did not speak or look at Maxwell, and his mind was racing. If the checks had been stolen, who had done it? How could a stranger have walked into the offices and taken the checks? It must have been someone from that town. Did a man named Salisbury actually open two checking accounts at that bank for such large amounts of money? If this had happened, why hadn't someone at the bank called the Merrill offices to verify the validity of Salisbury Construction Company? Who was this Paul Norris at Cameron National Bank?

Finally, Maxwell spoke and asked if he could take the company records back to his office.

Jenkins didn't answer him, but picked up the phone and called the cashier at Fidelity National Bank. "It looks like checks have been stolen from our office. We want you to close our overdrawn checking account immediately. As soon as we know what happened to cause this overdraft, I'll get back to you," he said.

Next, Jenkins called Merrill's bonding company, asking that they send a representative over right away. Still not looking at Maxwell, he said, "You may go back to your office."

As Maxwell departed, Jenkins grabbed the telephone directory and looked up a number. His next telephone call was to the Philadelphia office of the Federal Bureau of Investigation.

Chapter 9

On the morning that the investigators swooped down on Cameron National Bank, no one in the small town knew why they were there, no one except the bank president, Paul Norris. The investigators didn't speak to the bank employees unless they asked for certain records, and the employees hardly spoke to each other.

Normally, Serena would have asked Joyce and Phil if they had watched the television show, *All in the Family*, the evening before. She had been shocked months earlier when her husband, Fred, called her in from the kitchen to watch the first episode. The main character, Archie Bunker, referred to blacks as "Spades," to Hispanic people as "Spics," and to Jewish people as "Hebes." Now it was the only television program she tried to see because it reflected the common bigotry and narrow-mindedness that had never before been seen on a television show.

Serena hadn't heard anyone use these terms, but she knew people who thought like the Archie Bunker character—people who thought whites lost something when blacks, Hispanics, or Jews made progress. One of her customers at the bank had recently said he didn't know why Archie Bunker was considered funny. "He thinks the same way I do," he said.

She had passed the cement duck wearing unusual sunglasses that morning and predicted that the duck's strange appearance meant that she would have an exciting day. But when she saw the intimidating strangers in the bank, she completely forgot her prediction. And if she had remembered *All in the Family*, she wouldn't have mentioned it. A remark about a popular television show wouldn't have been appropriate on a morning when nothing was normal.

Before 9:00 AM and time to open for business, Serena, Joyce, and Phil talked about a possible sale of the bank.

At 9:15, Serena was at her window when the president, Paul Norris, buzzed and asked her to step into his office. She leaned toward Joyce at the next window and whispered that she had been summoned. Serena was almost overwhelmed with curiosity, but she tried to keep a blank expression on her face as she walked toward Norris's office. After she opened the door and stepped inside, a tall man pulled a chair out for her, and she sat down at a round table across from another man. The man at the table was looking down at papers, and Serena waited silently. The tall man stepped back and stood near the wall. Norris was sitting at his usual place behind his desk.

Finally the man at the table looked up and stared at Serena a couple of seconds. "My name is Trey Bowman. I'm going to ask you some questions about your job here at the bank. Tell me your name and how long you have worked here."

Bowman spoke quickly and succinctly, not like anyone Serena knew. His eyes were dark, and the black pupils in the center were like sharp pinpoints as he looked at her. Suddenly she became aware that her haircut was not stylish, and her dress was old and outdated. Slight confusion joined the curiosity in Serena's mind.

"My name is Serena Sheppard, and I've been here for almost twenty years."

"Do you know Jarvis Salisbury?"

"I know he is doing business with this bank."

"Have you waited on Jarvis Salisbury during any of the times that he has come into the bank?"

"The first day he came in, I greeted him and asked a secretary to show him to Mr. Norris's office."

"Had you ever heard the name Jarvis Salisbury before he came into the bank?"

"No."

"Have you heard any talk of the bank being involved in a major construction project?"

"No. Well ... Since Mr. Salisbury began coming to the bank I have heard people talk about a secret project. That's all. I don't know what the project is."

"What have you heard about the secret project?"

"Uh … well, not anything, just people saying that Mr. Salisbury is coming into the bank because of a secret project. No one knows him, and he always goes into Mr. Norris's office for his transactions. We don't know who he is or why he's here. I think that's why people have begun to say he's here because of a secret project."

Bowman looked down at his papers again. His black brows drew together above thick, black lashes.

"Have you always lived in Cameron? Do you know a lot of people here?" Bowman said, still looking at his papers.

"I don't live in Cameron. I live about twenty miles up the road. I was born in this county and went to school in the adjoining county. Working in the bank, I've met a lot of people including a few from the counties around us. I guess you could say I know a lot of people."

Maybe this man doesn't know that Georgia has 159 small counties, Serena thought. A person could drive fifteen or twenty miles from almost any county seat and be in another county, each with its own government and public school system.

"Give me details about Salisbury's visits to this bank," Bowman said, and Serena related her memories of the first visit.

The eyes pierced her again. "We need you to look at some photographs and tell us if any of these people are Jarvis Salisbury."

A gray-suited gentleman approached her with pictures in his hand. He showed her three photos, saying each time, "Is this Salisbury?"

Serena assured the strange man that she had never before seen any of the men in the pictures. She did not know that she had been shown pictures of three men who lived in Philadelphia: Sandy McMahon, a well-known con man; McMahon's burly bodyguard, Jan Godlewski; and James Maxwell, the head bookkeeper at Merrill Construction Company.

"Thank you. We'll let you know if we need you again," Bowman said, after Serena looked at the last photo.

"You can go back to your window and ask Joyce to come in," Norris said. No other words were spoken.

Serena walked out the door to Joyce's window and told her she was wanted. Serena did not say that she thought something was terribly wrong. She did not say that the atmosphere in Mr. Norris's room was so heavy that the air itself almost weighed her down.

After Serena and Joyce were back at their windows, they did not speak to each other again. Customers came in and conducted business, then chatted about family matters before going back out. Listening and talking with them helped both tellers push the bank's strange activity to the back of their minds.

Serena had once told Joyce that bank tellers could learn all they needed to know about what was happening in the world and in Cameron just by listening to their customers.

The high school was preparing for its homecoming game, and the young students had surprised the older population. They had chosen a beautiful black student named Marie Ivy as one of the five girls to serve in the court of the homecoming queen.

Integration of public schools had brought black and white children together during class hours in Cameron only two years earlier. The doors now were closed to Cameron's old black school, which served both elementary and high school students, and most of the school's administrative staff had lost their jobs, as did some of the teachers. On entering the formerly white school, the younger black children received school books that, for the first time, were new, but it was also the first time in their lives that they experienced deep prejudice because of the color of their skin.

Marie's father, Calvin Ivy, came into the bank, and Serena congratulated him on his daughter's accomplishment. "I want her to keep her grades up and get a college scholarship. That's far more important," Marie's father said.

Phil Anderson came out of his office and handed an envelope to Ivy. "Would you please give this to your daughter," he said.

After Ivy took the envelope without speaking and walked out, Serena said to Phil jokingly, "Are you trying to develop Mr. Ivy's daughter into a loan customer? She's only a high school junior."

Phil didn't acknowledge her comment and walked back into his office.

Both Serena and Joyce personally knew each customer, knew the members of their families, knew whether and where they attended church, and knew whether or not their children had been in trouble in school.

This morning, most of the customers were talking about bomb threats.

In distant major cities, bomb threats and plane hijackings were making the news on a regular basis. Only a couple of weeks earlier, a middle-aged man identified only as D. B. Cooper had boarded a Northwest Airlines plane in Portland, Oregon, carrying what looked like a bomb. He had opened his briefcase, shown a flight attendant the red sticks and wires, and hijacked the jetliner with forty-three persons aboard. After collecting $200,000 in ransom in Seattle, Washington, he had apparently parachuted out of the plane somewhere in the wilderness of southwest Washington State, and no trace of either him or the money had been found.

D. B. Cooper's clever ruse did no damage to another person and outfoxed law enforcement. He was rapidly becoming a folk hero, and now fake bomb threats had become a thrill for teenagers with raging hormones. A boy or girl could call a local school, say a bomb had been planted there, then hang up and listen to the local radio station as the announcer reported students being evacuated. No bomb was ever found, and all students enjoyed several hours or a whole day out of school.

In Cameron, more than once, a teenager had enjoyed the power of having the local school evacuated. Even the county courthouse had been evacuated twice just the day before, and the fake bomb threats were the main topic of conversation that morning at the tellers' windows.

It would be about a year before members of the news media, both radio and newspaper, would decide that reporting a fake bomb threat caused additional fake bomb threats. When the reporting stopped, the bomb threats diminished to almost none. Without hearing news reports of their action, the guilty parties sometimes never knew if they had caused the evacuation of a building. The fake threats stopped amusing teenagers.

But today, life was continuing as usual.

At lunchtime, Joyce left Serena on duty while she went to her house, which was only two miles from the bank, and made them both sandwiches of sliced chicken breast and mustard on whole wheat bread.

Back at the bank, Joyce handed the sandwich to Serena and said, "I hope we can talk after we get off."

They took turns hurriedly eating their sandwiches in the back room before going back to their windows. That evening the tellers left the bank at the same time, and Joyce said to Serena, "Come to my house before you go home."

Joyce and her husband lived in a white ranch-style house in the Cameron city limits. Serena entered through the back door and sat down in the kitchen before talking about the photographs and the questions she had been asked about Jarvis Salisbury. Joyce, who had poured two glasses of sweet iced tea, said, "They asked me the same thing. I didn't know the people in those pictures, either."

"This afternoon, I looked at those Salisbury accounts. One has a balance of about $2,000, and the other has a balance of a little more than $600. I didn't want to take too much time looking, but I think a lot of money has come through both accounts," Serena said.

"You know Mr. Salisbury always goes into Mr. Norris's office to do business. He always has that big briefcase, but one time I saw him come out of Mr. Norris's office with that large brown paper bag—you know, you saw him, too. It must have been stuffed full of money, but I never really thought about it until now. Another thing I've noticed is that truck from Atlanta has been here a lot more lately," Joyce said. She was referring to the armored truck from the Atlanta Federal Reserve Bank that had been making extra trips to the bank and always bringing cash in small bills.

The whole situation was a mystery to the two women. Why were those strange men in the bank? Why was Mr. Norris so intent about his work? He had not spoken a word to any of the bank employees all day. And who was this Mr. Salisbury, anyway? He had always been mysterious.

Phil had said Salisbury wore fake sideburns. That was after Salisbury's first visit to the bank, and everyone was talking about him. Serena had laughed at Phil, thinking he was a little jealous of the stranger's neat appearance. When Salisbury came in again, Serena had looked closely at his sideburns, and, if they were false, they had been well attached. They looked real to her.

"Would you like to hear something amusing?" Serena asked Joyce.

"Tell me if you think it'll make me stop thinking about the bank," Joyce said.

Serena told her about the costumed cement duck on the roadside. "You know how I'm afraid of anything with feathers. Well, each morning when I pass this certain house, I pretend that this cement duck is my special friend, and it's telling me what is going to happen during my day at the bank. Of course, I know it's silly. I know it isn't true, but this morning …"

"This morning, what?" Joyce said.

"I'm embarrassed to tell you. I really don't believe in such things. But this morning the duck had on the most unusual little sunglasses. I've never seen any like them before, and I told myself that the duck was forecasting a very unusual day at the bank."

Joyce did not smile. "Well, your duck was right. It's certainly been an unusual day," she said.

Chapter 10

After leaving Joyce's house, Serena went back to her home in the Batesville community and began making her family's supper. No one in or around Cameron ever referred to the day's evening meal as dinner. Dinner was eaten at noon.

Sometimes she wished they could have a supper of cold cornbread and either sweet milk, the southernism for plain whole milk, or buttermilk. She didn't prepare milk and bread for supper because Fred didn't like it, but it was the meal she had eaten many times as a child, and she still ate it now and then. She sometimes diced a ripe tomato into her bowl of sweet milk and cornbread or shelled parched peanuts and put a handful in her bowl. If she knew she would not have to worry about having an unpleasant breath odor, she liked to eat the slender, delicate tops of green onions with her milk and bread.

Serena's two daughters always stayed after school to practice basketball, and their father picked them up on his way home from work. When their first daughter had been born, Serena and Fred had named her Penny and immediately called her their "Lucky Penny."

Friends had joked about Serena working at the bank and then naming her child after a coin, so when the second daughter was born only fourteen months later, Serena had insisted on naming her Nicole. She liked the humor found in working at a bank and giving her daughters names that made others think of coins.

She and Fred had made decisions about their family when they first began talking about marriage. She told Fred that she thought children must always have both their mother and father in the home. Together, they decided that they would have only two children, so her gynecologist had tied her fallopian tubes after Nicole's birth.

Tonight the weather was cool, so it was hot oyster stew and crackers for supper. A few pieces of leftover pumpkin pie were available if anyone wanted dessert. At the table, Nicole teased Penny about a new boy at their school. "You're being silly," Penny said.

"But I see you talking to him a lot in the hallway. What's his name, anyway?" Nicole asked.

"He's Vernon Waters. His friends call him Vern."

"Where's he from?"

"He's from Florida. His parents are opening a store in Helen. He says Helen's going to become an important tourist town."

Helen was located about twenty miles north of Cameron, and a huge lumber mill began operating there in 1911. It had taken twenty million feet of lumber from the surrounding forest before it closed. A railroad track, the Gainesville and Northwestern, which was built to haul the lumber, went out of business in 1930. Now Helen businessmen were trying to revive the little gray mountain town by making it into a bright Alpine village. If they were able to make the mountain tourists stop there, the little town might come back to life.

"Oh, I know that some of the buildings there have been painted bright colors, but it will take more than that to make it become a tourist town," Nicole said.

After more discussion, they finished eating, and Penny and Nicole left the table to get their books. After supper on weeknights, the girls usually went to one of their small bedrooms to do homework and talk, and Fred left the table and went to the living room. Their home was small and had no den or family room as did some of the newer homes around Cameron.

Fred was leaving the table with the intention of smoking a cigarette or two and watching television while Serena washed dishes and cleaned up the kitchen. He was among those who had read stories about cigarettes being bad for a person's health, but, like most other smokers, he enjoyed his cigarettes and knew of no one who had been harmed by smoking.

"Please stay here. I want to tell you what happened today," Serena said.

She didn't ask Fred to help her because years earlier he had become angry when she almost begged him to help with housework. He said housework was not a man's job.

Fred's mother had never worked outside the home except for playing the organ each Sunday at church. His father, a postman, had never worked inside the home. They had moved to Forest Park, south of Atlanta, several years ago, and his mother's weekend church obligations, plus his father's job of daily mail delivery, meant that they almost never visited.

For years, Serena had felt a slow boil of resentment because Fred never helped her with housework, even when she was almost too tired to do important tasks. But her top priority had always been a good home for her children with both their mother and father. She didn't want to nag, and she didn't want to be constantly angry, so she tried to find a way to see her husband, the father of her children, in a positive light.

She once took a sheet of paper from Penny's notebook and made two columns about Fred. In one column, she listed Fred's personality traits that she viewed as positive, and in the other column she intended to list the traits she viewed as negative.

In the positive column she had written that he was a good father to his daughters, and that they adored him. He was steady at working every day and making the main cash contribution to their family. He cut the grass around the house every Saturday during summer and made sure the motorized equipment around the house—the lawn mower, her car, his truck, and her washing machine—were always operable. He was always at home each evening and did not drink White Lightning or any other alcoholic beverage.

For years, Serena had tried to help him in any of his tasks, thinking that he would return the favor, but the tactic failed. She also complimented and praised him, especially when he did something special such as the time that he surprised her by buying and planting new shrubbery. She wanted him to compliment her now and then because it would mean she had pleased him. But he had never complimented or praised Serena about a special meal or any other part of her work.

On the other hand, he rarely complained. At the beginning of their marriage, he had fussed about meals that were not like his mother's, and Serena had tried to comply with his requests.

After writing in the positive column, she turned to the negative column and wrote only one line. He never helped with daily housework. She did not write that having him sit and watch TV in the evenings while she did the housework made her feel like his servant instead of his partner. Somewhere during their years together, she had decided that moments of deep love and rapture between a man and woman never actually happened. Descriptions of such moments only made good reading in novels and good scenes in movies.

Fred never denied that her job and salary were important, but even more important was the hospitalization insurance for the family that Serena enjoyed as a bank employee. Getting sick and going into the hospital without insurance could cause them to lose all they owned. Employers such as Cameron National Bank could buy group insurance for employees, and the employees paid a small monthly premium to get coverage for their entire family.

Fred had not graduated from high school but had attended woodworking classes at North Georgia Trade and Vocational School, which eventually became North Georgia Technical College, and was located in Clarkesville about eight miles south of their home in Batesville. He made a decent living as a cabinetmaker, with his own small shop and one helper, but he could not afford group hospitalization insurance.

While Serena was examining Fred's contributions to their home life, she had to smile at their different focal points. She noticed everything that he did or did not do in their home, while he noticed everything that she did or did not do in the operation of their family automobile. The cores of their individual concerns apparently were perfect examples of male and female priorities in life.

After thinking about her unhappiness for a few days, Serena decided that it was her attitude, not Fred's, that was making her miserable. She had two daughters who were doing well in school and now helped with housework, and a husband with a list of good qualities. She had to find a way to stop feeling hurt. She had to be more positive about her personal life.

Eventually, she was able to get past the anger and stopped expecting help or a compliment from Fred about anything she had done. She started comparing her marriage to her work as the bank's head teller.

She wanted to complete her bank work successfully, and her marriage could be viewed the same way, as a personal project that she must complete successfully.

Despite all her efforts, she was never able to completely erase her resentment. She performed her duties and obligations as Fred's wife, but she no longer expected to find her own deep fulfillment.

Now Serena thought of Jack Hudson's neighbor who had lost his money because he thought his roof was leaking, and she remembered that Fred had successfully repaired their own roof.

Tonight, after being requested to postpone his television and early-evening snoozing, Fred lit his cigarette and remained at the table while Serena put dishes in the sink.

"You remember that Salisbury fellow I once told you about that came to the bank and opened those big accounts? Well, some strangers were in the bank today asking a lot of questions about him, and the accounts are closed. Mr. Norris acts like something is wrong, but nobody knows what's going on. I know thousands and thousands of dollars have been put in those accounts, and it's almost gone now, but the only checks withdrawing from the account were made out to Salisbury himself or to Salisbury Construction Company. I don't know what happened to all that money."

The next day Fred told Jim, his helper, about the mystery that involved "thousands and thousands of missing dollars and several strange men." The strange men were at the bank again that day and the following day. They began to be noticed by others, and, before the week was over, three-fourths of the population around Cameron was talking about the mysterious strangers at Cameron National Bank.

Chapter 11

Every weekday morning, a dozen or so of Cameron's white businessmen met at the Loudermilk Family Restaurant. A Cameron policeman wore his uniform, and the remainder always wore dark dress pants and short-sleeved, light-colored cotton shirts. In winter, an unbuttoned sports jacket, blazer, or Windbreaker was added. If Phil Anderson attended the gathering, he was always the only person who wore a tie.

Other members of the group were the assistant manager of the grocery store, one of the used-car dealers, the manager of the shirt factory, and the owner of the restaurant.

They gathered around a large round table, puffed on cigarettes, and talked while Annie, a waitress who knew the food preferences of each one, served them coffee.

The only worry previously revealed in the coffee table conversation had been about crime. For years, most local arrests had been for petty thefts or producing and selling illegal whiskey because bootlegging was a common crime. In the previous year, the revenuers working the southern Appalachian Mountains—six states plus north Georgia—had seized 5,228 stills, along with 86,416 gallons of illegal liquor, and 1.9 million gallons of mash.

Now deer-poaching arrests were described with amazement and a touch of disbelief. Deer had been considered long gone from the Georgia mountains. Now they were back in such large numbers that poaching arrests occurred frequently near Cameron.

Like whiskey-making, the poaching arrests didn't cause alarm in the general public, but, now, a number of strange things had been happening. A car-theft ring was causing everyone to lock their vehicles, which they have never done before, and rumors were circulating about airplanes flying low across the mountains during the night and dropping large packages into the Chattahoochee National Forest.

The coffee clique was worried that the packages contained cocaine or marijuana. "It couldn't be anything else," were words heard over and over again.

The distribution of illegal drugs was frightening. It was done by outsiders—people from distant large cities or even other countries. They were dangerous individuals who didn't know the unwritten rules of the mountains.

Talk of another low-flying plane was heard weekly, but no arrests had been made.

This morning, some of the caffeine drinkers were boasting about how the local high school football team had won its game on Friday night. No one ever publicly admitted it, but integration had significantly improved the sports teams at the high school, and a black student had scored two stunning touchdowns in the Friday night game.

The week before, there had been talk about the mysterious strangers at the bank, and now the subject came up again. The air became filled with more cigarette smoke than usual as the coffee drinkers speculated about the bank's sale.

Phil Anderson hadn't come for coffee since the strangers arrived. They couldn't quiz him, but if the bank was being sold, a group of strangers would come in for a detailed audit, wouldn't they?

No one in Cameron ever thought about bags of money disappearing from their bank. Money disappeared in bank robberies involving masked men and guns, and these happened in big cities like New York or Chicago. No one in this southern mountain town had ever once suspected that strangers from a distant northern town would travel to Cameron and quietly take more than a million dollars from their bank while business was being conducted as usual.

Some of the men remembered the long-ago failure of the first bank operated by the older Norris and the losses suffered by their fathers or grandfathers. But that was when banks were failing all across the nation.

"I remember my father talkin' about it. He said he didn't see how anybody cudda had much money to put in a bank. He had a little money when he worked at that big lumber mill in Helen, but it closed and moved to Mexico. He got a job at a much smaller mill, an' life was hard," said Glenn Loudermilk, the restaurant owner.

"Sometimes I wonder what people did a few years ago to make an honest livin'," said another man.

"I was able to take business classes at Habersham College, an' I worked on tha campus farm to pay tuition," Loudermilk said.

Habersham College had existed only five years and was part of President Franklin Delano Roosevelt's National Youth Administration. The students built their shop buildings, used four mules to cultivate a 310-acre farm, and even used a ceramics class to make the dishes used in the school's dining hall. It closed in 1943 after Congress ended funding of the National Youth Administration. One year later, the campus became North Georgia Trade and Vocational School, the place where Fred had learned his cabinetmaking skills.

Today, members of the coffee clique were curious about what was happening at their bank, but they saw no reason to be concerned about personal loss. If the subject of personal loss had come up, they might have talked about all banks carrying the letters "FDIC," indicating that they were members of the Federal Deposit Insurance Corporation.

The Federal Deposit Insurance Corporation had begun guaranteeing deposits of $2,500 shortly after the stock market crash of 1929. More than forty years had passed, and the guarantee had been increased four times. Now it insured deposits up to $20,000 for each depositor.

"I don't see any reason for y'all to spend the whole mornin' talkin' about what's happenin' at the bank. Let's talk about somethin' else—anything else. I was up in Blairsville yesterday, and I seen an amazin' sight," said Dick Hoyt, the used-car salesman, referring to a town deep in the mountains. He took a deep draw on his cigarette and exhaled before he said, "I heard about these people before, but I thought it was somebody's exaggeration. I ate lunch in that little country cafeteria 'cross the street from the courthouse, and some of 'em were there. I heard others say that these people prove how isolation of families in the mountains once caused interbreedin'."

"Who are you talkin' about?" someone said.

"Seven of the nosey Neals, four women an' three men. I cudden help but stare at 'em."

"Whaddaya mean?"

"There's a little community somewhere around there where everyone has very large, pointed noses. They look strange. When you look at one of 'em in profile, all you see is the nose. Everybody calls 'em the nosey Neals."

"Did you talk to 'em?"

"No. I mighta been able to talk to 'em if they'd went to the cafeteria line to get meat and vegetables, but they came in, went straight to a big table, and ordered from a waitress."

"It'd be hard fer strangers to talk to 'em anyway 'cause they don't ever look at ya and give ya a chance to speak.

"Actually, I don't believe I'da noticed just one of 'em, but seven of 'em together; that 'as impossible to ignore. The feller who told me about 'em a couple o' years ago said their last names wudden Neal, but the first person with such a nose was a Neal."

"I guess he cud always tell what his sperm was producin' if they all looked like 'im," said Loudermilk.

"I don't see how a man kin leave his mark on all his descendants, and one that's so obvious. The children I been claimin' as mine don't even look like me. Listenin' to what you're sayin' makes me wonder if they're really mine," Tony Stone, the policeman, said with sarcasm.

"Well, maybe the people who came up with the name of Cameron for our town had funny noses. I read somewhere that Cameron is the Scottish word for crooked noses. When you think about it, 'crooked noses' is a good definition for Cameron people who always want to dig into other people's business," said Taylor McIntire, manager of the shirt factory.

Others laughed at his remark, and the table became quiet.

Stone decided it was time to tell a joke. "Have y'all heard about the two guys walkin' down Main Street and seein' a dog lickin' his balls? The first guy said, 'I wish I cud do that,' and the second guy said, 'Why don't ya pet him? Maybe he'll let ya.'"

Speculation about the strangers at the bank returned as soon as the laughter died. Stone said, "Well, Paul Norris may be installin' a' instant teller. Have y'all heard about the automatic teller machine at the

First National Bank of Atlanta? They're callin' it 'Tillie the All-Time Teller.'"

"I heard 'bout that teller, and I also heard that people are afraid of it. It cost that bank a' arm and a leg, and now nobody's usin' it," Loudermilk said.

"Speakin' o' them strangers at our bank, a stranger showed up at the nursin' home yesterday and caused complete turmoil."

Every face at the table turned toward Allen Mote, the grocery store's assistant manager, as they waited for an explanation.

"Tha stranger was my mother, and she just wanted to he'p people who're unable to he'p themselves," he said.

"What happened?" asked another man.

"It was her first day as a nursin' home volunteer, an' she got there really early before the residents woke up. She wanted to make a good impression on her first day, and she went in all their rooms and took the false teeth they had sittin' in containers beside their beds. She took 'em to the kitchen sink and scrubbed 'em with a brush and special cleaner she brought from home. They was really clean when she finished."

"What caused the confusion?"

"She didn't know which teeth belonged to which person."

Before the ensuing laughter died away, someone said, "Oh, bullshit. Ya know ya mother didn't do somethin' like that. Jes' thinkin' about someone else's false teeth in my mouth is makin' me a little sick."

"Well. Believe me if ya wanna. It happened, an' if they tell my mother she can't volunteer any more, it'll break her heart."

"Don't worry about ya mother. Nursin' home patients have been known to lose their teeth when the remains on their food trays are dumped in the trash can," another man said.

"Well, I hope they make sure a trained employee is with anybody who cleans teeth in the future."

"Somebody needs to watch tha nursin' home while we watch tha bank. I got savin's there, and I wanna know what's goin' on."

"My nephew works with the Georgia Bureau of Investigation, an' he says we got a groupa hard gangsters operatin' in this area now. They think nothin' o' killin'. He calls 'em the Dixie Mafia," one man interjected.

"My neighbor's car was stole last week, and they still ain't found it," another man said.

"I don' know what this world's comin' to," said another, grinding his cigarette butt in the ash tray. "It's gettin' ta where ya can't trust anybody anymore."

Chapter 12

The next day the cement duck was still wearing a black pilgrim hat with a gold buckle, which had been put on its head before the recent Thanksgiving celebration. The tiny hat was perfectly shaped and evidently had not been harmed by the damp morning mists.

No change in the duck's attire means everything is going to be the same at the bank. The strangers are still going to be there, Serena told herself.

That same morning, the *Wall Street Journal*, the nation's respected financial newspaper, was delivered to Allen Mote's residence early, as usual, and it carried its first article about the little "back country bank" in Cameron, Georgia.

Mote always glanced at the paper's headlines before he left his house. Because this story was only four paragraphs, he casually read it. The article said a big construction company in Philadelphia had been bilked of more than one million dollars with bogus checks being run through the Cameron National Bank in north Georgia.

Mote caught his breath. He couldn't actually comprehend the amount because one million dollars was more than three hundred times his annual salary. He didn't know anyone in Philadelphia and hadn't heard that town mentioned since his high school history class.

He didn't want to believe the printed words, but knew the *Wall Street Journal* was a widely trusted newspaper. After hurriedly putting on his clothes, he drove to the grocery store. Inside, he went straight to his office and, on the store's new copy machine, he made ten duplicates of the story.

He didn't want to say a word about it to anyone until he had told his friends in the coffee group. He couldn't go to the restaurant immediately because the coffee clique didn't get together until about nine thirty. He waited until he knew his friends were there, then drove to the restaurant, walked inside the front door, and strode to the table without speaking to anyone. At the table, he silently handed out copies of the story. His friends could tell by his face that something was terribly wrong. Each began reading his copy of the newspaper article, and all were silent.

Finally, one of the men said, "This must be some kinda mistake."

Another asked, "How cud our bank here in Cameron become mixed up with somebody in Philadelphia, 'specially a big construction comp'ny?"

No one responded. According to the article, someone had lost more than a million dollars. Was it the Cameron bank? "Now I guess we know why all those strangers are here. Now we know why Phil's not been comin' for coffee," Mote said.

The men were silent again, and all were deadly serious as each pair of eyes darted around the table to this face and that face. If laughter and jokes were at one end of the spectrum of emotions, their attitudes this morning were near the opposite end.

Stone said, "Well, my daddy liked to quote President Roosevelt, who said money was safer in a bank than under tha mattress, but I don't wanna take a chance."

He got up to leave the table, and others also got up to begin walking to the front to pay. No one stayed to talk.

Within fifteen minutes, Mote, Stone, and Loudermilk were at the bank, glancing at each other somewhat sheepishly. Only Stone had admitted his intentions, but all three were there to withdraw their funds and close their accounts. The fact that their deposits were insured did not matter to them. Money had disappeared from the bank, and they wanted to withdraw theirs as quickly as possible.

Mote followed Loudermilk at Serena's window, and, before he closed his accounts, he handed her his last copy of the *Wall Street Journal* article. She glanced at the paper long enough to see the headline and the words "Cameron National Bank." They were both silent, and she read the entire article as soon as he left. It shut down her mind. She handed the article over to Joyce, and neither spoke.

The three men were the first of several people that day who came by the bank and withdrew all their personal funds.

The next morning, the bank did not open its doors. Reporters from several newspapers joined a number of depositors on the sidewalk, and occasionally someone would try to see inside, but the glass front and all windows had been covered. No one inside was visible, although their cars were outside in the parking lot.

Serena, Joyce, and other employees reported to work as always, but they had nothing to do. Occasionally they heard someone beating on the door or a window and shouting demands that the bank be opened.

That afternoon, the *Daily Times*, a newspaper in Gainesville, reported the swindle, saying that seventeen fraudulent checks from Merrill Construction Company in Philadelphia had been written on a check-writing machine between the dates of September 7 and October 1. The checks had been deposited in the Cameron National Bank, and, during the following days, large amounts of cash were withdrawn from the account several times.

An Atlanta FBI agent was quoted in the article who said, "It's probably the biggest and smoothest thing that has happened in this area."

The article also said authorities weren't releasing names or suggesting suspects.

A man had walked into the bank on September 7 and opened two accounts, the report said. "US Assistant Attorney Jack Newsom described the man as five feet six inches tall, weighing 135 to 140 pounds, and twenty-eight to thirty-two years old. 'He spoke perfect English and appeared to be well educated. He had longish, wavy black hair combed straight back and a Fu Manchu beard,' Newsom said."

Newsom, who was in the US Attorney's office in Atlanta, said the case would be presented to a federal grand jury. "This man Salisbury said he had an address here in Atlanta, and we don't know if he was using his real name. No one has been able to find him yet," Newsom was quoted in the article.

The next day the Salisbury bank statements, which had been mailed to the Atlanta address Salisbury had provided, were returned to Cameron National Bank with the words "Insufficient Address." Serena handed the returned mail to an FBI agent, and she later learned that the street number given by Salisbury was on a vacant lot.

The daily newspaper in Gainesville ran Cameron National Bank stories each day, and, although it was the talk of the town, the weekly newspaper located in Cameron didn't report anything about the bank's problems.

The publisher of the *Cameron Record* used his pages to report minor happenings and could not report news about the bank that hadn't already been reported in the daily papers. Getting comments from local residents for an article about the bank would be almost impossible because people were intimidated and frightened. He also was afraid he would lose advertising by writing words about such a large robbery almost in his front yard. Board members of the bank owned other businesses in Cameron, and they could pull their ads out of the *Record*. The publisher was as shocked and perplexed as anyone else about the bank's problems, but he didn't want his newspaper to lose money.

The FBI called in the bank's board members and other citizens for questioning. Why would someone in Philadelphia select a little country bank more than 700 miles away to use for his dirty work? Who in Cameron was the insider in this swindle? Who was the real Jarvis Salisbury?

Chapter 13

On Friday, Serena, Joyce, Phil, and the other bank employees were told to wait at home until they were called. Their salaries would continue, but the bank was temporarily closed, and their services were not needed until it opened again. They were not told anything except to "wait at home next week."

Serena suddenly faced no set schedule. She felt like her future had been canceled, and her life was on hold. For twelve of her early years, she had gone to school, and, for the nearly twenty years since school, she had gone to work daily. Breaks in these routines had been planned well in advance. They were either for vacations or caring for a new baby. Now she faced empty days. She was alone in the house with no work, nothing planned.

On her first two weekday mornings at home, she went through the routine motions of getting her family off as if she herself was going to work as always.

She knew that she could visit other women in the area who did not work outside the home. But she didn't really know them and also knew that they frowned on her decisions as a working mother. They believed a mother should stay by her young children all day each day and breast-feed her newborn babies instead of using infant formula.

Being a good mother had always been Serena's highest priority, but her job was necessary. She had once been weighed down with guilt about not being a stay-at-home mother who breast-fed her babies. The fact that both daughters had thrived on infant formula did little to relieve her. She planned some kind of special family activity every weekend and paid Mrs. Parker, a neighbor, to care for her girls during the week. The neighbor cared for several children, including her own, and by the time they were walking, Penny and Nicole were enjoying having playmates.

When Nicole was born, fourteen-month-old Penny did not go to the neighbor's house for six weeks. But she had no one her age to play with at home. She liked to look at Nicole and frequently offered her a rattle to play with. But Nicole was a newborn infant who could not yet hold the rattle.

Serena did not realize how much the other children meant to Penny until she decided one day to visit Mrs. Parker. She wanted to arrange new day care for Nicole, and Penny began laughing and squealing with delight the minute she drove up to the front of Mrs. Parker's house. Instead of walking to the door with her mother, who was carrying her baby sister, Penny had hurried up the walkway as fast as her small legs could carry her.

Inside, young Penny stopped and stared silently at the other children. After about two minutes, she walked slowly over to one of the other toddlers. The other child, who was slightly older, smiled, and Penny must have interpreted it as a friendly welcome. She began to run here and there to the other children. If Serena wondered whether Penny enjoyed her day-care playmates, all doubts were removed when she took Penny's hand to lead her to the car. Penny burst into tears.

When Penny had her twelfth birthday, Mrs. Parker began paying her a small amount to help with the little children during the summer months. She later did the same for Nicole, and both girls loved to talk about having "a job."

Now, finding herself at home in the middle of the week without prior vacation plans left Serena at a loss. She had made no plans for any kind of activity. She liked to make clothes for herself, but she felt too unsettled to put dress patterns together. She didn't know what to do with her time.

She had read almost every book in the library when she was in high school. She knew she could find new books there now, but she didn't want to read because she knew she wouldn't be able to concentrate.

She called Joyce about ten AM and invited her to come and visit.

Before she could finish saying the words, Joyce invited her to come to her house in Cameron. "You should drive by the bank and see those people still standing outside," Joyce said.

Serena accepted the invitation, changed her housecoat for a cotton house dress with small flower print, put on a long-sleeved red cardigan, left her house, and drove to Cameron. She felt uncomfortable driving by the bank in the middle of a weekday morning, and she saw the people standing outside. One was Jack Hudson, and Serena wondered what she herself would do if she had been depositing every extra penny in the bank to give her children a college education. *I know Mr. Hudson is worried sick,* she thought.

She wondered who was seeing her as she drove by. At Joyce's house, she pulled into the driveway and hurried down the walkway. Joyce, dressed in jeans and a pullover sweater, met her at the door. At the kitchen table, she sipped a fresh cup of coffee as Joyce told her about some of the people she had seen pounding on the bank door.

"We've been told for years that our deposits are totally safe. Why can't Mr. Norris or someone announce that to the community now?" Serena asked Joyce.

"You know I can't answer that question. I feel like I don't know anything now," Joyce said.

"Do you have any idea where this Jarvis Salisbury came from? Have you heard anyone mention him or say they knew him?" Serena said.

"I've never heard his name anywhere except when he came in the bank and made those deposits and withdrawals," Joyce answered.

"On that first day he came in, Phil said he had fake sideburns, but I couldn't tell they were fake. Did you look at them?" Serena said.

"I barely looked at him when he came in. He usually came by your window and then went into Mr. Norris's office. He seemed so sure of himself and so different from our usual customers, I was glad I didn't have to speak to him," Joyce said.

"I wonder why he always had to have cash and so much of it. None of our other customers operates like that. It looks like Mr. Norris would have been suspicious of him," Serena said.

"Mr. Norris obviously thought it was okay for him to need so much cash. It looks like Salisbury was not his real name, and I wish the cash he carried out of our bank had not been real," Joyce said.

"Someone in this town knows who he really is. Someone brought him here to use our bank in the swindle. I just wish the FBI could find that local person and arrest him. Right now, people are looking at you and me and wondering if it's us," Serena said.

"I know," Joyce answered, and neither said anything for a couple of minutes.

"What will we do if the bank closes permanently?" Serena said. "I'll have to find another job, and I have to work at a place that offers hospitalization insurance."

"Surely the bank won't close. Won't the FDIC make the loss good?" Joyce said and answered her own question. "I wonder if it's the bank's loss or the Merrill Company's loss. I wonder if the FDIC covers phony checks."

Both women wondered aloud when the bank would open again for business.

Chapter 14

Leaving Joyce's house, Serena did not want to return home. She desperately wanted to find out who had taken all that money from Cameron National Bank, but didn't know how she could go about it. For the first time in her life, she realized how much she loved her home and the town where she worked. But someone in Cameron had helped steal more than a million dollars from the bank. She really didn't know the people of Cameron, after all.

Why would someone from Philadelphia ever come to the bank in Cameron? Why would they even know about the bank?

After all, strangers always cruised through Cameron without stopping. Unlike many of the other towns in northeast Georgia, Cameron did not have a downtown theme to attract tourists. It did not have a personality, like Helen, which was beginning to promote its Alpine theme, or Dahlonega, which had its gold-mining history and gold museum.

Travelers coming by Cameron looked at the local scenery as they motored to the mountains a few miles farther north and stopped only if they needed a gasoline fill-up or a quick bite to eat.

Instead of going home, Serena drove around Cameron on small streets she had never seen before and thought about Cameron and its people.

Located about 1,500 feet above sea level, Cameron was like all the other small towns in the foothills of the Blue Ridge Mountains, the southernmost portion of Appalachia.

If one of the local stores or services was doing business in Philadelphia, it had to be an action that did not come through the bank, perhaps something underhanded and deceitful. Serving a population of slightly more than 3,000 were two gas stations, a popular women's clothing store, a farm supply store, a gun shop, a small supermarket, two used-car lots, two quick-order cafés, the family-operated restaurant, a drug store where medical prescriptions were filled, the weekly newspaper, and the bank. The only department store had been in operation for more than fifty years and still had its original wooden floors, which were regularly oiled to prevent dust from being stirred up when the floors were swept.

These businesses in the core of town were all locally owned because big corporations with their chain stores did not think a business in Cameron would be profitable. *I've never seen the word "Philadelphia" or the name of any other distant city on the paper I handle,* Serena thought.

Life in all these small mountain towns was quiet, with no big surprises. Adults worked quietly, day by day, for what could be described only as "a livable wage," and a person who was described as "well-to-do" was a steady, dependable character plodding away at the same job he'd had for many years. Serena knew from her experience at work that the average annual salary in and around Cameron was lower than the state of Georgia's average, and Georgia was never far from the bottom when the US Census Bureau ranked states by annual per capita income.

A person in Cameron who wanted to steal money would be pleased with a hundred dollars and never think about taking a million. No Cameron person would have believed that the bank actually had a million dollars, Serena thought.

Cameron residents followed the same reserved lifestyle as their ancestors, with some of the local people still believing that the landing of Apollo 11 on the moon two years earlier had been faked by the Washington government. The last local mystery Serena had heard about was when bank customers were asking who had caused the train to stop.

Each morning and each evening, the Southern Crescent passenger train passed through Cameron on its 1,377-mile trip from New York to New Orleans. The diesel locomotive usually didn't stop and whistled continuous, lonesome cries to warn drivers on the highway who might be approaching the railroad crossing.

Commercial aviation and interstate highways had robbed both the trains and bus lines of most long-distance travelers, but the engineer sometimes stopped the train because he had been notified that a passenger wished to get either off or on in Cameron. This happened so rarely that people talked about it and wanted to know who had caused the passenger train to stop. Where were they going? Where had they been?

With so little happening in Cameron, information about a train passenger was passed around quickly before talk returned to what some politician was doing, something about the local football, baseball, or basketball teams or who was dating whom.

Cameron's largest employers—a shirt factory and a poultry producer—were also locally owned. Serena had cousins and former classmates working in both places. More than one hundred women operated the sewing or cutting machines and pinning tables at the shirt factory. Ten years earlier, when John F. Kennedy was campaigning for president of the United States, Serena had tried to talk about the election with women who worked in the sewing plant. The woman she contacted, Serena's former classmate, said she didn't know much about the election, only that Kennedy was a Catholic.

"My niece in Atlanta married a Catholic, and my whole family has been heartbroken," Serena's friend had said. "We don't never see her anymore. She's gone from our lives, and I can't never vote for a Catholic."

Serena, who had attended a Protestant church all her life, was a Kennedy supporter, but she decided it would do no good to explain his intentions as president.

"At work, we break for mornin' coffee or lunch, an' nobody never mentions politics or government policies. The only thing I know is I wud never vote for a Catholic," her former classmate said. "But we're all members of the Ladies Garment Workers Union," she added with pride.

Decades earlier, labor unions had gained better living wages for workers across the nation, and textile workers across the Southeast had become involved in the nation's largest strike in 1934. The strike had failed miserably, and, now, thirty-seven years later, southeastern workers remained unorganized and antiunion.

The Ladies Garment Workers Union had gained membership at textile plants such as the Cameron shirt factory only because it was fighting competition from foreign imports.

A couple of Serena's male classmates had found enough money to build one or two large poultry houses, both originally saying they wanted to grow chickens so they wouldn't have to take orders from other people. They now were doing well in the poultry business, but each had to exactly follow the producer's instructions for feeding and housing thousands of birds. They still were not their own bosses.

The poultry producer provided baby chicks and feed to the farm families who grew the chickens into meaty broilers. At market time, the weight of the birds determined how much the farmers would be paid. After slaughter at the producer's processing plant, the meat was cleaned, packed in ice, and shipped in refrigerated containers to other cities, other states, and other countries.

I guess frozen poultry products would bring distant strangers into Cameron if anything did, Serena thought. She had been amazed to learn that almost every portion of the broilers was sold for food, either for humans or for dogs and cats. She remembered laughing when a bank customer told her about the chicken feet being shipped across the Atlantic to become part of the cuisine for people in China and South Africa. In both these countries, the small bones in the feet were removed, and the cooked tendons and cartilage were eaten. In China, the fried, boiled, and marinated chicken feet were called "Phoenix talons." In the South African cities of Soweto and Durban, the boiled, seasoned, and grilled chicken feet were known as "walkie talkies."

Even the first travelers in this area 200 years ago did not stop in Cameron, Serena thought. Those travelers had lived on the sea coast but had wanted to be in the Georgia mountains so much that they made the 300-mile trip in wagons pulled by mules or oxen. They had gone about ten miles past Cameron to build summer homes near Clarkesville, the county seat of Habersham County. They had resided there from June until November each year in order to escape the hot weather and coastal diseases such as malaria. The visits continued every summer until the War Between the States and the following long years of economic hardship.

More than once, Serena had enjoyed visiting Clarkesville's historic churches, built by those first summer visitors. One was a small Episcopal church with a balcony built especially to serve the slaves.

Organized religious faith steers our community ship, Serena thought. After all, Habersham County was located deep in the Bible Belt, and many Protestant churches allowed residents a choice in denominations. Now, there was even one church of the Catholic faith.

All the homes Serena passed as she drove around Cameron were similar. They were typical one-story wooden structures painted white. Some had dark green or black window shutters. Serena knew the homes were all similar because even the smallest difference could mark a person, and residents wanted to fit in.

Turning up Highway 197 back to Batesville, Serena knew she wasn't any closer to finding an answer to her questions. *How could someone in Philadelphia have come to Cameron and used our bank for a giant swindle? Who in Cameron had friends or relatives in Philadelphia? Who in Cameron had the ability to perform such an unbelievable scam?*

Chapter 15

About nine o'clock Thursday morning, Serena decided to get in her car and go see her grandmother, who was the only mother she had ever known. The elderly woman, called Mama Tatum by almost all who knew her, lived near another of the mountain's "C towns."

Mama Tatum had once said she couldn't understand why so many towns in northeast Georgia had to be named a word beginning with "C." In addition to Cameron, there were the neighboring towns of Clarkesville, Cornelia, Cleveland, Clayton, Commerce, Cumming, and a little community called Clermont.

When thinking of the "C towns," Serena always remembered a little village in the mountains called Choestoe, a Cherokee Indian word that meant "Land of the Dancing Rabbits."

And she couldn't forget the beautiful Chattahoochee River winding down out of the mountains.

Children in the local schools always had to memorize a long poem about the river written by Sidney Lanier back in 1877 and called "Song of the Chattahoochee." The river originated in White County, flowed along the Habersham County line, splashed into the adjoining Hall County, and traveled on through the flat lands between Georgia and Alabama before it ended in the Gulf of Mexico. North Georgia residents valued the poet and "Song of the Chattahoochee" so highly that a man-made body of water, seventy-three square miles of surface, mostly in Hall County, had been named Lake Sidney Lanier.

Serena recited the poem's beginning words to herself as she thought about the stream.

Out of the hills of Habersham
Down through the valleys of Hall
I hurry amain to reach the plain
Rush the rapid and leap the fall.
Split at the rock and together again
Accept my bed or narrow or wide
And flee from folly on every side.

Today, Serena completely understood the last words for the first time in her life. She definitely wanted to flee from folly on every side.

Mama Tatum lived in the Nacoochee Valley near Cleveland. The word Nacoochee was a Cherokee Indian word meaning "evening star," and the beautiful Nacoochee Valley adorned its wooded mountain surroundings in the same way that the brilliantly white Venus planet, also called the evening star, sometimes adorned the nighttime sky immediately after sunset.

Serena drove toward Lynch Mountain and crossed Chickamauga Creek, a tributary of the Chattahoochee. Driving into the green Nacoochee, surrounded by blue and purple mountains, Serena thought of her childhood and the valley's long history.

She had spent many hours in the forest and along the streams when she wasn't in school or reading a book. She knew where the rare pink lady's slippers grew wild and knew where to find the orange wild azaleas in the springtime. In autumn, she knew where to find the biggest and juiciest muscadine grapes, both the black ones and the dark purple ones. She also knew the best places in the streams to find the larger minnows that they called horny heads. Once she even found a perfectly carved Indian arrowhead and for weeks dreamed about the Indian braves and maidens who, more than a century earlier, had walked along the same forest paths.

Now, the situation at the bank made her feel that doom was pending in her life. The Cherokee Indians, who once lived in north Georgia, had probably felt the same sense of approaching disaster before they were removed from their homes. Like Serena, the Cherokees faced misfortune because of acts outside their control.

When the first white explorers had come into the Nacoochee Valley more than 400 years earlier, a large band of Cherokee Indians had lived there and had buried their dead with enough wampum beads and pottery to use in the next world. Some of the burials had taken place under a large mound of dirt in the center of the village. The ancient mound had been created by another culture that lived there before the Cherokees, a people known only as the Moundbuilders. On top of the ancient mound had sat the Cherokee band's council house.

The Cherokees had welcomed the first white men and had given them dogs as gifts. Serena had read that the dogs presented to the white men had been trained to hunt bears, but all dogs she had ever known had been loving pets, and she imagined the Indians' dogs were the same.

Years later, the Cherokees emulated the white man's ways. An Indian named Sequoya had spent years creating a writing system for their language, calling papers containing the words "Talking Leaves." The tribe became literate and formed the first American Indian newspaper called the Cherokee Phoenix, first published in 1828. The Cherokee also adopted their own written constitution and formed their own sovereign nation.

The discovery of gold in northeast Georgia in 1828, the same year the Cherokee Phoenix was first published, brought vast change. People came from everywhere and entered the new Cherokee nation to dig for riches. The Georgia government began serious efforts to remove all Native Americans, who referred to this period as "The Great Intrusion."

Cherokee leaders fought back through legal means but eventually became discouraged and signed a treaty agreeing to depart. All the Cherokee Indians in north Georgia were herded together with Indians from adjoining states. History books said the total number of Cherokees was 16,000 and that 7,000 mounted US troops marched them 1,200 miles to land reserved for them in what later became Oklahoma.

It was 1838, and an estimated 4,000 of the Indians died on the trail.

Some of the educated Cherokees wrote letters to friends and family members hidden throughout the mountains. The letters told of the illness, starvation, and deaths, and the march became known as the Trail of Tears.

Mama Tatum's own great-great-grandmother had been a Cherokee who was married to a white man, but she had died before the march. Her half-Cherokee great-grandmother had also been married to a white man, and she was among the Indians who hid in the mountains of North Carolina.

These ancestors meant that a trace of Cherokee blood flowed in Serena's veins.

"Our nation's forefathers risked their lives establishing freedom for people in this country, but it was freedom only for white men. We are still struggling for freedom for women and people of other races," Mama Tatum had once said.

As a teen visiting at the house of one of her school friends, Serena had been shown a letter that had been carefully preserved in an old family Bible for almost 150 years. It had been written in English by one of the Cherokees on the Trail of Tears.

The handwriting was beautiful, the English grammar perfect, the words expressing the writer's grief because he was forced to leave the only home he had ever known. He asked his friends to take care of the house and garden that he had left behind. His letter sounded as though he hoped to return, but no Cherokees on "The Trail Where We Cried" ever returned to their Georgia homes. Many of their houses were burned, and his home probably did not survive.

Looking at what was left of the Nacoochee Valley burial mound where the Cherokees had buried some of their dead, Serena felt more than her usual sadness.

The mound was located in valuable farmland, and, after the Cherokees were gone, plowing had greatly diminished its original size. Many decades later, another family had bought the area and turned the burial mound and its surrounding acreage into green pastureland. The family put a fence around the mound and placed a beautiful white wooden gazebo on top. Almost like a crown, the gazebo had remained there after members of that family were gone from the valley. Everyone who passed now saw that the ancient Indian mound was protected and honored.

Unless the passersby knew local history, however, they did not know that the green valley had been loved by humankind for at least a thousand years, because that's when the Moundbuilders had piled up the dirt, maybe as a place for their council house or maybe as a place for their temple.

Today, Serena stopped thinking about the beauty and history of the valley when she turned into a dirt road toward Mama Tatum's house. She hoped her grandmother would be home and not out roaming her pastures. She always shared any major personal problem with Mama Tatum and depended on her words to help her make a good decision. This time she needed a better perspective on what was happening at the Cameron National Bank.

Chapter 16

On the dirt road between two green pastures belonging to Mama Tatum, Serena saw her grandmother's Hereford cattle, about thirty head. Mama Tatum sometimes lost money on the calves that the herd produced, but her life was centered on them, and she would have been lost doing anything else.

Mama Tatum's pastures were kept in top condition, and the cattle crossed from one grazing section to another through a tunnel under the road. A neighbor's bull was used to impregnate the cattle, and chemical hormones were used to get as many cows as possible ready to breed at the same time. This required the bull only once each year, and calves were born during the same time period.

The white frame two-story house with six large rooms had been Serena's childhood home, and her deceased mother had been born in the house more than fifty-three years ago.

Rufus, a big, brown mixed-breed dog, barked a message to Mama Tatum, then ran to meet Serena's car before she got to the driveway. The dog bounded happily beside the driver's door almost smiling through the window at Serena as she drove the last few yards and stopped.

Her grandmother walked out the front door and stood smiling as Serena walked up three wooden steps to the porch and into her arms.

"What a wonderful surprise!" Mama Tatum said.

"I just wanted to see you. I hope you have time for a visit," Serena answered.

"You ain't been to see me since Labor Day weekend, and you ain't been here in the middle of the week since you got married. Is something wrong? Come in the house. I'll make some fresh coffee."

Mama Tatum was seventy-six years old, but her dark hair had only the faintest traces of gray. She wore a pale blue cotton dress and a white sweater. Both the sweater and the dress had bulging pockets, probably filled with handkerchiefs, peppermint candies, and cough drops, all wrapped in cellophane paper, and maybe a couple of one-dollar bills with a few pennies, nickels, and dimes. Serena could see a red, shiny object in one sweater pocket. It looked like an apple—a Rome Beauty.

Mama Tatum looked the way she always looked—calm, comfortable, and prepared for any small emergency such as a tickling throat, a runny nose, or a hungry stomach. Serena felt better just looking at her.

"I already walked over the back pasture this morning. I'm gonna have to get Wilbur to come over and check the fence over at them chinaberry trees. It looks like we're gonna have trouble there, and I was just about to call 'im when you drove up," Mama Tatum said, talking about a neighborhood handyman who regularly helped her on the farm.

"Have you heard about the bank?" Serena didn't mean to blurt out the words without even asking about Mama Tatum's health, but they were out before she could stop.

"Which bank? What's the matter?" Mama Tatum said.

"The Cameron National Bank where I work has lost more than one million dollars. The FBI is here. They're investigating, and Mr. Norris sent everyone home. I can't imagine how this has happened. It doesn't seem real to me."

"Come in here and sit down. Ya can tell me about it while we drink some coffee," Mama Tatum said.

They walked through the house into the kitchen, and Serena's grandmother put fresh grounds and water in a percolator before she took two white china cups and saucers decorated with small pink roses from a cupboard.

"Let me go feed Rufus before we talk. He's waitin' fer me," Mama T said.

Both women were seated at the table with the cups of hot coffee in front of them before either spoke again.

"If all of this at the bank is true, who did it? I guess that's what bothers me the most. Who did it?" Serena said.

"Just start at the beginning, and tell me about it," Mama Tatum said.

Serena told about the disturbing man with a Yankee accent and the mustache who had opened two accounts, then evidently withdrew cash in small bills and carried it away.

"He called himself Jarvis Salisbury. He never did business with anyone except Mr. Norris. Mr. Norris took his deposits, and when he came in for cash, Mr. Norris would have it ready for him. It was a strange situation from the beginning. I don't know why he had to have a lot of small bills. One time he took the bills out in a big brown paper bag. But I can't believe Mr. Norris knew the money was going to disappear," Serena said.

"I guess yer feelin' bad now 'cause you really don't know who ta believe. You don't know which one o' yer friends ya can trust," Mama Tatum said.

"You're right. At this moment, I don't know which person is my real friend. And they don't know if I'm their friend. I don't know which person I can talk with about this. I don't know which way to turn."

Mama Tatum looked at Serena and didn't answer immediately. Then she said, "I felt thataway once. It happened here in the valley. Sometimes I still worry about it."

"What could have made you feel that way, Mama T? Haven't you always worked here on the farm?"

"Oh, sure. I always worked on tha farm, but I also did business with a lot of people off tha farm. What I'm talkin' about happened about twenty-five years ago. I think you were in grammar school at the time, and I probably didn't talk to ya about it. I'll tell ya now if ya feel like listenin'. I don't know if it'll make ya feel better er not."

Serena stood up, went to Mama T, and put her arm around her thin shoulders. "It makes me feel better just to be here with you. Please tell me."

"Well, back in tha '50s, a man here in this county started lookin' through deeds at the courthouse and found some valuable parcels of land that were privately owned but didden have clear titles. They were located either inside or bordering the Chattahoochee National Forest. I don't know how he did it exactly, but I believe taxes hadden been paid on these properties for two or more years. He'd file a quitclaim deed on tha property conveyin' tha supposed ownership ta 'is brother. He and 'is brother would start payin' taxes on tha property, all without the real owner knowin' it. A few years later, the second brother ud sell tha land back to tha first brother for 'one dollar an' other valuable considerations.'

"He 'as able to get title to some valuable property thataway, an' I had a widow friend who lived on a prime piece o' mountain property beside the Chattahoochee River. You could sit on her front porch an' watch tha river go by. She'd heard rumors about this man's deceitful actions, an' he knocked on her door one day an' wanted ta buy her land.

"She refused 'is offer, an' somebody started botherin' her. She started findin' big logs across her driveway, too big fer 'er to move. Each time, she cudden get her car out 'til she called somebody an' paid 'em to come move tha log.

"Her telephone ud ring in the middle of the night, but, when she answered, tha caller ud hang up.

"She was elderly, lived alone an' had no children. Of course, she became a bundle of nerves. She suspected tha man who wanted to buy her property. Maybe he thought that if her life became miserable, she'd sell her property ta him and move away. Several times she asked the sheriff to do somethin', but there wudden anything he cud do 'less she took outa warrant. She cudden take outa warrant fer this man without real proof that he uz the one.

"I was really worried about her, an' I knew one o' tha sheriff's deputies that I cud trust. I told 'im about this land problem my friend was havin', and he began investigatin'. I think he was findin' real evidence of some kind of major land swap skullduggery involving the federal government and tha national forest lands. But he died. He never hadda chance to do anything about what he found."

"Was he sick?" Serena asked.

"No. No one has never come up with a believable story about his death. He had a wife and young child. One morning, 'is wife left tha house to take their kid to school. When she got back home she found 'im in the floor, dead, with a plastic bag over 'is head. The sheriff said he committed suicide. But you tell me—would it be possible to keep a plastic bag over yer own head long enough to completely stop breathin'? The bag would haveta be airtight, an' I don't know how that cud be done. I still think about 'im and about his wife and child. She moved away, and I don't know where she is today."

"Did you feel responsible for his death because you got him to look into the problem?" Serena asked.

"Not really responsible, but I asked 'im to he'p my friend. What happened to 'im? I don't believe it was a suicide. I know how interested he was in exposin' those land-grab deals with the quitclaim deeds. I know how much he loved his family. It was so hard fer me to believe he woudda committed suicide," Mama T said.

"If there is someone around here who murdered that deputy, do you think he's involved in the missing million dollars at Cameron National Bank?" Serena said.

"Oh, no. My friend's problems with her land ended shortly after the deputy's death. Now, too much time has passed. I'm just tellin' ya about this 'cause I was real scared back then. I didn't know who I could trust, the same as ya don't know who ya can trust today. It's amazin' that if ya suddenly don't know who ta trust, yer life instantly becomes topsy-turvy. Ya begin ta feel like a ship without a rudder."

"Mama Tatum, you always help me put things in perspective. There are a lot of evil people in this world who can make the rest of us feel miserable," Serena said.

"Now, wait a minute, honey. Don't think for one minute that the world's fulla evil folks. We talked about two incidents here this morning, and I guess maybe we talked about one-tenth of one percent o' the population. No, not even that many. We talked about maybe two or three people who're evil among the thousands o' folks who go ta church ever' Sunday an' try to live good lives. Folks who don't go ta church also do good stuff for others. Air lives are filled with good people."

"But I hear so much about bad, evil people," Serena said.

"It's 'cause we need ta know as much as we can about what the bad people are doin'. It's air duty to prevent 'em from hurting other folks. We talk about evil people a lot, and the newspapers and radio stations always have stories about crimes o' bad people. That's 'cause they scare us, and we have ta guard against 'em, not because there's a great number of them," Serena's grandmother said.

Serena took another sip of coffee and didn't respond.

"Ya need to go back home an' get ya family ready for Christmas. Ever'thang'll be okay."

"I love you, Mama T. I'm so lucky to have you. But I won't be able to think about Christmas or anything else until I know who caused this disaster at the bank."

Chapter 17

The next day Serena decided she would do something really special for her family. After all, it was Friday, and she didn't have to be away from the house.

She took out her recipe books and began planning a very special supper. She would cook a small beef roast, candied sweet potatoes, and green beans, prepare a fresh green salad, and make a fresh coconut cake. She rarely made such a cake because it took so much time and effort, but today she had no excuse.

She would make vegetable soup in the Crock-Pot for the following week. She could serve it with fresh, hot cornbread.

Her spirits rose as she began to make a list for the grocery store. Making plans about what she would do kept her busy and kept her from thinking so much about the bank and her job.

At the grocery store with her list, she realized that she couldn't remember a time in the morning in the middle of the week that she had been at the grocery store with a long list of items to buy. She picked up a flat container holding thirty eggs and placed it in the cart. Next were a head of iceberg lettuce and the sweet potatoes.

It was not the season for vine-ripened tomatoes, so the salad would have to be only a wedge of lettuce. She would make a special dressing that the girls always liked. It was a mixture of tomato ketchup, mayonnaise, diced boiled eggs, a dash of salt, and a spoonful of sugar.

Serena stopped to look at the coconuts, and a woman came close to her and whispered, "They finally caught Paul Norris, didn't they?"

Did I understand this woman? What is she saying?

"I don't know what you're talking about," Serena said.

"Ever'body 'round here knows Paul Norris took that money, and the FBI oughta see that he pays for what he's done," the woman said.

"I don't know what you're talking about," Serena repeated. "Paul Norris has not done anything wrong," she said, as she quickly moved away.

"I guess y'all were he'pin' Mr. Norris," the woman said louder. "Ever'body knows somebody in tha bank is friends with somebody at that Philadelphia construction comp'ny. They ain't no other way them checks wudda been put in the Cameron bank."

Serena couldn't believe her ears. The woman didn't do business with the bank, and Serena wanted to get out of the store and away from her immediately. She didn't want to change her plans for supper, however, so she picked up the remaining items on her list as quickly as she could. She could feel the woman watching. She felt as if everyone in the store was watching.

At home she prepared the potatoes and onions to begin cooking the vegetable soup. Lima beans and whole kernel corn came from the canned goods in her cabinet. She used the home-canned tomatoes that Mama T had given her over the summer. The beef roast came from the freezer, a product of one of Mama T's grain-fed Herefords. At least one heifer was always kept for the family and fed a finishing diet of corn grown especially for it. This roast would be tasty and tender because it was perfectly marbled.

When she was a child, Serena had tried to make pets of the calves as soon as they were born on the farm. She had become strongly attached to one big-eyed bovine that she called Beauty. She always gave the calf pieces of lettuce or handfuls of grass, and Beauty followed her when she roamed in the pasture. She considered Beauty her special friend. When her pet heifer was loaded up with the others and taken to the auction barn in Gainesville, she had cried for days. Mama T had tried to console her by saying that more calves would come. But Serena had learned her lesson, and she never again grew attached to any of the cattle.

She prepared each dish for supper with special care, but she was almost in a daze. *Is everyone thinking the same thing that the woman at the grocery store was saying?*

She prepared her golden cake batter, poured it evenly into three nine-inch pans, and placed the pans in the oven. After cracking the coconut with a hammer, she removed the meat from the shell and grated it into a bowl. After the cake layers were cooked, she emptied them from the pans onto wire racks to cool. While the cake layers were cooling, she put four egg whites, corn syrup, sugar, cream of tartar, a pinch of salt, and water in the top of a double boiler. She beat the mixture with a hand-held electric mixer until it became shiny and thick, then added vanilla flavoring. Placing the cake layers on a plate, she carefully sprinkled each one with a teaspoon of the fresh coconut milk, which was followed by the white frosting and grated fresh coconut. With the three layers stacked, she covered the edge of the cake with the remaining frosting and coconut.

Throughout the afternoon she thought of the woman at the grocery store and her comment about Mr. Norris and all the bank employees.

The roast, sweet potatoes, beans, and rolls were finished when Fred and the girls came in about five thirty.

Penny said, "Something smells good." Nicole said, "What have you been doing?"

"I've prepared a special supper for us," Serena said.

"Are we celebrating something?" Nicole said.

"Yes, we're celebrating being a family," Serena said, smiling at both of them.

Penny saw the fresh coconut cake and put her arms around Serena. "I'm so glad you're my mother," she said. "Me too," chimed Nicole.

Serena's pride had been deeply wounded by the words of the woman in the grocery store. Her daughters' words were like healing salve.

After everyone was seated at the table, Penny said, "Let's hold hands and pray. Mom, will you say the prayer?"

Serena, seated between the two girls, reached for each hand, while Fred did the same, and heads were bowed.

"Dear heavenly Father, thank you for this family, and thank you for our many blessings. Please be with Mr. Norris and the other people at the bank. Please let them get this problem solved quickly. Thank you for this food, and please help the FBI find the guilty party," Serena said.

"Amen," said Fred. "This is a good way to have our evening meal because everybody is wondering who at the bank took that money."

Chapter 18

The doors of the Cameron National Bank were closed to the public for only one week, and Serena and the others were back to perform their usual duties on Monday, but customers were almost nonexistent. Signs announcing that deposits at the bank were insured had been placed on the bank's doors. Four suited strangers were still there, but they did not question bank employees again.

The cement duck was wearing a pale blue wrap and appeared to be carrying a tiny blue umbrella as Serena drove home on Wednesday evening. The weather forecaster must have said rain, and that would be good for the pansies she had planted in her yard the previous Thursday. She had stopped at a home with a sign in the yard advertising the flowers and bought stocky plants filled with buds. Pansies bloomed during the winter months, and she planted them in the full sun on each side of her rock walkway. Their tiny faces would welcome her home at the end of each workday.

At home, the vegetable soup, beef roast, and coconut cake were gone. Fred had taken a large portion of the cake to his shop to share with his helper. Serena took a ground beef casserole out of the refrigerator. She had made it during the weekend and planned to serve it two evenings during the week. This way, she wouldn't have to be in the kitchen so much after getting home.

The girls walked through the door in a heated discussion about an incident that had happened on the school bus. A boy they thought was cute had apparently whispered something to another boy, then looked toward them and laughed. Penny thought he was talking about her friendship with Vernon Waters, the new student whose family had opened a store in Helen. Nicole thought they were talking about her too-tight skirt.

"Mom, when are the FBI agents going to arrest someone about that bank robbery," Penny asked. "The other students are talking about it, and they stop talking when I get close enough to hear them."

"Me, too," said Nicole. "Sometimes I feel like they are saying that my mother is the one who did it."

Serena was surprised. She had not thought about the teenagers making an issue of the bank's problem. "You must try to ignore people who are saying things that they know will hurt you. They are not your friends," she said. "I'm sorry that you are experiencing this, but there is nothing I can do. We just have to hope that an arrest is made soon. When everyone knows who did it, people will stop talking."

Each of the girls grabbed cookies from a canister and went toward their room, still talking loudly about Penny's friendship with the Waters student. Serena didn't say anything else. There was no point. Her daughters would work their way through their intense discussion about why people act in certain ways. They were now at the age when they almost never wanted her help.

Serena had been thinking about the woman at the grocery store saying she had probably been involved in the bank robbery. Now she was pondering the quizzing by FBI agent Bowman almost two weeks earlier. *Why did he ask me if I know a lot of people around here? Why wouldn't I know a lot of people, for heaven's sake! I'm related to a hundred or so people. If I count my in-laws, maybe 200. I don't know anyone that I think would steal money. If a person knows a lot of people, what difference does that make?*

She put supper on the table and called Fred and the girls in to eat. The girls talked about their "awful homework," and Fred said to Penny, "I had that same teacher you've got when I was in school. She always gives a lotta homework."

After eating, Serena and the girls cleaned the table while Fred started back toward the living room and the television set. "When the FBI agent was questioning me week before last he asked me if I know a lot of people around here," Serena said before Fred got out of the room.

"How'd you answer?" Fred said.

"I said I've lived here all my life so maybe I do know a lot of people."

Fred, already in the next room, had turned on the television. He didn't say anything else, and Serena turned her attention back to the kitchen. The girls hurriedly washed the plates, and Serena told them to do their homework while she finished cleaning the kitchen.

A few minutes later, she put the clean dishes in the cabinets and cleaned the countertops.

She felt like a long relaxing soak in the tub with lots of bubble bath. Her life was full of quick showers and rushed completion of family duties. She couldn't remember when she had thought of giving herself a relaxing soak in the tub. She had purchased a bottle of strawberry-scented bubble bath for the girls a few months ago, and they had used only about half the bottle. She turned on the water and poured in plenty of the liquid soap. Lowering herself into the tub with the water still running, she slid down and watched the bubbles form a blanket over her legs.

For some reason, she began to think about what the investigators would see when they looked at her. What kind of first impression did her appearance give? If she could convey character qualities with her appearance, she wanted those qualities to be honesty and competency. She had never had these thoughts before and had no idea what her appearance conveyed. She had frequently been told that she looked like her grandmother, and she thought about the way her grandmother looked in a photograph made decades earlier.

A skilled professional photographer had captured Mama Tatum's large brown eyes with a dreamy expression. The perfect lighting revealed longish lashes, smooth brows, and a small smile showing straight, pearl-like teeth. Her hair had been arranged in the style of the day, bobbed just below the ears with shiny bangs across the forehead. She could have been a movie star. Although Mama Tatum was in her seventies now, Serena sometimes had to take a second glance at her grandmother's beauty, especially if she used lipstick and a little makeup.

When Serena got out of the tub, she looked at herself in the mirror and tried to see where she resembled her grandmother, but the only thing she could see that looked like the face in the photograph were her straight, white teeth.

The next morning as she began to dress for work, Serena took out the scissors and started to trim her long, thick hair, as she had done for many years. Then she stopped before cutting. She could afford to get a professional haircut, so she would call for an appointment later.

She decided to wear a black A-line skirt that stopped an inch above her knees with a white blouse and black shoes with two-inch heels.

From now on, she was going to pay more attention to the way she dressed and the way she looked. She did not want to feel disheveled and awkward again.

Chapter 19

At the bank, the customers continued to stay away, and Trey Bowman was back with the other men.

The employees had learned the day before that some of the strangers going over the bank records were federal bank examiners.

Paul Norris was so quiet it was hard to remember he was there. Serena found his actions unnatural. He didn't seem to be fighting for his reputation. He had always been kind and considerate of his employees. Now he wasn't talking to his employees, and he wasn't looking out for himself. She wondered why.

Serena was also wondering why she was there at work when she was summoned again to Norris's office, where she had been questioned almost two weeks before. The same two agents were waiting for her, and Bowman was standing behind the table.

He motioned to the other chair at the table with his right hand as he said, "Good morning. Please be seated." He sat down immediately after she did and said, "We'd like you to tell us again about the day Jarvis Salisbury came into the bank."

"I don't know what I can say that I haven't already said," Serena said.

"Just tell us every detail you can think of as it occurred on that first morning he came in," Bowman said.

"Well, I was going over the night deposits, and I looked up just as he parked outside. I could see his car, and it was a new Cadillac. I guess you could say it was a tan color, no, more of a golden color. It looked like it had just been driven from the showroom floor.

"Of course, I wanted to see who was driving such a nice car, and I watched him come in the front door. He walked quickly, with long strides, and came straight to my window. He said he wanted to see the president of the bank, and I immediately knew that he wasn't a local resident because he had a Northern accent."

"Can you describe his accent?" Bowman said.

"He just sounded like a Yankee," Serena allowed herself to smile a little as she said the word "Yankee."

Cameron residents still liked to find an excuse to curse Yankees because of the stranglehold the Northern states had over the Southern states more than one hundred years earlier. Lives of strong and industrious Southerners had been lost in the War Between the States, and all dignity had been lost during Reconstruction. Southern historians wrote that the South fought the war to regain states' rights. Northern historians wrote that the war was to free the slaves in the South.

The ancestors of only two or three Cameron families had owned slaves, while others had resented the aristocratic attitude of all slave owners. Many of the Southerners who lost their lives defending their homes and families had opposed slavery. The following long years of Reconstruction and federal military rule had left a lasting image of Northern domination and oppression. Cameron elders, like longtime residents all across the South, passed along the strong distrust and fear of Yankees that they had learned from their ancestors.

But blame for this latest damaging invasion by Yankees was never known because local residents believed that one or two of their own had executed the giant swindle. They were not aware that anyone from outside Cameron might be involved.

"What do you mean? Are you talking about the Yankee baseball players?" Bowman asked. He obviously did not know Southern culture.

"No. He just sounded like he was from one of the Northern states," Serena answered. She stopped smiling when Bowman did not smile with her.

"Would you say he was from New York? Did he sound as if he was foreign-born?" Bowman asked.

"All I can say is that his words were short and fast. No, he didn't sound as if he was foreign-born."

Silence filled the room.

"Can you think of anything else?" Bowman said.

"He was very nicely dressed in a dark suit and a tie with red in the design. His shoes were what I call Italian-made, and, of course, he had what we refer to as a Fu Manchu beard." Serena knew she was simply repeating her words of two weeks earlier.

Bowman wrote on a white paper tablet before reaching into a briefcase beside him.

"I need you to look at some more photos to see if any of them look like Salisbury," he said.

He pulled at least a dozen black and white photographs out of a briefcase and placed them on the table in front of Serena.

"That's not him," Serena said, looking at the top photo.

"Look at the rest of them," Bowman said.

Serena took the stack of pictures and stared at one after another for a minute or more. She could not select any one of them as a photo that could have been Salisbury.

Suddenly she placed her hands over her eyes, and she still had more photos to examine.

"Okay. Let's take a break. Do you have a coffee machine in this building?" Bowman said.

"No. But I can go into the back room and make a fresh pot of coffee if you would like a cup."

"I'd like that. Do you drink coffee? Will you have some too?"

"Yes. I'll have it ready in about five minutes," Serena answered.

She hurried into the little room, put fresh coffee grounds into the Drip-O-Later, and poured water through the back, watching a minute later as dark liquid began to drip through. Then she stepped through the back door into the alleyway and took several deep breaths in the cold, refreshing air.

Back inside, she used a paper towel to wipe the small table, then took two six-ounce white Styrofoam cups from the cabinet. She was pouring coffee into the cups when Bowman walked into the room.

"Do you take cream and sugar?" she asked.

"A half teaspoon of sugar," he said.

She put the sugar in the coffee and handed him the cup, complete with a red stir stick.

After taking the coffee, he stuck his head out the back door and looked toward the sky. "This is the first time I've been in this state," he said. "Well, actually, it's the first time I've been in the Deep South. I'm afraid I had already formed an opinion about the area that may not be accurate."

"What did you think it would be like?" Serena asked.

"Someone told me a few years ago that everyone in the South, particularly in Georgia, went barefoot all the time, always ate something called grits, and ate biscuits with something called sorghum syrup."

Serena was standing beside him looking out the door, and she was surprised to hear her own hearty laugh. It was a relief to be amused, if only for a moment.

Bowman turned toward her. "I take it that that description is far from the truth," he said.

"Oh, I don't know. I do eat grits, and I have eaten biscuits with sorghum syrup and butter. I recommend that you try both while you're here. But I wear shoes." She held out her foot with her trim nylon-clad leg going into a neat black pump.

This time Bowman laughed. His black eyes were dancing as he looked straight into her eyes for the first time. They each took another sip of coffee, and Bowman said, "Let's go back and begin looking at those pictures again. We've got to get a lead on this Salisbury. Think back. Is there anything else?"

"Well, there is one more thing."

"What?"

"He had longish dark hair coming just to the bottom of his ears, and Phil Anderson, who works here in the bank with me, said he had fake sideburns."

Bowman stared intently at her.

"I don't know if they were fake or not," she said.

They walked back into the examining room, and she looked closely at the remaining photos. None of the pictures looked like anyone she knew. Finally, she went back to a photo and said, "If I have to pick out one that looks most like Salisbury, it's this one."

"You are making this interesting," Bowman said in a tone of dismissal and stood up. She got up and left immediately. Her nerves felt almost raw, and her whole body tingled.

Chapter 20

Serena concentrated on continuing her life as usual and forced herself to look at roadside scenery as she had always done while driving to work on State Highway 197. The twenty miles to and from work had always been her time for private thinking and planning because she had no one waiting on her to perform some task. On the road, she made plans such as menus for family meals, family activities during weekends and vacations, and clothing to recommend to her daughters. She contemplated personal or family problems and tried to work out solutions.

She knew every yard along the old, narrow road. It wouldn't be long until the trees were completely bare of leaves, and, when cold arrived, she knew where camellias, winter-blooming plants, could be seen with their waxy, roselike blossoms in pink, red, or white. In springtime, jonquils and forsythia made yellow splashes here and there. After the yellow blooms were gone, pink and red colors blazed across yards as the azaleas blossomed.

At the same time, a wild wisteria vine with its grapelike clusters of flowers draped color over the tallest trees in one wooded area, creating the illusion of a lavender waterfall.

In other wooded areas, blooming white dogwoods looked like fluffy clouds hiding among the brown trunks of the taller pines and hardwoods. In the yards, an occasional pink dogwood reminded Serena of the cotton candy her grandmother had bought her years earlier when the little roadside carnival operated for three days in a pasture on the outskirts of Clarkesville.

At one home along her route, the owners elaborately decorated their house and lawn for Christmas, Independence Day, and Thanksgiving as well as National Flag Day, Mother's Day, and Father's Day.

Another nearby home was where she found the duck figure with personality. In addition to regular daily attire, it was dressed for each holiday. On Halloween the previous year, the duck had worn a tiny black pointed witch's hat on its head and an orange kerchief around its neck. A small black stick broom stood propped against its wing. At Christmas, it had worn a red cape, and a small red Santa hat, complete with a white fluffy ball, had been perched on its head.

Serena always looked with anticipation to see if the cement duck's attire had been changed. Every time she looked at it, she remembered the "exploding" sunglasses the duck had been wearing on the day the bank investigators came.

Laughing at fear is the best way to overcome it, she told herself, and it was silly, but fun, to pretend that some strange psychic medium in another world had noticed her, Serena Sheppard, and was using a motionless, featherless fowl to forecast her future.

Serena would stop driving anytime, anywhere to move a slow-moving terrapin from the danger of oncoming cars or to help any injured animal. She once suffered a bloody punctured thumb because she was trying to rescue a gray squirrel that had been hit by a car. It had only been knocked unconscious, and when it awakened in Serena's hands, it bit her to regain its freedom.

She didn't hesitate to rescue any animal without feathers but could not imagine helping a chicken, wild turkey, or any kind of bird. She feared all feathered creatures because a Bantam rooster that her grandmother once owned had acted like a guard dog that considered every person a menacing stranger.

Her grandmother had bought the banty when it was a small pink chick. Easter was approaching, and some enterprising person had dyed fuzzy baby chickens different colors and sold them as gifts for small children.

When the pink Easter chicken became a brownish adult rooster with a dark green tail, it flogged every person it found in the yard.

Serena suffered flapping wings in her face more than a few times and began to view all birds as winged attack creatures.

When the spurs on the banty's feet grew to more than one inch and easily drew blood, it had cut Serena's right cheek near her ear. The next day, its spur stabbed the underside of her left arm. Serena's grandmother became frightened herself, and she also became angrier each day. She tried more than once to shoot the bird, but failed, then asked the neighbor to come with his gun. He killed it on the first shot.

As an adult, Serena and Fred had gone to Gainesville to see *The Birds,* a horror movie by the entertainment world's suspense genius, Alfred Hitchcock. She had hoped the movie would relieve her fear of feathered creatures, but she had sat in a hypnotized state during the movie's first bird attacks and screeching sounds. She could not stay for the whole film, and, instead of helping, the movie had changed her fear to real horror.

If she used the cement duck to poke fun at herself, maybe she could learn to laugh at her fear.

Today, the duck wore a miniature, red, wide-brimmed hat as if it needed protection from the December sun, and a red polka-dot scarf was tied around its neck.

The scarlet color means my heart will be touched, and the polka dots mean there will be more than one heart-touching incident, Serena thought.

Upon arrival at the bank, she and Joyce sat down for their usual cup of coffee together in the back room before going to open their cash drawers.

Serena searched her mind for something interesting to talk about that would keep them from worrying aloud about the bank investigation. Phil came in to greet his coworkers, and Serena asked him about "Pistol Pete" Maravich, who had been added to the Atlanta Hawks team about a year earlier. "Have you ever actually seen Pistol Pete Maravich play basketball?" she said.

"You know I went to Atlanta last season and watched him in a game. I told you about it. He's amazing in the way he handles that ball, but I guess that can happen if your dad's a basketball coach. How are your girls doing in basketball?" Phil said.

"Basketball is all they think about," Serena said. "They love being on the school team."

After a few more words about basketball, Phil went into his office, and Serena and Joyce rinsed their long-used personal ceramic cups, dried them with a paper towel, and placed them in the small cabinet before going toward their windows, wondering if they would have customers.

Today, Mrs. Belinda Lockwood, a widow in her mid-seventies, was at Serena's window less than two minutes after it opened. This was the first heart-warming incident that Serena had predicted that morning with the duck. "I believe what y'all say about that FDIC insurance," she whispered to Serena, before adding that she had held a yard sale and now had $105 to put into her savings account.

"I sold my old wood cook stove, my wringer washin' machine, and a lot of other junk," she said, chuckling at her unexpected success. "My children give me an automatic washin' machine last Christmas and a' electric stove the Christmas before. I wudda sold those old things a long time ago, but I didn't think anybody ud buy 'em.

"Now I'm gonna move to a small house much closer to muh daughter, and I don't have a choice. I had to sell a few things."

Mrs. Lockwood, who walked with a slight limp since a car accident years earlier, was always in good spirits. Today, she wore a homemade hat made of black and white checked cotton gingham. She had fashioned the crown with a smocking stitch, left almost two inches for the brim, and perched it directly on top of her head. Her bright, intelligent eyes looked out from underneath the brim.

Hats had lost their popularity about twenty years earlier, although men sometimes wore baseball caps that they respectfully removed as they entered the bank doors. Most women did not even wear hats to church anymore, so it was always fun to see what kind of hat Mrs. Lockwood would be wearing.

"My cosmos plants have made seeds now," she said to Serena. "Wud you like some? They're easy to grow, an' they bloom in white an' two or three shades o' pink."

"You can bring some seeds to me next time you come in. I know just the place I can put them," Serena said.

Mrs. Lockwood, who had picked up her deposit receipt and begun limping toward the exit, stopped to look back at Serena. "You'll have to wait till spring to plant 'em. I always put my seeds in tha freezer till plantin' time. They do better thataway," she said.

The morning moved slowly as Serena worked three overnight business deposits and served two customers who wanted to withdraw all their funds.

Lunchtime had almost arrived when Joe Ward, who ran a small grill down the street, came inside the front door of the bank and almost shouted. "'Rena, the Goat Man is in town. Didn't you say you'd never seen 'im?"

Chapter 21

Serena motioned for Joe to come across the lobby to her window so she wouldn't have to raise her voice. "No, I've never seen him, but I've heard a lot about him," she said. "Where is he, exactly? Maybe I can see him on my lunch break." Joe was suggesting an unusual diversion, and her heart began to feel lighter.

Joe said the Goat Man and his goats were camped out in a grassy area just outside of town. "He's travelin' with a young man this time. I think it's 'is son, and he must be about eighteen years old. He may be young, but he's almost as gray as 'is father," Joe said. "I'll get a hamburger ready for you. Come an' get it as soon as ya get yer lunch break, and then you kin go see him."

The Goat Man was a stranger who had stopped in Cameron in previous years. Before televisions became affordable to the masses, the Goat Man's arrival stirred more excitement than the annual carnival. Excited telephone calls and the area's radio announcer let residents know he was back in town. People who earlier had seen him and the goats pass along the highway always said he had not changed except that he was older. Today, despite televised entertainment, he was still a unique attraction.

The Goat Man said he had traveled in forty-nine states and expected someday to reach Hawaii, the fiftieth. Nine of the largest billy goats of indeterminable breeds pulled two connected box-shaped wagons, one much smaller than the other. Two larger billies with seven large nannies were fastened behind the last wagon. The goats' harnesses and tethers were hand-stitched pieces of leather and rope.

Some of the goats in the rear pushed when going uphill, and all acted as brakes when going downhill. A long piece of metal on top of the largest wagon was also used as a brake. When going downhill, the metal was lodged against the back wheels and slid with the wheels. About seven young goats, including still-nursing kids, frolicked along beside the caravan when traveling and climbed into or on top of the wagons when stopped.

The wagons rolled on large iron Pullman wheels, which seemed ready to fall off the axles at any minute, and more such wheels were fastened to the side of the wagon as spares. A countless collection of other items fastened on the wagons made them into traveling junk piles—buckets, plastic jugs filled with water, assorted pieces of furniture, rusty automobile tags from a variety of states, bales of hay, gray rags, pots, and pans. Among all these items were plastic barrels filled with pieces of tin, glass, plastic, and other items scavenged from the roadways. They bounced, swayed, or banged as the wagons rolled along. Aged tree limbs and tire recaps, foraged from the roadways, were stored on the wagons and used in campfires. One well-worn kerosene lantern bounced along with the rest but was surviving the rough ride.

On top of the large wagon stood a hand-lettered, highly visible sign that said, "Jesus wept."

A deep aura of mystery traveled with the Goat Man. Said to be rich, he was rumored to live in a town somewhere in middle Georgia. He drew swarms of people—the curious, the amazed, and the appalled.

Serena thought she must be the only one in town who had never seen this mysterious man. She went by Joe's grill, bought the hamburger for thirty-five cents plus a penny tax, and went to her car, which was parked at the train depot. Eating the hamburger as she drove, she took the last bite as she arrived at the place Joe had described to her. The cars of other curious townsfolk were already parked along the roadway. Parking and getting out, she walked beside the cars before stopping to talk with Bill Harrison and another armed Cameron policeman. Harrison said they were there to watch for vandals.

At the main wagon, the sights and sounds began to lift the darkness of Serena's thoughts about the bank investigation. The large goats were grazing in the grass where they had been staked, and the young goats were jumping around beside them. The Goat Man was sitting on a low, three-legged stool beside his wagon. He held an open Bible in his hands. Soot had blackened his face and hands, and faded, dirty, blue denim overalls with a gray, soiled, long-sleeved shirt covered his lanky body. His gray hair flowed down beside his face to his shoulders, and a long, gray beard brushed his chest.

The stench around the wagon made breathing difficult. Maybe it was the Goat Man's lack of bathroom facilities. Maybe the goats had urinated too many times on the wagon wheels. The Goat Man might need a bath. Whatever it was, it was almost overwhelming.

The Goat Man might need donations to buy food for himself, his son, and his goats, but he didn't have to buy gasoline or pay utility bills.

About eight people had gathered around him, while at least a dozen others stood farther back. He was saying, "A boy in Indiana asked me if man ud come from monkeys. No, man didden come from monkeys. That's the silliest thing I ever heard. God created man, then sent his son, Jesus, to save us from our sins. Ya just got to believe in 'im." He raised his voice for the last words.

Serena watched and listened, trying to place the man's accent.

The Goat Man shut his Bible, gathered up a bleating kid to hold in his crippled left arm, and stood beside the wagon. Seeing that he was selling picture postcards and booklets to tell about his life, she bought three postcards to take home to Fred and the girls. The Goat Man added a yellowed booklet without charge. "This tells about my life," he said.

"Where are you going?" Serena said.

"I'm goin' to Washin'ton to see Mixon," the Goat Man said.

Serena was about to ask him if he was talking about President Nixon when a barefooted young man walked from behind the wagon and stood beside the Goat Man. After about thirty seconds, the young man stooped over and reached underneath a male goat. He grabbed the goat's penis and pulled it hard. The goat reared up on its back legs, bleating, and moved as far away as its tether would allow. Both the father and son laughed loudly.

The Goat Man stirred her curiosity, but the young man's action was disgusting. Serena quickly turned and walked back toward her car.

As she passed the last cluster of people, a young man took a step toward her and said loudly, "Have y'all checked out the comfort of our jail? Tha whole town is waitin' for somebody in yer bank to be arrested."

Serena stopped and stared at him before walking quickly on. There was no way she could forget the bank investigation. Relief would come only when the crime was solved, and the guilty party or parties had been arrested.

Back at the bank, she didn't tell Joyce about the young man's comment because Joyce had heard similar remarks, and Serena didn't want to add to her worries. She told Joyce about using her lunch hour to go see the Goat Man, whom Joyce had seen on one of his previous visits. "He could have been sixty or seventy years old. He made me think of the California hippies and Jesus people. I think he's just a harmless nomad who has an unusual lifestyle," she said.

"The only thing I know is that he gets attention wherever he goes," Joyce said. Then her facial features drooped to indicate repulsion. "My neighbor told me that he milked one of the nannies while she was watching. He used a dirty quart jar, then turned the jar up and drank it while the milk was still warm."

"That makes me nauseous," Serena said before she turned back to her window.

After dinner that evening, Serena shared the three postcards with Fred and the girls. "He was selling cards for twenty-five cents each or three for one dollar," Serena said. "Oh, my goodness. That was no bargain," she admitted quickly. She had not realized the increased price of multiple-card purchases until she said the words. The cards had cost an additional eight cents each when she bought three of them.

"I can't believe you were swindled by the Goat Man," Fred said, laughing. "You, the head teller at our bank, who handles money all day. I hope the bank investigators don't find out that you can't count."

Deeply embarrassed and hurt by Fred's remark, Serena said, "I wasn't paying attention to the price." Then she got up and went into their bedroom.

Fred did not understand that she had been trying to forget the bank's problem and see into the mind of this man with the goats. The Goat Man didn't have to stay in any one place but could travel wherever he wished, and, since the bank investigation had begun, she frequently wished she could be somewhere other than her home in northeast Georgia.

The next day, she wanted to thank Joe Ward and was leaving to go to his grill for lunch when Phil Anderson came out of his office.

"Have you heard? After the Goat Man left here early this morning, a transfer truck crashed into the wagons, killed him, and left dead goats all over the highway. I heard it happened on one of those bad curves north of here," he said.

"When the Goat Man came through Cameron before, someone started that same rumor. I believed it then, but later I heard about him being in another town. The rumor was not true," Serena said.

"Yesterday, Bill Harrison was there at his campsite. Bill said vandals had turned his wagons over in another town and killed two of his goats. The Goat Man's travels are a real pain for law enforcement, according to Bill. Police or state patrolmen try to protect him from accidents or more vandalism. He doesn't hurt anyone, and I don't want to hear falsehoods about him," she said.

"Well, the bank investigation may show us that the Goat Man is not the most unusual stranger who ever stopped in Cameron," Phil said.

Chapter 22

On Wednesday morning, Serena got a call from Charlie Young, a second cousin she hadn't seen in years. He reminded her how they had once played together at Mama T's, before asking if she could visit him at his home. "You must come alone," he said.

Serena didn't ask him why she had to come alone because she didn't want to hear the answer. This cousin's call was another strange happening, and she didn't want to know the reason behind the call.

"I'll try to drop by some weekend," she said, attempting to end the call without promising to drop by.

"You must come as soon as you can. You won't be able to turn into my driveway. You'll have to come in the back way on the logging road that comes through the forest."

Serena did not respond. She didn't know what to say. Then it occurred to her that Charlie might have some important information about the bank robbery. If that was true, she had to see him and find out what he wanted to say.

"Please say you will come," he said. "It's extremely important. You'll understand when you get here."

After a minute, Serena said, "I'll try. I'll have to check with Fred and the girls. Then I'll call you and tell you when I can come."

On the way home that afternoon, she thought about what she would say to Fred. About four miles had passed before she remembered Mama T telling her that Charlie had been in the hospital. She would simply tell

Fred about Charlie being ill and say she was going to drop by his house. Fred had known Charlie when they were all in school together.

She wouldn't tell Fred that Charlie had called and almost begged her to come. She wouldn't say that he had asked her to come alone because Fred would demand to know why, and she didn't have an answer.

If she could help solve the bank robbery, she would be repaying Paul Norris for his kindness to her through the years.

At home, the girls reminded Serena that they would be going from school to their friend Susan's house on Friday for a spend-the-night party, and she decided that she would drop by Charlie's the same day. She would make sure leftovers were available that evening if Fred wanted to come home, or he could stop and get a bite to eat in Clarkesville.

On Friday afternoon while at work, Serena called Charlie and got directions to his home. As she left the bank at 4:00 PM, she was glad that the sun would remain above the horizon for at least another hour. She didn't want to drive along a forest logging road in the dark.

Georgia had changed to daylight saving time five years earlier, and she still found it a little strange to move the hands of all the family's clocks one hour forward each April and one hour back each October. Now she wished that it was April and daylight savings time had begun because the change each spring gave her one additional hour of daylight after she finished work at the bank.

Soon she arrived in Martin County where Charlie lived, and, following his directions, she turned down a narrow blacktop road to the place where the logging road entered the forest. There, an old pickup truck was parked off the road with someone sitting at the steering wheel. She could see a rifle across the back window, and a big black dog standing in the back of the truck watched as she steered her car around it and onto the logging road.

Serena felt extremely uneasy as she drove along the road's two dirt tracks through the dark and looming Chattahoochee Forest. She wanted to turn around and go back, but there was no place wide enough for that. She would have to back her car out, and who was the man in the truck at the end of the logging road? If she was accosted, who could she go to for help? No one else was anywhere around, only trees and more trees. She decided to keep going until she found a place to turn around.

After about a mile, she arrived at a clearing with an old mobile home and stopped in the high grass in the backyard. She held her breath in anticipation. It might be Charlie's current home, but she didn't know for sure.

The back door of the home opened, and she was very relieved to recognize her cousin as he stepped out.

"Come in. Come in," Charlie said, and Serena got out, walked through the grass, up the small steps, and through the door that he was holding open for her.

Charlie's wife, Christine, welcomed her and said she would get her a piece of pound cake and a cup of coffee.

Charlie asked her to sit at the small dining table.

"Serena, I didn't wanna ask you to come here an' see me, but I didn't know anything else to do. Someone told me you been talking to an FBI agent who's investigatin' the bank robbery. I hope you can get 'im to he'p me."

Serena wanted to deny access to an FBI agent, but she said, "What's the problem?"

"Come over here and look out this window," Charlie said as he got up and opened the drapes at the front of the room. Serena walked over and looked out at Charlie's long driveway stretching to the blacktop road in front of the mobile home. A brown rusty contraption with big iron wheels was sitting across the driveway.

She didn't have to go near the ancient tractor to know that manually pushing it out of the way would be impossible. It would have to be pulled off with a big truck or wrecker. Whoever put it there wanted to make it impossible to use the driveway.

They sat down again at the table and Serena looked closely at Charlie for the first time. He had recently undergone a triple heart bypass and was on medical leave from his job with Martin County. He looked like he hadn't shaved in three or four days, and he needed a haircut. He nervously ran his hands through his hair as he talked.

He told Serena how he had seen a plane more than once dropping packages on top of the mountain behind his house during the night. "We had a bright full moon almost three weeks beginnin' in November, and now the December moon's bright and full again. If I hear a plane overhead, I look out the back door, and I've seen large objects fallin' from the plane three different times. I don't know if it's always the same plane," Charlie said.

He had called the local sheriff's office to report the objects falling from the sky, and now someone was calling his house with threats in the middle of the night. He had no idea who had parked the old tractor across his driveway. He and Christine couldn't get their car out quickly now if they had an emergency and needed to get to the doctor. It would take them longer, but at least they could drive around to the back of the house and go out the logging road.

"Whoever's droppin' them packages knows I called the sheriff's office. I been hearin' law enforcement people say a Dixie Mafia's operatin' in this area, and that's good words for what's happenin'. I can't call the sheriff anymore, and it don't do no good anyway. I know them packages contain illegal drugs 'cause it cudden be anything else. If you'll tell the FBI agent, he can do somethin' about it."

"I believe he's looking for any kind of information that will help him solve the bank robbery," Serena said.

"Maybe it's the same people," Charlie said.

"That's possible. There's a man in an old truck at the end of this logging road. Do you think he's connected with the packages?" Serena said.

"I don't know if he is or not. I didden know anybody was there, but I don't know anythang anymore," Charlie said. "Please just tell the FBI agent what's going on here. He'll know what to do."

Serena had taken only one bite of the pound cake and one sip of coffee, but she didn't want to stay another minute.

"I have to get home, and I don't even know if I'll see the FBI agent again. If I do, I'll tell him what you have told me," she said.

"Please get 'im to he'p if ya can. I'm scared. I don't wanna live any more. Before they operated on my heart I think I died in the hospital emergency room, and I'm sorry they brought me back to life."

"What makes you say that?" Serena said.

"I musta died 'cause I rose to the ceilin' and looked at my body layin' on tha operatin' table. Then I saw a bright light. I followed the light an' saw my long dead gran'daddy standin' by a purty river. He motioned me ta come join him, but then he 'as gone. I learned later that the doctors used shock treatment, an' my heart started pumpin' again. I wish they hadn't o' brought me back ta life. I think 'bout seein' my gran'daddy all the time. I hope he'll be waitin' for me ag'in next time I die," Charlie said, and his face crumpled. He was about to cry.

Serena got up from the table and took his arm as she said, "Please don't be so depressed. I'll do everything I can."

Charlie's face straightened again as he escorted her out the door and to her car. "Be careful goin' home. I don't feel safe anywhere anymore," he said.

Charlie's desperation had frightened Serena, and she was more afraid driving out on the isolated logging road than she had been driving in. It was totally dark when she arrived again at the blacktop road. As her car lights hit the old pickup, she saw that the hood was raised, and the man appeared to be working on the motor.

Was he pretending car trouble so he could watch the traffic going into Charlie's house?

Now I'm becoming suspicious of all persons, even those sitting in cars parked on the side of the road. What is happening to me?

Chapter 23

Christmas arrived, but Serena could not feel the holiday spirit. Fred brought in a live, green fir tree from a farm just south of their home, and its aroma wafted through the rooms. The girls helped Serena decorate it with items that the family had made through the years. When the girls were infants, Fred had made small ornaments such as stars and bells from scraps of wood for one of their first family Christmas trees. Serena had painted the girls' names on each one, and they still used them. Shiny sequins were falling off one small star, and two other items were tattered and worn, but each had sentimental value. White crocheted snowflakes made by Mama Tatum were always the last decorations they hung on the tree.

Serena wrapped four gifts, one for Mama Tatum, one each for Fred, his mother, and father, and placed them under the tree. Fred later placed a gift for Serena, which had been wrapped at the department store, with the other four gifts.

Years earlier, Serena had told the girls that if they didn't believe in Santa Claus, he could stop visiting them. Each year since that time they assured her that they still believed, so Serena always kept their gifts hidden and placed them under the tree during the night. The girls opened the presents after they woke in the morning while their parents watched, then opened their own gifts.

Serena and Fred always drank warm, spiced tea made with apple cider on Christmas morning. The cinnamon and clove spices were not a taste that appealed to the girls, but Serena made the tea anyway. She called it their Christmas wassail drink, just as her grandmother had done. For her, it was a Christmas morning tradition.

Penny and Nicole both got new clothing that they had been admiring, as well as new music recordings. Nicole gave Penny a recording of "Knock Three Times" by Tony Orlando and Dawn, and she laughed about the words "Knock three times … if you want me." Nicole explained that Penny's new friend, Vern, knocked on his desk three times so Penny would know to meet him in the hallway after class.

The girls gave Serena a recording of "Indian Reservation" by Paul Revere and the Raiders. The song, especially the words, "They took the whole Cherokee nation, put us on this reservation; took away our native tongue, taught their English to our young," especially touched her.

Serena gave Fred a new electric circular saw because she knew his old one was beginning to skip. She tried to respond with enthusiasm when he presented her with the stylish forest green suit that she had suggested he get for her.

One week later, she made the same New Year's resolutions she always did, but without enthusiasm. She vowed to become better organized, both at home and at work; to struggle against her own prejudice or prejudgment of another person without trying to understand them; and to make sure that Penny and Nicole were getting prepared to go to college. She reminded them constantly that college was ahead, because she knew they didn't hear their classmates talking about such plans.

Penny and Nicole were practicing basketball every afternoon and playing one or two games a week. Serena and Fred attended all the games, even when the girls were playing at a school on the other side of the mountains. Both girls were on the varsity team, and, although they were winning, attendance was low at the games. The girls' team always played early in the evening, and the boys' team played during the hours when people most likely would attend.

Serena's family life had not changed, but her job at Cameron National Bank had always sheltered her with a layer of safety and comfort. She had never been aware that her job provided such a sense of peace, but now the feeling was gone, and its absence overshadowed everything else. Her longtime coworkers at the bank were her second family, but someone had arranged the swindle. Someone in her bank family could not be trusted. Who was it? In addition to worrying about trust, she constantly wondered if her job would soon be gone. What would she do if this happened?

Serena had not passed on Charlie's information about the airplanes to Trey Bowman because she had not seen him since the day she had spent so long going over the photos.

The banking officials and remaining FBI agents left a few at a time, and Cameron became a quieter place.

Business continued almost as usual, but no new depositors came in, and, almost every week during the first months of the new year, one or two longtime depositors came in and closed their accounts. It was almost as if they didn't want to be disloyal, yet were afraid of what might happen to their life's savings.

Paul Norris had not been seen at Cameron National Bank since just before Christmas, and he had not told the employees he was leaving. Jim Robocker, a stranger from Atlanta, was now acting as bank president. No one at the bank had heard the name of the new president before he was introduced to them his first day on the job.

The new bank president was personable and outgoing. He had immediately begun to change the record-keeping procedures and the way loans were made. Only two people had applied for loans, and each was from a different nearby town. Serena suspected that they already had been turned down at their hometown banks. They filled out long forms and had to wait several days while calls were made to every place they had ever owed money. One of the men was approved for a loan of $5,000, and he had to use twenty-five acres of land that he owned as collateral.

When Paul Norris was bank president, he had decided if someone could get a loan based on whether or not he knew the applicant's family and whether the applicant had a steady job. Occasionally, he would demand collateral, but not always. His method had worked well before Salisbury appeared on the scene.

No new announcements were made about the missing money, and, without new information, speculation and gossip became rampant. Every person in town seemed to have a different story to tell about the real identity of Jarvis Salisbury, and those who did not personally know Paul Norris believed he had arranged the whole scheme.

Serena's days became routine on the surface, but questions had not been answered. Suspicions of coworkers would jump into her mind when she least expected it, even though she tried to avoid such thoughts.

Joyce asked for a week off in April, whereas she had previously always asked for a week off in June. Questions flew into Serena's mind before she knew Joyce's reason. Why was she changing her vacation time? Where was she going, and who was she going to see? At the same time Serena went over these questions, she scolded herself for being suspicious.

Joyce said Albert, her husband, who was an insurance agent in Gainesville, had won a trip to Miami, Florida, and they had to take it in April. They had not been given a choice. Joyce and Albert had no children, so they wouldn't have to wait until school was out for the summer so their offspring could join them on vacation.

Several years earlier, Joyce had said she didn't want children, and Serena had asked her why. Joyce said that her own mother and father had argued and fought constantly when she was a child. They finally divorced when Joyce was a teenager, but the fighting had continued. Joyce said she had lived with one parent, then the other, and her life was miserable until she married. "I wished many times that I had never been born, and I don't want to bring a child into this world," she said. Joyce was obviously saddened by the subject, and Serena never talked to her about it again.

Phil was his usual quiet self. How did he spend his personal time? Did he have any special friends? Why did he never talk about girlfriends? Why did he never mention the bank's problems? Why did he always want to talk with Calvin Ivy? Why did he now refuse invitations to lunch with Serena and Joyce? Before they knew about the swindle, Phil would sometimes eat lunch with them in the back room, but now he seemed to be in a world of his own.

Phil had come out of his office more than once to talk to Ivy, and Serena found this strange. Ivy didn't have a loan with the bank, only checking and savings accounts. He never went to Phil's office, except the one time that Phil had escorted him to his desk. Ivy had stayed only about three minutes before coming out and leaving the bank. He was the only regular bank customer with whom Phil always made an effort to talk.

In May, the bank had closed early as usual on a Wednesday afternoon, and Serena was leaving when Phil came up to her. "My uncle is hosting a really big party in a couple of weeks, and we need help waiting on tables. It'll be on Saturday, and it may be fun. Would you and your daughters like to help?" he said.

Chapter 24

Phil's uncle owned an old fishing lodge about thirty miles north of Cameron. A popular and somewhat exclusive location in the mountains, it was on a hillside overlooking Lake Burton. Occasionally, a large canopy was raised at the edge of the lake and across the highway from the cabins and dining hall. The canopy served as a temporary pavilion for large numbers of people gathered for family reunions or for the meetings of large organizations. Long tables lined with chairs were placed underneath.

This time, the canopy had been raised for a political gathering. The commissioner of the Georgia Department of Agriculture was hosting a fish fry for his many financial contributors in the area. Almost two hundred people had been invited, and it was not an invitation to be turned down. The commissioner was better known than the governor, and he had been in office much longer.

Serena was glad to be involved. The event would require a different kind of activity and would be a good experience for Penny and Nicole. Phil asked them to wear blue jeans with pale blue cotton shirts. His uncle would provide small, white cotton aprons for each table server, and he wanted them dressed as nearly alike as possible.

Serena's favorite long-sleeved, blue cotton shirt was faded enough to be in style and had a big goose flying across the back, one she had embroidered herself. "My heart goes where the wild goose goes. My heart knows what the wild goose knows." She sang the familiar lines to herself as she put on the shirt. The old song was the reason she had chosen to stitch the goose pattern into her shirt a couple of summers earlier.

Her faded, size ten jeans with the stovepipe legs were a little snug, but passable, and Penny and Nicole looked neat in theirs. She pulled her professionally cut, mahogany-colored hair back to the nape of her neck and fastened it with a wide, red clasp to add some color. She powdered her face, put a light covering of black mascara on her lashes, and made sure her lipstick matched the hair clasp.

She had not heard comments lately about the bank's missing money, and it was almost possible to put it out of her mind. Working as a waitress for a political gathering was going to provide a refreshing change.

When they arrived at the fishing lodge, the only cars there were parked near each of the little tin-roofed cabins on the side of the mountain. They belonged to guests who had spent the night in the cabins, and Serena wondered if acorns from the large oak trees had fallen onto the roofs during the night. She remembered spending the night in one of the cabins about a year after she and Fred married. She had been awakened three times during the night when an acorn had banged onto the tin roof and clattered its way to the edge.

The man-made lake was full, with no red clay banks showing around the edge. Mountain laurel bushes around the water and along the highway were full with pink blossoms. Serena wondered if the commissioner had asked that water not be released at the Georgia Power Company dam before this event, making sure that the surroundings were as perfect as possible.

Breakfast had already been served at the lodge, but it was still early in the morning. The surface of the lake was mirror smooth, and a pale mist hovered, with one cloudy fingerlike spiral dripping down to the blue-green water almost like a loving touch.

Fishing boats and the big flat pontoons were in their separate slots at the marina. The people usually out fishing at this time were either invited to the fish fry or were staying away because they knew the commissioner and his guests were coming.

Phil greeted Serena and her daughters and introduced them to another blue-jean–clad duo, another mother and daughter who would also be table servers. Serena was glad to see Eloise, a woman her age whom she already knew, and the woman's daughter, Susan, was a best friend of her own daughters. Four other trim, smiling young women joined the table servers, and work was about to begin.

One of the young table servers was Marie Ivy, the black high school senior who had been a member of the high school homecoming court the previous autumn. She was a willowy figure with skin the color of caramel. Her black hair was extremely short, and worn close to her head. The cut drew attention because other young African-Americans were wearing Afro hairstyles. Afros required curly hair that was stretched out from the scalp to form a cloud of black around the head. Marie's hairstyle was the opposite. It looked like a glistening, tightly fit cap on a perfectly shaped head. Marie was using pieces of mountain laurel to make low, pink flower arrangements for the center of every table.

Phil smiled broadly as he introduced Marie, and Serena was immediately impressed by her open, confident smile. She evidently had completely understood the James Brown song from a few years earlier that featured the words, "I'm black and I'm proud." Serena could see why the young woman was breaking social barriers.

Phil was right. This was going to be a fun experience.

The servers worked together to spread snow-white cotton cloths over about twenty long tables. Five chairs were placed of each side of the tables with just enough room between them to keep the diners from feeling crowded. They placed white cotton napkins on the cloths with stainless steel utensils, a glass of ice water, and a piece of chocolate cream pie. Additional glasses were lined up on a side table to be filled with ice for sweet tea.

Usually, plastic utensils and plastic glasses with paper plates and napkins were used at a lakeside gathering. These dishes were white porcelain. The lodge didn't have enough dishes for such a large group and had probably rented them from some distant place. This was definitely not the usual fish fry.

The first cars began to arrive, and a handful of men were already standing on the marina dock talking when two state patrol cars drove up. One patrol car parked on the side of a curve of the old mountain highway about 300 yards north of the tents, and the other car parked on the side of the road about 300 yards south. Both cars activated the blue flashing lights on their roofs.

Drivers of the few cars passing by on the curvy road would see the flashing blue lights, then immediately slow down and drive carefully past the lodge and the tent, making it safer for people walking across or beside the narrow mountain highway.

The commissioner's car arrived, accompanied by several other cars, and more followed. Robocker, the acting president of Cameron National Bank, arrived with his wife, Edie. Serena saw Robocker shake hands with people here and there, including the president of a bank from an adjoining county.

The table servers were watching from the lodge, and Serena smiled to herself as she saw a well-known preacher chatting with a man known for his bootlegging habits. The bootlegger had recently served two years in prison and was probably still on probation. But he was also a member of the church where the preacher was currently employed. As she thought about how the preacher had to condemn alcoholic beverages to be considered good at his job, Serena suppressed a small smile.

Two hundred rainbow trout still containing their heads and fins had been soaked in salted milk and dipped in flour before being fried. Phil's uncle believed that the good natural flavor could be preserved by gutting and cleaning each fish but otherwise keeping it whole.

Now the fried trout were placed on the plates with coleslaw, whole kernel corn, green beans, and a golden-brown yeast roll before the servers carried the plates to the tables. Two small baskets of hush puppies were also taken to each table. As the servers placed the plates before the diners, they asked if they wanted iced tea or coffee. Serena set one plate down, asked the question, then set another plate down.

As the second guest looked up and said, "I'd like coffee," Serena found herself looking into the eyes of Trey Bowman. Her mind immediately focused on the bank robbery and the fact that no one had been arrested, meaning the employees still were under suspicion. The surprise showed on her face as her breath almost stopped, and he grinned.

"Hello," she said.

"Hi. Have you stopped working at the bank?"

"No. I'm still at the bank. I'm just helping out here today."

Her body grew slightly warm as they stared at each other a few seconds. Then she smiled at him, attempting to act as if he was a friend the same as any other, and moved away to get more plates.

Chapter 25

As the guests finished their meal, the state agriculture commissioner made a short speech thanking them for their faithful and generous support through the years, then promised to continue to serve them with the same dedication he had always shown.

Three other people got up to make brief comments about what a good job the commissioner was doing. They talked about his enforcement of the seed and plant protection acts as well as the food protection act, especially as it applied to liquefied and dried egg products. Everyone stood up to applaud loud and long, and then they began to talk with one another as they slowly moved away from their tables.

Serena was cleaning near the head table when a man grabbed the commissioner by his arm and said, "How can I get mountain oysters on tha market?"

The commissioner chuckled and said, "Are you talking about hog testicles?"

"Yes. If you cook 'em right and serve 'em with cocktail sauce, they're delicious. I have a hog farm an' I could sure use some extra income."

The commissioner continued to laugh as he walked away. Looking back at the man, he said, "Well, if you can get a lot of people to buy them, get in touch with me, and we'll see what we can do."

Serena smiled to herself as she continued cleaning tables. She had heard people talk about fried hog testicles, which they called mountain oysters, but she had never known anyone who ate them.

The majority of the people finally got into cars and drove away, but others didn't hurry to leave. They stood and talked while the dishes were collected, along with the tablecloths and napkins.

Serena was wondering if she should begin gathering the folding chairs when Phil walked up to her and addressed her, using a shortened version of her name. "'Rena, do you want to make more money today? Smith Jackson has invited a few people over to his house, and he's asked my uncle if he can provide a table server there."

"Doesn't he have a place on the lake? Do you want three servers? I have my girls with me."

"Three aren't really needed, only one. I'll see if I can find someone else."

Nicole, standing nearby, heard the conversation. "Mom, go on, if you want to. Penny and I want to go home with Susan. Her mom has already asked us. We're going to shoot some hoops."

Serena looked at Phil. "Basketball! My girls spend all their free time playing basketball. Okay, I'll help you. Doing housework in someone else's place will be a nice change," she laughed. "And, of course, I can use the extra money because I'm saving to make a trip with the girls this summer."

Phil explained that Smith Jackson had a beautiful, old two-story summer home on the northern part of the lake. The house had originally belonged to his father, and Jackson had totally remodeled it and had the grounds professionally landscaped about two years ago.

"We're going to take people up the lake to the Jackson place on pontoons. You and I will follow the pontoons in that motorboat. Wait here while I get the pontoons ready."

The large, flat-bottomed pontoons, which floated on closed, round cylinders or barrels, could hold eight or ten people and moved slowly through the water.

Phil walked away and Serena began to fold chairs and stack them. "Can I help you?" asked a voice behind her. She turned and found herself again face-to-face with Bowman.

"I'm getting paid to do this. It's extra money for a special vacation this summer."

"I'll help you," Bowman said as he began to fold the chairs and stack them.

"Can you tell me who this Smith Jackson is?" he said.

"He's a state senator. His family has been in this area a long time, and he was a state representative before he ran for the senate. He's invited the commissioner and some other people to his house here on the lake."

"I know. I've been invited, too. I just wanted to know something about the people who are going to be there."

Serena looked toward the people gathering on the dock to get on the pontoons. "I see Frank Fowler, the president of First National Bank over in Martin County. And there's Newt Ganos. He's a chicken farmer, but I guess I should tell you he's served time for bootlegging. Everyone around here knows that."

Bowman laughed as he started a second stack of folded chairs. "Making bootleg liquor is an occupation everyone in this area seems to know about."

"Everyone may know about it, but everyone doesn't do it!" Serena said.

"I didn't mean to imply that," Bowman answered. After a brief pause, he said, "Tell me about life here in the mountains."

"I personally have had a good life. I haven't traveled and seen the world, but lately it's felt like the world is coming here to us." She talked while she stacked the chairs.

"I guess you're referring to the people coming into the bank?" Bowman asked, stopping to look at Serena.

"Yes," she said and stopped her work. "I must tell you something else. My cousin is having problems because he reported small airplanes dropping packages on the mountaintop behind his house. He's getting strange calls in the night, and his driveway has been blocked. He thinks it might be connected with the bank robbery."

"The airplanes and package drops in this area are being investigated," Bowman said before turning away to get more chairs. He made it obvious that he had nothing else to say on the subject.

Motors began to rev up, and the first pontoon operated by Smith Jackson moved away from the dock, followed shortly by the other.

Phil yelled toward Serena and Bowman, "You two come over here and go with me."

By the time they arrived at the dock, Phil was in the motorboat, motioning for the two of them to sit in the middle while he sat back beside the engine. They stepped into the boat and sat down just in time to take the life jackets Phil extended toward them. "Got to follow the rules. The local game warden is on one of those pontoons, and he can fine anyone who doesn't have a life jacket," Phil said.

"We don't have to put these on unless you want to. We can just keep them near," Serena told Bowman.

The boat moved out into the open lake and traveled slowly, staying a distance behind the pontoons. The two pontoons and the boat were the only floating objects in view, and, after they moved out of the small bay, the narrow lake stretched out around them.

The mountains seemed to begin at the very edge of the shores, with the nearest a deep blue-green color and the more distant mountains a purplish hue. Summer homes dotted the shoreline here and there, and some of them were grand showplaces.

Some of the homes had two-story boathouses with chimneys coming out of the roofs. They obviously had fireplaces. Another boathouse had a strip of wood containing carved bears underneath the roof edge on its three visible sides.

Their boat passed a fisherman with his line in the water, and the man threw up his hand.

"Do you know him?" Bowman asked Serena.

"No. People just have a habit of waving when they're passing someone on the lake," Serena said.

"This is one of the most beautiful places I've ever seen," Bowman said.

"I never get tired of just looking at the scenery on this lake," Serena answered. "If this boat could stop today and just float in the middle of this lake, I could look at the mountains and blue sky and forget all my troubles." She emphasized "forget all my troubles" to indicate that she was exaggerating.

Bowman smiled. "Did you grow up here?"

"No. Actually I grew up in White County. I was raised by my grandparents." *Now, why did I tell him that? He doesn't want my life history.*

"What a coincidence. I also grew up in my grandparents' home. When I was a child, I felt ashamed because I didn't have young parents to introduce to my friends. Now I know I was very fortunate. Someday,

I hope I can bring my grandparents here to see this beautiful area. They love their home in Philadelphia, but they like to travel and see different parts of the country," Bowman said.

"My grandmother still lives on the old home place in White County. My grandfather is dead. I hadn't thought about it before, but I hope she'll go with me and the girls when we make our trip this summer. I want to take them to Washington, DC. That's why I'm glad to work today and make a little extra money."

"Have you been to Washington before?"

"Yes. When I was a senior in high school, the whole senior class made a trip to Washington and New York City. We caught the train in Cameron, and I'll never forget it. I want to take Penny and Nicole because whole senior classes don't make trips together anymore. And my grandmother has never been. She would enjoy it as much as the girls," Serena said.

The pontoons were stopping at a dock in front of a beautiful white house with two rows of windows. Phil landed the boat near a small beach, and Bowman jumped out to pull it farther up on the land. He held his hand up to Serena. She let him help her jump down to the ground, and Phil jumped out behind her, then ran to help dock the pontoons.

Chapter 26

Smith Jackson was leading the way from the lake and going up wooden stairs to a two-story house that might have been made of glass. Its windows facing the water went from one end of the house to the other on both floors. Except for Phil and Trey Bowman, Serena didn't really know anyone present. She knew some of the men only by name and had never seen the others before. She was the only woman present. She was glad she would have work to do because she didn't want to be forced to stand around and make idle conversation.

Inside the first level of the comfortable home, Jackson showed Serena where glasses and serving trays were located. Newt Ganos walked into the kitchen and set a gallon glass jug of clear liquid on the counter. "Here's some triple-filtered top-of-the-line," he said.

Serena concealed her surprise. She did not know Ganos was so open about his sideline business. He could only be charged with breaking the law if he sold his liquor, and this time he appeared to be giving it away. Serena felt uneasy and unsure of what she was supposed to do.

Phil came into the kitchen with a case of Coca-Cola in glass bottles. He went back to the boat for two bags of ice, and two cans of salted peanuts brought from the lodge. As he returned, Smith Jackson followed him, chuckling. "Let me fix these drinks for Ganos. I know exactly how to do this," he said.

He got small glasses from the cabinet and filled a tray. After pouring about half an inch of the clear liquid into each glass, he took the tray back into the main room. "We're fortunate today to have some of the best brew made in the mountains. I've poured some for everybody," he announced.

In the kitchen, Serena got larger glasses and filled them with ice. Then she found small glass bowls to fill with salted nuts. The situation was strange to her, but she felt she could handle it as long as Phil was there to advise her.

She slowly poured Coca-Cola into the glasses of ice, went into the other room, and served one to each person. She returned to place bowls of nuts here and there and went back into the kitchen. After a short time, Jackson came in and asked her to pour the liquor from the gallon jar into a glass pitcher, then bring it in and serve the guests. Serena did as requested, and, one at a time, each man held up his small glass for a refill. She remembered to pour half an inch of liquid.

When she got to Bowman, he shook his head so slightly Serena had to look hard at him. She looked at his larger glass half-full of Coke and didn't see a small glass. She moved on with a sense of relief.

Conversation grew louder and louder in the main room, while in the kitchen Serena had found a Ladies Home Journal magazine with Elizabeth Taylor on the cover. She was reading an article about an unknown couple called "Can This Marriage Be Saved?"

Suddenly she heard someone say, "He knew what was goin' on. He hired the man himself. He's plannin' to completely disappear after all this is over. I know who his partner is."

Serena stopped reading to pay attention to the conversation in the other room. The voice belonged to the president of the Martin County bank.

A lower voice said, "You don't know what you're talkin' about, Herman. You ought to keep yer mouth shut."

Herman Fowler answered. "Oh, yes, I know what I'm talkin' about. Paul Norris's partner in this scheme came to me first. I told him quick to get lost. Money don't mean that much to me. I'd never do that to my family."

Everyone in the room was quiet except Fowler and Smith Jackson. Jackson said, "If you know so much, Herman, tell us who tha partner is. I think people need to know what's goin' on an' who's behind it."

"I can't tell you his name, but I can tell you this much. He moved up here from Florida a couple o' years ago, an' he has a landin' strip for airplanes at his house. That's all I'm gonna say."

"You don't have to say anything else. Everyone knows about the man in Martin County with an airplane landin' strip in his pasture. I always wondered where he got all his money," Jackson said.

"He came to see me about nine or ten months ago and said he wanted to talk to me about a project he was workin' on. I told 'im I was busy, and he acted like he was insulted. I've not seen him in my bank again, but I see planes headed toward his place ever' once in a while. I don't know what's goin' on over there, but it's profitable. There's no doubt about that," Fowler said.

Another voice chimed in. "I hear rumors all the time. I once heard that a sheriff's deputy was findin' real dirt in some land-grabbin' activities, an' then he was found dead with a plastic bag on his head."

Fowler said, "That was a long time ago. I don't think that has anything to do with what's goin' on today. The coroner ruled that death a suicide, but, of course, everybody's always wondered how he cudda done it himself."

Still another voice. "Someone told me they've seen planes flyin' over the mountains durin' the night and droppin' out packages of illegal drugs."

"You know that's been happenin'. Don't you remember that incident up near the Tennessee line? Bears or some kind of animal tore into a bag of cocaine an' scattered it in tha woods. That man in Martin County's probably into illegal drug smugglin'. There's no doubt that somebody's doin' it."

In the kitchen, Serena felt like she had fallen from the sunlight into a black hole. She already had heard some of the talk about the man in Martin County and about the planes. But the Martin County banker was indicating that Paul Norris had willingly partnered in the swindle at his bank.

Bootlegging and moonshine liquor were almost as old as the mountains. But illegal drugs and airplanes dropping packages in the mountains were alien. Such activity did not fit into her life and did not fit the life of anyone she knew. She wanted no part of it and didn't want to be near people who obviously enjoyed talking about it. She especially didn't want to hear negative talk about Paul Norris. *Herman Fowler's words could not possibly be true.*

She could not read anymore and didn't know what to do.

"I don't wanna end this party, but I gotta get back to the lodge," Phil announced.

Was Phil purposely ending the conversation? Serena didn't know, but she gratefully went into the main room to gather the glasses. Back in the kitchen she rinsed them and placed them in the dishwasher as Smith Jackson had instructed. "My whole family's comin' up here next weekend. We'll wait till then to run the dishwasher," he said.

Bowman walked into the kitchen with the three bowls still holding a few nuts. Serena picked up one of the cans, poured in the leftover nuts, and refastened the plastic top. "I certainly haven't done very much," she said to Bowman, "but I don't know anything else to do."

"Don't worry about it. Come on, let's go back to the boat," he said, holding the kitchen door open for her.

She didn't know why, but Trey Bowman didn't seem threatening anymore. It was actually comforting to walk toward him and have him escort her back to the boat.

They assumed their places in the middle of the boat while Phil helped load people onto the pontoons.

"Who is this man in Martin County with the landing strip at his house?" Bowman asked Serena.

"I don't remember his name. I don't know him," Serena said.

"Has he ever been in Cameron National Bank?"

"If he has, I didn't know it. Do I have to answer questions about the bank? I don't know anything except how to do my job. The Norris family has always been good to me, and I appreciate having a job there."

"Don't get upset. I have a job to do, too, but I won't ask any more questions today," Bowman said.

Phil was back at the motor and started the engine. Again the boat followed the pontoons down the lake.

"May I tell you that you are a beautiful woman?" Bowman said softly to Serena.

The words were as unsettling as the questions about bank activities.

"You make me very nervous, and it's not because I've done something wrong," Serena tried to laugh.

"I said what I was thinking. Maybe you don't want me to talk to you."

This time Serena did laugh at the same time her whole body grew hot. What a strange day this was.

She looked toward Bowman and saw the sheen on his black hair and the way it tried to curl toward the smooth, olive skin of his face. She wouldn't describe him as handsome, but his face showed confidence and something else that she couldn't describe. It was foreign, something she had not seen in a man before. "Are your ancestors Greek?" she asked.

He laughed wholeheartedly. "No, my father was a half-blood Seneca, an Iroquois Indian, and my mother was of English descent."

"We have something else in common. My father was not an Indian. He had a Scottish ancestry. But a grandmother, four generations back on my mother's side, was a Cherokee Indian."

"What happened to your parents? You talk like they're no longer living.

"I never knew them," Serena said. She wanted to change the subject fast and said, "Let's talk about you. Are you staying in this area while you do your investigation?"

"I'm returning to Philadelphia tomorrow, but I'll come back here in a few days. I have several leads, and I'm determined to get to the bottom of this and find out exactly who got that money, but it's very slow."

They were silent until Phil pulled up at the dock a few minutes later. He thanked Serena for her help, tied up the boat, and jumped out to go to the pontoons while Bowman helped Serena from the boat.

He held on to her hand a minute and said, "I guess I've secretly always expected Southern women to be beautiful and industrious, like Scarlet O'Hara in *Gone with the Wind*. You haven't disappointed me, Mrs. Sheppard."

Serena pulled her hand away. Her mind was jumbled, and she could only glance quickly at Bowman before she turned and walked away without speaking.

Bowman stayed on the dock beside the boat.

-    -   -

At home that evening Serena told Fred that she had been paid one hundred dollars for the work she and the girls had done. The going rate for waitresses was fifty cents an hour plus tips. This meant she should have received about twenty dollars for the work she and the two girls had done. She felt guilty and wondered if she had accepted some kind of hush money.

She did not tell him about going to Smith Jackson's house, nor did she repeat the conversation she had overheard. She didn't even want to think about it. After they were in bed with the lights out, she thought about Bowman's return to the area. He was a striking man, she had to admit, and he must be about five or six years younger than she was. Why was he saying such personal things to her? Did he think she knew something she wasn't telling, and maybe he could get to her by flattery? Why did recalling his personal comments to her make her feel uniquely beautiful and smart? Why did it make her whole body turn warm?

Chapter 27

The entire area was buzzing on Monday when Serena arrived at work.

The house that Phil Anderson had rented, moving out of it only a week before, had blown up the previous Friday night. The unoccupied house, located in Hall County just south of Cameron, had exploded into tiny pieces. The cause of the explosion was not yet known. Everyone was wondering if the exploded home, which was formerly occupied by a Cameron bank employee, and the missing money were connected. Too many strange things were happening in what was once a peaceful, quiet area. Residents were edgy and instantly suspicious of anything that happened, unusual or not.

Serena wondered if Phil had friends, and, if so, who. She knew he went to have coffee with other men at Loudermilk Restaurant, but she had never seen him with another person anywhere else. She thought about Phil inviting Marie Ivy to work as a table server at the fish fry. It was so like Phil to include a black girl among the waitresses, when almost any other person would have been afraid to do so. Serena hoped she and Marie could become friends someday.

A few weeks earlier, Phil had become upset at the morning coffee and returned to the bank spouting words about how much he disliked prejudice and bigotry. After she asked him why he was so upset, he said, "Tony Stone told a horrible racist joke. I've never liked racist jokes. Such so-called jokes are part of the barrier between races. They keep people from trying to know people in the other race. We have an obligation to respect each other, to work together and understand one another, or at least do nothing that denies opportunity," Phil had said, hotly.

Inside the bank, she had seen him talking regularly only with Calvin Ivy, Marie's father, but if he had become upset again with the bigotry found all around them, she hadn't heard him mention it.

Work inside the bank was becoming almost normal again because customers were beginning to believe the announcement that the bank's bonding company and Merrill's bonding company were going to absorb the million-dollar loss. The bonding companies were fighting it out in court, and representatives from both companies said their company would not pay more than one million dollars. If one company's lawyers agreed that the entire loss was their client's responsibility that would leave an unpaid loss of $229,000.

All duties and responsibilities at the bank were being changed, and employees were finding their jobs changed drastically. Even the paper forms long used by the bank in routine operations had been reworded and redesigned.

Employees had been selected, one or two at a time, to spend a day at an Atlanta bank recommended by Robocker, the new president. Serena left home one morning at six o'clock to visit the Atlanta bank and watched a teller operate a computer bookkeeping machine. She had been fascinated by the fact that checks had special magnetic numbers and could be encoded with the dollar amount before being scanned and debited from the proper account. She was especially interested in how the machine did its own balancing and printed each depositor's statement. She returned home after 7:00 PM, knowing that computers were going to bring more major changes to the Cameron bank operation.

Robocker also offered a free electric toaster to anyone who set up a new checking account and arranged free coffee and doughnuts one morning a week to draw people into the bank. He also announced plans to offer free peach ice cream to all visitors one afternoon as soon as the local orchards produced ripe fruits. He joined the employees in greeting and welcoming all visitors to the bank.

Whenever Robocker's name was mentioned, local people said, "He's gonna straighten things out," and a few more people came in for loans. If nothing else happened, the bank might return to the profitable side.

Serena had stopped worrying so much about losing her job and was concentrating on doing exactly what the new president expected. Joyce was doing the same, and they frequently talked about details of the new procedures to be sure they both understood.

No arrests had been made for the bank swindle, and rumors had died down. The disappearance of Paul Norris had left the impression that he was guilty, and townspeople were waiting until the FBI agents gathered up enough evidence to make his arrest.

Trey Bowman was traveling between Cameron and Philadelphia and concentrating his efforts on the bank swindle. He had been successful in other investigations and earlier had been named top agent in the Philadelphia FBI office. He was determined to be successful in the "Merrill Mess," the sobriquet used by the agents.

Bowman also was enjoying brief explorations of northeast Georgia. During his first week in Georgia, Serena Sheppard's laughter at his description of Georgia people had been like holding a lighted match to a fuse. His investigative nature went into overdrive, and he immediately wanted to know as much as he could about the area. All his previous work had been in or around Philadelphia, a totally different place, with very different people. Philadelphia was the social and cultural center of America's first thirteen colonies. There, the ideas and subsequent actions of people long ago had given birth to the American Revolution and the nation's resulting independence. The city now was a metropolis full of art, science, and history museums.

On hearing that he would be working in Georgia, Bowman's first thought was about racial prejudice. Although it was found across the nation, racial prejudice made up the soul of the Deep South where Cameron was located. It was much more than simple fear of a person who is different.

Bowman checked out library books to recall his knowledge of slavery. When slavery first came into the United States, it flourished across the North as well as in the South, but only the South's economy depended on slavery. Slaves were eventually released in the North, but it took the terrible War Between the States to free slaves in the South. The war had happened more than one hundred years earlier, but the damage it caused still remained in the minds of Southerners, both whites and blacks. Whites in the South lost everything in the war—livelihoods, national status, pride. Blacks gained freedom from slavery, but remained tangled in the history of their race. It was a history that also burdened white people.

People seeking influence in the South began to openly play the races against each other, and politicians continued to make promises that benefited whites to the detriment of blacks. At the same time, blacks almost always approached white strangers as if they expected bad treatment.

Bowman and his fellow agents in Atlanta had talked at length about attitudes in the South. Bowman learned that pointy-headed Ku Klux Klan members in white sheets and other signs of racial hatred still appeared on the Cameron scene now and then. These public demonstrations were rare, but they raised fear in the whites as well as the blacks. The whites feared that people such as the Klanners were going to cause unnecessary violence between the races. The blacks feared for their own well-being.

Martin Luther King Jr., the brave black Baptist preacher from Atlanta who successfully led the nation's nonviolent protests against discrimination, had been assassinated in Tennessee three years earlier. For thirteen years, he had been the main leader seeking equal treatment of all people, and his death was devastating for black people everywhere. He had been their Moses, the man leading them to a promised land.

Bowman believed that spouting words of hatred toward a different race allowed people such as the Klanners to feel power, an emotion that gave them a sense of self-worth. These fervent, loud-mouthed, sometimes violent, radicals were full of fear, and they eased their discomfort by condemning people who were different from them. "It is probably this fear that keeps Klanners from succeeding in life because they almost always reside in low-rent areas with few material possessions," said one of the Atlanta agents.

Most residents in the small mountain towns avoided association with any sheet-wearing radical who appeared on their local streets.

The agents also talked about Philadelphia's Liberty Bell monument, comparing it to monuments in northeast Georgia. Bowman told his fellow agents about Gainesville's plans to build a monument to a chicken. He had read in the *Daily Times* that the Gainesville mayor wanted such a monument because decades earlier his city declared itself the Poultry Capital of the World. Another agent said that Cornelia, a town near

Cameron, had a monument to apples. Bowman and the Atlanta agents had chuckled about comparing Philadelphia's historic Liberty Bell to a chicken and an apple.

But later, Bowman thought about their conversation as he drove to Cameron.

The Philadelphia bell was a monument to freedom and independence. It first rang on July 8, 1776, to announce the first public reading of the nation's Declaration of Independence. Engraved words on the bell were taken from Leviticus 25:10 and read, "Proclaim liberty throughout all the Land unto all the inhabitants thereof."

In Gainesville today, almost 200 years later, people were planning to build a monument saluting poultry. Bowman learned that residents in the area began growing chickens by the thousands in the 1930s. During the 1950s, chickens helped Gainesville produce more millionaires per capita than any other town, and the city declared itself the Poultry Capital of the World. Now people wanted to salute the industry that made their riches possible.

In Cornelia, the apple monument had been dedicated on June 4, 1926. At that time, Habersham County's prize-winning apples were being loaded onto the train in Cornelia to be shipped all over the country, and Southern Railway donated the monument to show appreciation of the business. Constructed of steel and concrete in Virginia, the apple weighed 5,200 pounds, was seven feet high, twenty-two feet in circumference, and was painted bright red. It was located at the train depot, mounted on top of a white concrete pedestal eight feet high and six feet square at the base.

The three monuments were a lesson in America's history, in a citizen's right to own property and to conduct business. Cornelia's big red apple monument and Gainesville's proposed poultry industry monument confirmed the freedom declared by the Liberty Bell in Philadelphia. *I wonder what monuments demonstrating freedom I can find in other cities*, Bowman thought.

Back in Cameron, the explosion of the Hall County home was one more brick on a very heavy load for Serena. When she tried to talk to Phil about it, he said he had no idea what caused the explosion and then shocked her by saying she was acting too much like Trey Bowman.

Serena sometimes could put unpleasant things out of her mind, and she tried to erase thoughts about both the explosion and the change in Phil's attitude. As she drove home that evening, she was looking forward to seeing if the cement duck had different attire from what it had worn that morning.

The duck's attire had changed to a somber black cape with a wide-brimmed flat black hat. If it had worn a black mask across its eyes, it would have looked like Zorro, the swash-buckling Spanish superhero who used his favorite weapon, a rapier, to make his distinctive Z mark. Instead, it only looked dismal, gloomy, and cheerless. *Its costume manager is having a bad day*, Serena thought.

Looking at the duck, she did not see a large truck loaded with giant logs, a common sight on north Georgia roads. She did not notice that the truck was coming too fast toward her on the curve ahead.

*   *   *

The next thing Serena knew, she was trying to see who was standing at the foot of her narrow bed. She had opened her eyes and found herself flat on her back with her hands tied down. *They have put me in jail and tied me down,* she thought.

The strange figure in her room was dressed from head to foot in an unusual sage-green color.

She looked at the stranger and said, "Where am I?"

"You're in tha Gainesville hospital, honey," the figure said, and the voice sounded exactly like her grandmother's.

"Why are my hands tied down?" Serena said.

"That's because you've been trying to pull out the tubes," her grandmother's voice said.

The figure came to the side of the bed, and Serena could see that it really was her grandmother, but she was wearing a green smock and a green cloth over her head. It was the same thing that doctors wore when they were in the operating room.

"Why are you dressed like that?" Serena said.

"You're in intensive care. You had a wreck, and you're injured really bad. The doctors wudden let me come in here and see you unless I put this on first," Mama Tatum said.

"It was the bird."

"Whaddaya mean, honey?"

"It was a big, black bird."

"Honey, I don't know anything about a bird. A loada logs fell offa truck right in front of yer car, and you plowed into 'em. They wudda fallen on top of yer car if it 'ad gone forward one more second. The car's a total loss, and, at first, the doctors thought you wudden live, but yer strong. Yer gonna make it, honey."

"What is today?" Serena said.

"It's Tuesday. You been here five days," Mama Tatum answered as she patted Serena's arm.

Serena glanced down and saw a tube coming across her stomach from somewhere near her neck. She could see another tube sticking out of her side. Her eyes closed again, and she did not know anything else.

Chapter 28

The next time Serena was aware of her surroundings, the tubes were gone, and the incisions made for tubes in her throat and side were closed with fresh stitches.

Two nurses came into her room and said that she was going to be moved out of the intensive care unit and into a private room. But first they would have to wheel her bed into the X-ray laboratory. They wanted more pictures of the bones in the lower part of her body before they put her legs into either orthopedic tractions or casts.

The bed was rolled down the Northeast Georgia Medical Center hallway and into an elevator. After the elevator dropped a couple of floors, the bed was pushed out and rolled down another hallway. In the X-ray laboratory, Serena was lifted onto the cold metal table, and the nurse carefully arranged her legs in the appropriate positions. A large camera was positioned over her lower body for pictures, first of one leg then the other.

The resulting negatives verified the simple fracture in the femur or thigh bone of one leg and the dislocated patella or kneecap in the other.

Cotton bandage saturated with plaster was carefully rolled around her knee. After an aide wet the bandage, it began to harden into a close-fitting cast that would hold her kneecap in place.

Back in her private room upstairs, she was lying in her bed totally exhausted when a white-coated doctor and his male assistant came into the room. The assistant carried a small black bag.

"We want that broken femur to heal the right way," the doctor said, looking down at her leg.

The assistant took a hammer and slender metal pin out of the black bag and handed them to the doctor. "This won't hurt," the doctor said. The assistant took her leg and again held it in the right position while the doctor hammered the silver pin through her knee. Serena knotted her fists and gritted her teeth, expecting to feel more pain than she actually did.

The pin protruded from both sides of her knee, and the doctor attached cords on each end of the pin. The cords went through small pulleys on a metal frame and ended below her foot. Iron weights were added at the ends of the cords to pull the thigh bone back into place.

Serena had never verbally expressed fright or alarm about accidents or the deaths of loved ones. She had always put her thoughts on hold if a problem came up that she couldn't solve—as, for example, when her grandfather died suddenly when she was ten years old.

He had been warning her, her younger brother, and her grandmother about work that was under way to replace the porch and steps on the back of the house. "You can't go out the back until it's finished," he said. Minutes later, a man delivering feed had sounded his truck horn at their barn, and her grandfather had dashed out the back door. The resulting fall had broken his neck, and he had died three days later. At that time, she had said nothing about her own heavy sadness but had immediately tried to think of ways she could help Mama T.

Now she was waiting again, waiting to be whole, waiting until she could go on with her life just as before.

After the doctor finished putting her right leg in traction, she went to sleep once again. She woke when Fred, Penny, and Nicole came into the room.

"You have really given us a scare," Fred said. Both girls came to the bed and kissed their mother's forehead.

"We don't want to hurt you," Penny said.

"Does your mouth hurt?" Nicole said.

"No," said Serena. Her head felt strange, and she didn't wonder why Nicole had questioned her about her mouth.

"Are you going to school? Are you doing your homework?" Serena asked slowly.

Both girls assured her that they were keeping up with everything at school. "We missed school only two days," Nicole said.

"Daddy came and got us the night they brought you to the hospital, and we stayed here in the waiting room all that night and the next day. We were afraid you were going to die, but after the doctors told us you were going to make it, we went back home and went to school the next day," Penny said.

"You ought to see your car. No one knows how you came out alive," Fred said.

All was silent in the room for a minute. None of the family knew exactly what to say.

"We've only got one more week, and we'll be out for summer," said Nicole, who was never without words for long.

"You must study to pass your finals," Serena said. Penny would be in the twelfth grade next year and would get her driver's license that summer. Nicole would be in the eleventh grade. But Serena still could not think well enough to remember these details.

Fred said he had been asked to build expensive black cherry cabinets in the kitchen and two bathrooms of a home, adding that it was for a farmer who raised chickens for a living. Then he said they must leave, and this time he came to the bed and kissed Serena on the forehead before he left the room. Nicole and Penny said, "We love you, Mom," as they stepped out and closed the door behind them.

The next morning, a nurse's aide gave Serena a mirror and asked her if she wanted to comb her hair. It was the first time Serena had seen the stitches in her lips or her missing front tooth, and the fact that she had bandages on one side of her forehead. But the rest of her face was just as she remembered.

Later that day she summoned a nurse to her room to tell her about severe pain in her chest and back. A doctor was called, and a quick examination revealed that she had a collapsed lung. Although she had not been moving, a rib broken in the accident had punctured her lung, and now air was filling the space between the collapsed lung and her chest wall.

The nurse pulled her over onto her left side and held her there while a doctor inserted a needle into her back between her ribs to withdraw the air.

The days passed slowly, and the television beside her bed didn't help pass the time. The severe concussion had left her mind muddled, and a bruise on her brain had damaged her vision. A hospital volunteer came to her room daily with magazines loaded on a cart. But Serena couldn't see well enough to read the stories, and she stared long and hard at cards from friends who were wishing her well. Vases with flower arrangements and get-well wishes were brought in almost daily, and they eventually filled the shelf at the bottom of the large window and covered the bedside stand.

She could use electric buttons to raise the head of her hospital bed, but when she did, the weights on her leg pulled her whole body toward the bottom of the bed.

She could never eat the food that was brought to her bed, and Fred went to the hospital kitchen and placed a special order to provide her with a sirloin steak. But steak was his favorite food, not hers, and when it was delivered for her evening meal she couldn't force down the first bite.

Joyce came in to see her and brought a shiny apple—a Red Delicious from the grocery store. Despite her missing front tooth, she bit into the apple, ate every morsel, and got praise from the nurses.

She still had not summed up everything in her life and reached a solid conclusion as to why she was in the hospital.

Days floated past, and she began to remember the details of her job and the last months at Cameron National Bank. She had been in the hospital a month, and it had been nine months since the money had been discovered missing. Maybe someone had now been arrested for the giant swindle.

She finished eating a few bites of her lunch one day, and the aide walked out with the tray when she heard a soft knock at her door.

"Come in," she said.

The door opened and a man came in wearing a navy blue shirt and khaki-colored cotton pants. His face was familiar, but Serena could not immediately remember who he was.

Chapter 29

"Hello," the visitor said, and warm memories flooded into Serena's mind as if a curtain had been raised to let in the sunlight. It was Trey Bowman, the FBI agent.

"Hi," she answered.

"How do you feel?"

"Much better. I'm getting better every day."

"I've talked to your doctor, and he said I could come here and talk to you, but only if you feel up to it."

"I feel like talking, and my memory is coming back day by day, but it's still not the best. Have you found out who took the money?"

"No."

"I still don't remember everything, and I don't know if I can help you," she said.

"If you feel like having me here for a while, we'll just talk about life. I'm enjoying learning about this part of the United States, and I want to learn as much as I can while I'm here. If you remember something that you think is important about the missing money, just tell me when you think of it," Bowman said.

"Okay. Maybe just talking about life will make my mind work better. My family is always so busy, no one has time to just sit here beside my bed and talk," Serena said.

Trey picked up a chair near the wall and moved it close to the bed before sitting down to look at Serena.

"You told me you grew up with your grandmother in White County.

What was your childhood like? Did you have pets? Did you have brothers and sisters?" he said.

"You're serious. You really want to know, don't you?"

"Yes, I want to know."

"Well, I didn't have sisters, but I had one younger brother and plenty of second cousins. My brother is married now and lives in North Carolina. The second cousins were actually grandchildren of my great aunt, my grandmother's sister. They were always coming to Mama Tatum's house, and I was never lonely. They always called her Mama Tatum or Mama T, so that's what my brother and I called her, too, even though she was the only mother we had."

"What about pets?"

"When I was a child, I liked to collect wild animals and have them for my pets. I love almost all the Earth's creatures, but I don't like birds."

"What's wrong with birds?"

"My grandmother had a bantam rooster that fiercely attacked me and other people. It used the sharp talons on its feet to draw blood. It was so bad that she had to ask a neighbor to kill it."

"I've seen pictures of bantams called fighting cocks. I don't doubt that a bantam could make you dislike birds."

Serena wanted to tell him that she didn't just dislike birds, but was terrified of all feathered creatures. Instead, she said, "I had a flying squirrel named … wait, I'll think of his name."

"A flying squirrel?"

"Yes, he was dear. I had one blouse with a pocket, and I never wanted to wear anything but that blouse so he could hide in the pocket. I know—his name was Grayboy. I was about twelve years old and had really enjoyed a library book about a medieval knight called Sir Graystone. I think that's why I named him Grayboy. He liked to stay in my blouse pocket and raise his head up barely enough to look around with his big eyes."

"What does a flying squirrel look like? I've never seen one," Trey said.

"That's probably because they're active at night and sleep in the daytime. They are the size of a chipmunk and have a thin furry skin between their front and back legs. They glide through the air between trees almost like birds, and they make wonderful pets," she said. "Have you ever seen a lightning bug? Have you ever played with a June bug?"

Bowman laughed as he said, "Did you play with insects, too?"

"I wish you could be here in Georgia on a soft summer evening just as the sun is setting. Tiny flashes from lightning bugs or fireflies begin to fill the night. They're sending signals to other fireflies."

"Do June bugs send light signals too?"

"No, they're just beetles. We would catch one during the day and tie a sewing thread to one of its legs. Then we held the thread while it flew around us."

"How big is a June bug?"

"Only about the size of your thumbnail. But it was fun for us as children to think we were controlling their flights."

Serena didn't want to do all the talking, so she asked him questions about himself. "You said your grandparents also raised you. Do you have brothers and sisters?" she said.

"I have a sister. She works for the Bureau of Indian Affairs. We both always wanted to do something that we thought would benefit other people, but I think she's helping others now more than I am," he said.

"You told me you have American Indian blood. Can you tell me about your Indian ancestors?" Serena said.

"My ancestors on one side of the family were Iroquois Indians. The name Iroquois refers to a league of five—later six—Indian nations located around the Great Lakes area. My father was a Seneca, which is one of the Iroquois tribes. His mother, my paternal grandmother, was a French-speaking Canadian, and his father was a full-blood Seneca. I was reared by my mother's people, and I've never really known my father or his people.

"My mother was a secretary at the University of Buffalo, and she met my father when he was there working his way through college. They had planned to have three children, but Mother decided I would be the last child, and that's how I got the name Trey. It means "three" in French. She died of cancer when I was eight years old, and I have only vague memories of my father. Someday I'm going to look for him and his relatives. I want to know more, but at the same time I'm hesitant. I want to know as much as I can about my own personal strengths before

I look at the accomplishments or failures of my ancestors," Bowman said. It was obvious that he had given much thought to investigating his heritage.

"Before you start looking, do you want to know you can deal with any frightening ancestry you might discover?" she said.

"That's one way of putting it. You seem to understand what I'm saying," Bowman said.

"Maybe I do. Maybe I've felt the same way. I guess we both wonder what traits we might have inherited, don't we?"

Bowman got up and walked around the bed to look out the window.

"Trey," Serena said, softly. It was the first time she had ever spoken his name. He looked at her.

"I remember a house exploding in Hall County just about the time I had my accident. Was it their gas stove? What made it explode?" Serena said.

Bowman turned his face back to the window, and they both were silent for a few seconds before he said, "It might not have been accidental. I'm not sure, and the local law enforcement officers are investigating. People are saying a small bomb was detonated underneath the house by someone in a plane overhead."

Serena tried to absorb what he had said. "Do you think the explosion is connected with the missing money?"

"I don't know what to think. I'm just trying to gather all the pieces and see if anything fits together."

"I'll be relieved when it's all done, whatever the outcome. Our lives in Cameron have changed. I've been looking at different people and wondering if he is the one or she is the one who stole the money from Cameron National Bank. I know people are looking at me and wondering if it's me. Do you have any real leads yet? Can you talk about it?" Serena said.

"I can't talk about it. When the pieces begin to fit, I'll be making a case to be used by the court prosecutors," Bowman said.

"If you want me to talk about the bank again, I'll try, but I don't think I can remember anything that I haven't already told you," Serena said.

"I'm going to come back and bring pictures for you to look at. I guess you think you've looked at all the pictures, but I need you to look again. I'll give you a little more time to recover. I don't think another week will make me lose anything. It's been nine months since I began looking at this check-writing caper. I don't think the guilty parties are going to try it again anytime soon. May I come back to see you while you're still here in the hospital?" Bowman said.

"Please do," Serena answered.

He walked out the door, then stuck his head back in and said, "I'll be back on Monday."

Chapter 30

That evening, Serena tried hard to concentrate on a television program and decided she would be able to think much better if she could find a program that captured her mind. She had three stations to choose from and a skimpy television schedule on the bedside table. A movie was going to be shown on one of the stations in about five minutes. It was based on a novel by Emily Brontë that she had read in high school.

The black-and-white movie, *Wuthering Heights,* produced thirty years earlier, was set on England's Yorkshire moors in the eighteenth century. It told of an orphaned boy named Heathcliff who grew up to fall passionately in love with his foster sister. The sister was played by Merle Oberon, and Heathcliff was played by Laurence Olivier. Olivier's shiny dark hair and chiseled face reminded her of Trey Bowman's. It totally captured her attention, and, despite the couple's thwarted love, which resulted in contemptible, bitter actions by the Heathcliff character, she was sad when it ended.

She vowed she would find things requiring concentration and try to exercise her mind. Maybe it would speed her mental recovery and make her feel clear-headed again.

Serena was attempting to work a crossword puzzle in the daily newspaper when Fred brought Mama Tatum and the girls by on Wednesday evening. The hospital was almost forty miles from both Mama Tatum's home and Serena's home. It was not easy for Fred to bring them and still put in a full day of work.

Penny and Nicole soon found Serena's unfinished crossword puzzle on the table beside her bed. They had never seen their mother engage in this type of activity and began to question her.

"This is about entertainment, and it's supposed to be an easy puzzle, but I'm already stuck, and I just began," Serena said. "What is a five-letter word for 'Studio 54 and its Man in the Moon' dance floor? I think it begins with a *d*."

"Would that be 'disco'?" said Penny.

"Yes. I believe you're right," Serena said. She penciled it in and laid the newspaper back on the hospital's tray table.

The girls had passed their finals and were getting ready to welcome Serena back home. They would be out of school and would be able to stay at home with her until she was completely recovered.

On Sunday afternoon, Fred and the girls came back for an hour.

Later that day, Phil Anderson came by to give her news from the bank. He told her he had seen Paul Norris's wife, Carolyn, leaving the grocery store but didn't have a chance to talk to her. "I went by the feed store twice, trying to see the Norrises' son, but he's always traveling," he said. "He never comes into the bank anymore."

"It's not a good idea for an innocent person to change his way of doing business. It makes him look guilty. He should still come in the bank and do business the same way he always has," Serena said.

"Yes, you're right," Phil said.

Both Phil and Serena wondered aloud about Paul Norris and what he was doing with his time. He and Carolyn evidently were staying close to home because no one ever saw them. Phil did not mention the exploded house or the FBI agent and neither did Serena.

On Monday, Bowman returned to Serena's room shortly after lunch, as he had done before.

They greeted each other, and before he could ask how she was, Serena told him she was probably going to be dismissed from the hospital that Friday. The cast had been removed from her left leg, and her right leg, which had the broken thigh bone, was out of traction, the silver nail having been removed from her knee. A new fiberglass cast now covered the leg from her toes to her hip.

"I'm glad you're going home, but that means I won't have a captive audience when I want to talk," Bowman said, smiling.

Serena laughed. "If you just want to talk, you'll find someone," she said.

"I don't enjoy talking with just anyone," Bowman said. He did not tell her that he would have liked to talk to her even if she had never worked at the bank.

Again he pulled the chair away from the wall and placed it near her bed before sitting down. He had brought his briefcase in with him, and he reached in to pull out a file.

"Do you feel like looking at pictures again?"

"I'll look, but …"

"Here, I'll place them on your tray table," Bowman said.

He placed in front of her the photo that she had chosen as being closest to her memory of Jarvis Salisbury. As she looked at it, he placed a clear piece of plastic over it giving the image longer sideburns, longer hair, and a Fu Manchu beard.

Serena stared at it and then raised her eyes to look at Bowman. "That looks a lot like my memory of him," she said.

Bowman pulled out four more photos and went through the same procedure with a different plastic overlay for each one, but it didn't work as well with the other photos.

The first one was still the closest to a likeness of Jarvis Salisbury.

Serena decided to question Bowman while he was putting the photos back in his briefcase. "Do you remember back at the fish fry when we were at Smith Jackson's lake house? Do you remember Herman Fowler, the president of the bank over in Martin County?" she said.

"I remember him well," Bowman said.

"He said he knew Paul Norris was in on the scheme from the beginning to get that million dollars. My grandmother says Herman Fowler is known for his bragging, and I don't believe he was telling the truth that day."

"I've been checking into Fowler's background, and I can tell you this much. I've come to the conclusion that Herman Fowler likes to be in the spotlight, even if it's for the wrong reasons. I'm beginning to think he made up what he said about the man who approached him before he went to Norris. I think he said those things just because he didn't want Norris to have all the attention," Bowman said, chuckling.

"I know it's impossible for me to look at this objectively, but I can't believe Paul Norris knew that money was going to be stolen," Serena said.

"No, you can't be objective," he said conclusively, indicating that the subject was closed for the moment.

"We haven't made any arrests in the bank swindle, but you'll be glad to know that yesterday your sheriff broke up a car theft ring. He and the Georgia Bureau of Investigation arrested four people who have been operating from an old farm in Banks County. They had a chop shop in an old abandoned chicken house and were stealing cars all over this area. They took them apart and sold the pieces, everything from the radio and seats to the transmissions and wheels."

Banks County, like Martin, White, and Hall counties, was located on the Habersham County border. The chop shop probably had been only fifteen or twenty miles from Cameron.

"I'm glad I don't drive a popular car. If I drove a Ford Mustang, I'd be worried all the time," Serena said.

"You're right about that. They found the remains of two disassembled Mustangs in the chicken house."

"The arrests are good news. We never had so many car thefts before, and, of course, everyone was wondering if the car thefts and the money thefts were done by the same people," Serena said.

"No. The people arrested in the car theft ring probably haven't even visited Philadelphia. The people involved in the money theft, the ones we think did it, make their homes in Philadelphia," Bowman said.

Silence filled the room as both wondered who the local person was that the investigators had not yet identified.

"What are you going to do when you're dismissed from the hospital? Can you walk yet?" Bowman said.

"I'm walking a little with crutches. I'm not walking fast, but I'm walking," Serena said. "My girls will be at home with me, and we'll all be fine."

Bowman left without saying much, and Serena wondered if she had said something to insult him. On Thursday evening he was back again.

"I didn't come back especially to talk about the bank. I've got to go back to Philadelphia, and I just wanted to see you again and wish you well before I left," he said.

"I'm glad you came back," Serena said.

"For some reason, I feel like you and I have been partners in a past life. I feel like we are old souls who have found each other again," he said. "Maybe it's because we were both raised by our grandparents. Maybe it's because I've enjoyed discovering things about this area through talking to you.

"I told you something about my background and my parents, but you haven't told me about you. You don't really have to tell me, but I'd like to know where your parents are. Why were you reared by your grandmother?" he said.

Years earlier, Serena had listened when her grandmother had talked about her mother and father, but she was only about fourteen years old the last time she heard them mentioned. She had never before discussed with another person the details of what had happened to them.

Now she hesitated, but, for some reason, she felt she had to be totally honest with Bowman on any subject. As she started to speak, she could literally feel a movement in her chest as if her heart had opened. "The only things I know about my parents are what my grandmother and grandfather, my mother's parents, told me. My grandmother is still deeply hurt about what happened, and I'm sure the information I have is one-sided."

She stopped talking, aware that he was looking at her intently, but he waited patiently.

"My father was very jealous of my mother. He shot her and killed her, then turned the gun on himself."

"I knew it was going to be a tragedy. For some reason, I knew," Bowman said. "Where were you when this happened?"

"I was barely four years old. He and my mother had a terrible argument, and then he left. I don't know what they were upset about. After several days passed, my mother took me and my baby brother and went to my grandparents' house.

"One day a man, whose family lived near my grandparents, came by and asked my mother if she wanted to take a ride in his new car. He had been working in Atlanta and was considered very successful. The year was 1942, and new cars were rare in this area, so riding in one was a special treat for my mother.

"My mom picked me up and got in the car. He drove us all the way to Clarkesville, which earlier was a popular resort town for people who lived on the coast. He parked near a gazebo, and they talked for a few minutes, then he left the car and went into a drugstore to get ice cream cones.

"Mama Tatum said my father saw us as soon as the car came into town. When my mother's friend went into the store, my father came to the car, pulled out a pistol and shot her in the chest, then shot himself in the head. He ended her life and his."

"Was your mother holding you in her lap?"

"No, I was sitting beside her. We both were sitting in the passenger's seat." To Serena's surprise, tears rolled down both her cheeks.

Bowman looked at her with great tenderness, but did not move. "I'm glad you were not older," he said.

"Sometimes I think I remember it. Sometimes I'm afraid I'm going to remember it." She used both hands to wipe the tears hastily from her face. "Someday I want to know more about my father. He was from Oregon, and I don't really know anything about him or his family."

"Tell me about your husband and your daughters."

Serena told him quickly about how she had always known Fred, about his cabinet-making business, about her daughters, and how she jokingly had named them Penny and Nicole because, when Penny had been born almost sixteen years ago, Serena had been childishly proud to have a job at the bank.

"Whatever it takes, whatever I have to do, I want to provide my daughters with a stable home complete with both their mother and their father," she said, looking intently at Bowman.

"You must be a wonderful mother," he said.

"I'm trying my best to do what I think is right."

"Are your daughters planning to go to college?"

"I hope they will. I hope they can get some kind of scholarship. They love basketball, and they're good at it. Sometimes I think how wonderful it would be if college sports scholarships were available for females the same as they are for males. I think they will be, eventually," she said.

Serena had heard about efforts to open female sport scholarships to women, but she did not know that a bill called Equal Opportunity in Education was already being considered by the US Congress. It would become known simply as Title IX and would deny federal funding to any program in the field of education that was not open to both sexes.

"Many things are unfair in this world," Bowman said, and they were both quiet for a moment before he spoke again.

"I'm going back to Philadelphia, but I plan to be back here sometime this fall. Take care of yourself and take care of those daughters. They're lucky to have you. I hope I can see you again when I come back," Bowman said.

"You know where I work," Serena said, smiling and exposing her missing front tooth.

She wanted to say, "Please don't leave," but only watched as he walked out the door without looking back.

Chapter 31

A couple of weeks after Serena got home, her mind was almost back in full form, and she had only the one cast on her right leg from her hip to her toes. She could move short distances with crutches and hopped a short distance several times each day in an effort to increase her stamina.

She had been afraid she and Fred would be saddled with a huge hospital bill, because they had learned that the man who owned the log truck didn't have insurance and didn't own much more than the big truck.

But the health insurance at the bank and the policy they had on her car had paid the entire hospital bill and provided money for a down payment on another car for Serena—a five-year-old gray Ford LTD with an automatic transmission. The premium for their car insurance, both collision and liability, had been due once a month, and sometimes it had been a strain to pay. Now Serena was deeply grateful that she had never missed a payment.

The summer months were hot, and they used electric fans to move the air in the house both day and night. Serena knew that using the fans meant having to dust the furniture more and wash the curtains much more, but she opposed air-conditioning. She believed fresh air was important.

The long-planned trip to Washington, DC, had to be postponed. Despite being very nervous, Penny got her driver's license the first time she took the test, and, with Serena at home, she wanted to drive somewhere every day. Serena would drag her cast into the passenger seat of the newly purchased car while Penny got under the steering wheel.

Her right leg still was in its fiberglass mold when Serena went back to work in late July. Luckily, the Ford LTD's automatic transmission meant she could drive using only one foot. She threw the unbending right leg across the seat toward the passenger side and used her left foot to operate both the gas pedal and brakes.

Back at the bank, it was as if her life had made a small, complete circle and was back to its starting point again. Every employee was still at the bank except Paul Norris.

Robocker, the gregarious president who was quick to make friends, was still there, and the bank was still recovering from the losses it had suffered when so many people withdrew their funds. It was still not back to the point where it had been when the check fiasco had occurred, and apparently some unknown person was going to get away with a million dollars because no arrests had been made.

*   *   *

In mid-October, the trees across the northeast Georgia mountains were at the beginning of their annual color exhibition before they retired for the winter.

Serena had been without the cast for almost three months, a dentist had replaced her tooth, and her health was almost back to its former condition.

One Sunday morning, she and the girls attended their little country church. Hearing the preacher's message and seeing friends on Sunday morning always seemed to refresh her mind and renew her spirit for the following week.

This Sunday, they wanted to hear the visiting preacher from Florida. Serena knew that a visitor would not be preaching about stealing, with vague references to the bank. Joyce had told her about a local preacher who had said so much about money and thievery that he had made it sound sinful to be employed by a bank.

In his sermon, the Florida preacher had talked about times of darkness in personal lives and the darkness Jesus Christ faced in the Garden of Gethsemane before he was arrested and facing crucifixion. "His disciples were confused and made wrong decisions, but they were forgiven. We also can be forgiven for the wrong decisions we sometimes make," he said.

As Serena left the church, she spoke to people she knew. One woman said, "How is Mr. Norris?"

"I haven't seen him since he left the bank. I hope he's well," Serena said.

"I also hope he's well," the woman answered, and Serena was relieved. Then the woman said, "But I'll be glad when they find out who took that money. It had to be someone in the bank." Serena's relief disappeared.

Earlier, before the visiting preacher began his sermon, he had described trying to find the little church. The story revealed the tourist attractions of the mountains and amused Serena so much that she repeated it later at work.

To get directions again, the preacher had stopped at a telephone booth at a service station and called the deacon chairman, who was responsible for his visit. After having the directions repeated, the visiting preacher asked why there was so much traffic on the roads.

"It's people coming to the mountains to see the leaves," the deacon had answered.

"What are the leaves doing?" the visiting preacher had asked. He had lived all his life in Florida and did not know about the beauty of the mountains when the hardwood trees turned red or yellow and colors in between. But he was a man who could laugh at himself, and, after the deacon told him people were coming to see the autumn colors, he had laughed, then laughed again as he told the congregation about asking what the leaves were doing to cause so much traffic.

Each day, Serena drove to work and looked at the roadside scenery as always. One Friday, as she passed the cement duck, she saw that it was wearing an elaborate necklace containing what appeared to be large rhinestones. As with the little sunglasses months before, the necklace was like nothing she had ever seen before. This time, she could not imagine what it might be predicting. A wild night on the town? A new and rebellious experience?

That same weekend, Clarkesville was having its annual autumn festival with booths on the square, and Serena and her two daughters had volunteered to help, as they did each year. Artists and craftspeople were displaying clever woodwork, needlework items, and skilled oil or watercolor paintings of mountain scenes. Cars had come through town in a steady stream, and people—both local residents and tourists—had crowded around the booths throughout the day.

Children carried helium balloons of every color, and occasionally one would accidentally be released to become a colorful orb floating across the blue sky. Some of the youngsters were pulling wooden ducks on strings. The ducks quacked almost like real ducks and raised their feet to waddle forward. *I guess my cement duck and its big rhinestones were letting me know that Clarkesville was going to be filled with joy*, Serena thought, with a mental smile.

She worked at a food booth for the high school and spent much of her day sitting on a stool. When she was getting ready to leave, she began to look for Fred. He was nowhere to be found. Finally, she saw one of her neighbors, who said, "Fred said to tell you he was going home early."

She had ridden to the festival with her daughters and one of their friends, but they wanted to go into Gainesville for a movie, so she had told them she would ride home with Fred. Now she was tired and stranded ten miles from home.

She looked around through the crowd but saw no one with whom she could ride, and it would soon be dark. She gathered her purse and started walking along the only sidewalk in town. A gas station with a public pay phone was located about four blocks away, and she could use a dime there to call Fred.

Before she got more than a block from the square, a car stopped on the street beside her. It was a black sedan, and FBI Agent Trey Bowman leaned across the seat to open the door on the passenger side. "Can I drive you?" he asked.

Serena had thought about Bowman more than she wanted to admit since the last time she had seen him. Seeing his face again made her heart beat faster as she got into the car. "When did you get into town?"

"Yesterday. I've been looking for you. I have a lot to tell you," he said.

"I want to hear it, but now I'm trying to get home. I'm going to the station up here to use the telephone. Fred'll come back for me, but I'm glad to ride to the station. I'm really tired."

"I'll drive you home," Bowman answered. "You'll have to show me the way."

"I don't live near Clarkesville. It's about ten miles north of here."

"That's okay. I'll drive you," he said again.

He turned the car around at the gas station and drove slowly back through the square. String music was flowing from a temporary wooden bandstand as a young man played his guitar and belted out words from the new bluegrass favorite, "Rocky Top."

"I've had years of cramped up city life
Trapped like a duck in a pen
All I know is it's a pity life
Can't be simple again."

A few couples were dancing together on the pavement, and Bowman seemed to be in deep thought.

"This reminds me of a festival I used to go to in a suburb of Philadelphia," he said.

"Turn left up there," Serena said, and they turned onto Highway 197.

The car soon crossed the Soque River. The field beside the river was filled with vines, withered after fulfilling their purpose, and ripe orange pumpkins waiting to be made into jack-o'-lanterns for Halloween.

"How do you pronounce the name of this river?" Bowman said.

"It's sew-quee, with emphasis on the second syllable. It's an Indian name, and the river originates here in Habersham County and merges with the Chattahoochee River at the county's border. It exists only in this county," she said.

Serena suddenly realized that she was staring at Bowman's striking profile, at the way his shining black hair wanted to curl toward his face, and at his strong, tan hands on the steering wheel. She turned her head away. "It's good to see you," she said. "I'm anxious to hear what you have to tell me."

"You'll have to work me into your schedule in the next couple of days because I won't be here after that," he said.

She said, "I'll try," and was so aware of his presence beside her that she could think of nothing else to say. She sat quietly as the car went up a steep hill, then slowed down for deep curves.

"This must be what you call a mountain road," Bowman said.

"It's a unique road," she answered. "Before we get to my house we'll pass a place where a stream flows across the pavement. It may be the only paved road anywhere with a stream that you have to ford."

More deep curves were lined by forests and, now and then, a green pasture. Then the road began to curve beside the Soque River as it twisted and splashed over gray rocks.

"You're almost to the place where the side stream crosses the pavement," she said, and he slowed again.

The car topped a little rise, then went downhill to the stream. "You're right about this road being unique. I've never before had to drive into a stream that flows over a paved road," he said. "Why doesn't the water go underneath the road?"

"This place has an interesting history like so many other places around here," Serena said.

Bowman drove the car carefully across the stream, then pulled over and stopped. "Let's get out, and you can tell me about it."

They both got out of the car at the same time, and Serena said, "I think there's still enough light that we can see where an old corn mill used to be."

No longer tired, she began to step through the roadside's low weeds, and he said, "Let me have your hand."

He clasped Serena's right hand as she came around the back of the car, and she led him across the road to where the water splashed over the edge and down into the Soque. The afternoon sun was shining through the trees, softly touching them with early-evening shadows.

"Can you see that wall there?" she said, pointing down to where the water was spilling over. "You can still see a little bit of what once was the bottom of a chimney. It was part of a corn mill back at the turn of the century.

"An elderly woman who lived near here told me about riding to Clarkesville in her daddy's wagon when this road was dirt. The mules would always stop here and get a drink of water. During autumn the front porch of the mill would be filled with baskets of apples. They would buy a basket and eat apples on the way to town," Serena said.

"You like history, don't you?" he said.

"I love these old mountains and the wonderful stories they have to tell," she said, slightly embarrassed. They were still holding hands, and she didn't want to pull away.

"When this road was paved by President Roosevelt's Works Progress Administration, the woman at the mill here insisted that the water continue running across the road, not under it." She felt shy and spoke in a low voice. The only other sound was the splashing water.

Bowman didn't say anything.

The little stream tumbled into the river, and the river rushed on to its destination, while beside it, two people stood silently holding hands and watching. The trees in the forest stood like silent sentinels, and the sky grew darker. The surroundings were almost hypnotic.

Finally, another car came down the road and broke the spell. After it passed, Bowman started toward his car, still holding Serena's hand. He opened the door for her and shut it after she was seated. He went around the front of the car and opened his own door, getting in under the steering wheel. But instead of starting the engine, he turned toward her without speaking.

He put his hand on the back of her neck and pulled her face toward his. Slowly he put his lips on hers. The kiss was gentle, sweet, natural.

"I have wanted to do this since the day we were on the lake. I can't get you out of my mind," he said slowly, almost whispering.

With a hand on each side of her head, he moved his face inches away to look at her again. "I have missed you. When I'm with you I feel as if my life has come full circle. It's like I've looked and looked for something, and now I've found it," he said.

"And I've missed you," Serena said.

He kissed her again, hungrily.

Serena felt as if she were on another planet, a world containing only her and this man. Awareness intensified in every inch of her body. She felt as if she were floating, falling, and soaring, all at the same time.

She began to put her arms around him, when somewhere in her mind the images of her daughters and Fred floated to the surface, and she pulled away. "I can't do this," she said. "This is not possible. I must go home."

Bowman turned away slowly and started the engine. He pulled the car back onto the highway, and a few minutes later she said, "Turn left up there. Our house is on the right about three hundred yards down this road."

Bowman followed her directions and pulled into the graveled driveway of the white frame house. He didn't turn off the engine, and she didn't invite him inside.

She got out, walked around the front of the car to his window and said, "I'm sorry." She was sorry she had to push him away. She was sorry that she couldn't invite him inside.

"I'm not sorry, and you have nothing to apologize for," he said.

"Thank you for bringing me home," she said, moving away from the car.

He sat silently, letting the car lights shine on the gravel as she walked up to the walkway of flat rocks that led to her front porch. The front light was on, and she opened the door and went inside.

She heard Fred shutting the refrigerator door in the kitchen, and she leaned back against the front door. She felt drained and weak as she listened to Bowman's car back out of the driveway.

Chapter 32

"Can you meet me at the train depot?"

These were the words Serena heard the next day when she said, "Hello, this is Serena" into her telephone at the bank. It was Bowman's voice.

"I want to tell you some of the things I've learned," he said.

"What time?" she asked.

"Can you meet me when you get off at four o'clock?" Bowman asked.

"Yes," was all she said.

Bowman probably knew that Serena parked her car at the train depot every day. The depot was a large building with an office selling rare tickets for the Southern Crescent passenger train and also handling services for two freight trains. The employees of the bank and several other businesses used the parking lot in back.

Serena's last customers that day were identical twin sisters, Hortense and Drucilla Gooch. They always came in together, but they had separate checking and savings accounts. They had been Serena's classmates throughout elementary and high school, and each time she saw them she recalled what a third-grade classmate, a boy, had said behind their backs. "There goes Horse Sense and Draw Silly. Where did their parents get those names?"

Serena later learned that they were old family names passed down through the generations. The family believed that each name always brought success to the individual; when they had twins, they wanted them both to be successful. The names had met expectations; the twins operated Cameron's small women's dress shop and had a good customer base. They always looked as if they had just stepped out of a fashion magazine, and they had never questioned the bank about their deposits.

Taking care of their requests took only five minutes, and when the bank closed at three, Serena hurried through the balancing and closing procedures, attempting to be ready to leave a few minutes before four. She did not tell Joyce where she was going and hurried out the door.

The depot was only three blocks from the bank, and she saw Bowman sitting in his car parked across the lot from the place where she parked every day. She got into her driver's seat with the intention of driving over and picking him up, when she saw him getting out of his car. He walked across the lot, opened her door, and said, "Come and go with me. I'll drive around while we talk."

After escorting Serena to his car, he opened the passenger door for her. Feeling free and at ease, she sat down and pulled her feet into the car.

"I've got some news to share with you, but the bank case hasn't yet been solved," Bowman said as he settled in behind the steering wheel.

"We'll just drive around while we talk, but you'll have to give me directions," he said.

Whenever Serena wanted to think about a problem, she never failed to drive toward Mama Tatum's house. Now she gave Bowman directions to get his car traveling that road.

"First, I wanted to share news about the planes that dropped packages in the mountain forests and that man in Martin County who had the personal airport at his house," Bowman said.

"Oh, good. Please tell me," Serena said.

"It's already been reported in the Miami newspapers, so it will be reported here soon. The man with the busy airport was one small part of an international drug-smuggling ring."

"An international drug-smuggling ring? I know that President Nixon declared war on drugs some time ago, but I didn't know ..."

"Of course you didn't know what was happening here. The drugs— more cocaine than marijuana—were coming out of Colombia, South America. It hasn't been verified yet by the medical profession, but cocaine is highly addictive, a lot more than marijuana, and it's extremely dangerous. The people who bring it into this country are called 'death messengers'."

"Who is buying these drugs?"

"The drugs were being transported from South America into Miami, either by plane or boat. From Miami, they were being flown into northeast Georgia and into a rural area of Arkansas. From this area, they were going to southern cities such as Atlanta, Charlotte, Nashville, Richmond, and Washington, DC. From Arkansas, they were going to Chicago, Denver, Los Angeles, San Francisco, and other Western cities."

"How do you know all this?"

"I told you. It's being reported daily in the Miami newspapers. I have friends there who have called me and mailed me copies of stories because they mention this area. They know I'm working on the bank case here."

"How did law officers learn all of this?"

"One of the smugglers was gunned down outside a homeless shelter in Miami about six months ago. According to the reports, he was a gun runner, a drug trafficker, and a covert informant for the Central Intelligence Agency. That hasn't been confirmed, but he held a significant post in the drug ring. When agents went to his residence, they found a complete set of books documenting his activities. They even found his bank records, sometimes showing deposits of $50,000 a day in a Caribbean bank."

"How did they learn that the man here in Martin County was involved?"

"The informant had code words for both the drop points and details about the exact locations. Planes didn't fly to the Martin County man's landing strip until they had dropped their packages. The code for Martin County was Susanna. The drop point in Arkansas was coded Jezebel. I wanted you to have this information because I know how much you were concerned."

"Has the man in Martin County been arrested?"

"He's in prison in Atlanta."

"You know I told you about my cousin in Martin County who was seeing packages dropped on the mountain behind his house. After he reported it to the sheriff, he found his driveway blocked and began to receive calls in the middle of the night, but the caller would hang up when he answered. Do you remember me telling you about it?" Serena said.

"Yes, I remember. I'm sure these arrests will end the drops that he saw. You can tell him that the smugglers have been caught," Bowman said.

"He and his wife have moved away, and they didn't tell us where they were going. He was a bundle of nerves, and I hope he's better now," Serena said.

"A parachute was found hanging in a tree in the Georgia mountains only a month ago. It had been there for a while, and it had duffel bags attached that contained more than 200 pounds of cocaine. The little green luminescent sticks that children carry at Halloween were fastened to these packages so the ground crews could find them easier. US customs agents, National Guardsmen, and state and local officials searched the forest for more drops, but nothing else was found," Bowman said.

"I'll be glad when this is reported in the local papers so everyone knows."

"These drug smugglers have been captured—at least the leaders are caught—but more will step into the vacuum they're leaving. This is a money-making activity that touches more people every day," Bowman said.

"I don't want to think about more drug smugglers coming in."

"At least airplanes won't drop any more packages in these mountains any time soon; the car-theft ring has been broken, and neither one of these criminal activities is connected with the bank swindle. That's the riddle I have to solve," Bowman said.

"At least the drug smugglers weren't local people, but the guilty parties must have had local people helping them, and they must have had a direct line into the sheriff's office," Serena said.

"You may be right, but I have to concentrate on the bank swindle. We have the evidence we need to make arrests in Philadelphia, but we still don't know the person or persons in Cameron who were involved. I know you have no way of knowing about arrests in other states, and when the Philadelphia arrests are made, I'll make sure you know it."

Chapter 33

The car moved toward Nacoochee Valley, and neither one spoke. Serena was relieved because planes dropping packages might stop, and members of the car-theft ring had been arrested, but she was still uneasy about upcoming arrests concerning the bank. At least one of the bank arrests would have to be in or near Cameron. That person would be the one who led the Philadelphia swindlers to the Cameron National Bank.

"What is that supposed to be?" Trey asked as they passed the Indian burial mound in the Nacoochee Valley.

"That's where the Indians once buried their dead. I understand it once was much, much larger, but that's all that's left of it now. A man who once lived here in the valley and owned the land is the person who put the gazebo on top of the mound," Serena said.

"Do you ever study the beliefs and history of our Indian ancestors?" Trey said.

"I've read all the books I could find and did essays on Cherokee history when I was in high school. I plan to study it more when I have time," Serena said.

"I haven't been able to trace my Seneca ancestry, but I've studied the history of the tribe. When you told me about your animal pets and your flying squirrel, you made me think of Grandmother Twylah, who said all living creatures are one with the Earth."

"Your grandmother?"

"She wasn't actually my grandmother. She was a direct descendent of the Seneca chief called Red Jacket. Chief Red Jacket also said things that I never forget," Bowman said.

"I want to hear about Chief Red Jacket, but now we are nearing my own grandmother's house. It's where I grew up and where I had so many wild animal pets. I guess I wanted you to see one of my favorite places," Serena said.

Cattle stood near the fence on one side of the dirt road. "Do those cattle belong to your grandmother?"

Serena told him how Mama Tatum still made a little money raising beef cattle and how she still liked to get out and check the fences. As they passed the house, Rufus stood up in the front yard and watched them go by. He would probably shake himself well and lie down again as soon as they were out of sight. The front door was open, as were all the windows. As they passed, they could see all the way through the house, and it looked like someone was outlined before a back window.

"That was Mama Tatum," Serena said.

"It's good to see where you grew up," he said.

Silence filled the car as the miles rolled by.

"We'll soon be back to Cameron. I don't want to be back so soon. Is there any place where we can go and have a soda? Maybe a Big Orange?" Bowman grinned at Serena as he used a term he had picked up in Georgia. It was a term made famous almost twenty years earlier by Andy Griffith, a North Carolina school teacher who now was the star of a popular television show. He had used it in a humorous monologue called "What it Was, Was Football."

Serena smiled back. Trey Bowman made her feel special, and it wouldn't hurt anything to feel special for another half hour. She had already told Fred she would be late coming home.

"I guess we could go to Clarkesville. We're only about four miles from a restaurant there."

She directed Bowman to the Rock Creek Grill. Inside, Bowman held a chair for her to sit down and told the waitress they each wanted a Big Orange, emphasizing the words. At first the waitress seemed slightly annoyed, because it was an attempt at humor she had heard too many times before. Then she joined them in laughter as she said, "I'll see if we have some."

"Thank you for showing me where your grandmother lives,"

Bowman said. "I must tell you: you have a beautiful voice, and you don't pronounce words exactly the same as some of the other people here."

Serena laughed. "I love the soft, slow English words we hear around here, but I know that success in business depends on the way you talk. I was very proud to get my job at the bank, and I wanted to be successful. I bought a tape recorder and spent about a year recording my voice and listening to my pronunciation. I also recorded radio announcers on television and tried to say the words exactly like them."

"Seeing where you grew up helps me think about my own childhood, and I needed to think about life in general for a while," he said.

"Can you tell me about Chief Red Jacket?" she said.

"He was a member of the Wolf Clan, and they were the philosophers of the Iroquois nation. I learned two important things when I studied about him and the Iroquois. The tribes had female leaders, and they worshipped the Great Spirit, but they never fought about their religion."

Although she had often read about the Cherokee Indians when she was in high school and before she had children, Serena had never before talked with a person who was interested in Indian history. She said, "Please tell me more."

"Chief Red Jacket lived about 200 years ago. He believed the Indians and the white people could have lived in peace if the white people had respected the red man's religious beliefs. He also asked why the white man quarreled and fought so much about religion."

"I think quarreling about religion probably happens because every person is searching for God's truth. I have always attended a Protestant church, and the teachings inspire me, but I'm still personally searching for the truth. When people find a group that thinks like they do, they become absolutely certain that they have finally found God's truth. I think it's the 'absolute certainty' that causes problems," Serena said.

"You're right. All faiths teach kindness to other people and say 'do not kill,' but these people who believe they are absolutely right will kill others because they're certain they know God's will," Bowman said.

"Then we have Communism in the Soviet Union, where the government says God does not exist and will kill people if they follow a religious faith," Serena said.

"The Great Spirit told the red man to be thankful for all favors, to love each other, and to be united. History tells us that the Indian tribes fought about hunting lands and about beautiful maidens, but they never battled about the Great Spirit," Bowman said.

"I like the way all Indians referred to God as the Great Spirit. I have a friend who says he does not believe in God. I find it hard to understand how he cannot believe, but I haven't been able to convince him. I asked him what he would do if he learns after he dies that God does exist after all. He laughed and said he wouldn't be nearly as disappointed as the man who depends on God all his life and then dies to learn God does not exist," Serena said.

"Grandma Twylah referred to God as 'the Great Mystery,'" Bowman said. "Chief Red Jacket asked the missionaries why they believed that God's word was given only to them and not to all people. He didn't get an answer."

"Calling God a Great Mystery fits the way I believe. I look around at the beauty and complexities of Mother Earth and am amazed at how it all works together. Each item and each creature has a purpose, and they are all intertwined. I have great respect for this beauty, and I know all life had to be created by something or someone much bigger than us," Serena said.

"Chief Red Jacket spoke his words about religion at a council called by the white missionaries. It's found in books, if you want to know more. For now, let's get out of this deep discussion. I know you have to get home," he said.

Back in the car, both were silent as Bowman drove back to Cameron.

As they approached the depot, Serena said, "The problem at the bank has brought me one good thing. I've met you." She couldn't believe the words had come from her mouth.

Bowman's eyes seemed to envelop her. "I am thinking the same thing about you," he said.

Serena wished she could just sit and look at him without talking. When she first saw him at the depot, she had noticed how the green striped shirt he was wearing enhanced his complexion.

Back at the depot, Bowman jumped out of the car, walked around, and opened her door. She slipped out and stood up, looking into his eyes, at his lashes, his hair, his lips, his neck at the opening of his shirt. She wanted to drink in everything about him.

Escorted to her car, she sat down under the steering wheel and looked up at him. They had not touched, not even to hold hands, but she felt as if they were holding each other now.

"I'll see you again, my beautiful Serena," he said.

"I hope so," she said, feeling a tug as if she were tied to him by invisible cords. He shut the door, and she turned the ignition to crank her car.

Chapter 34

Serena had to get groceries before she went home, so she stopped at Ramey's Superette.

She didn't have time to cook for supper, and there weren't any leftovers. She bought flour, corn meal, grits, eggs, a whole chicken, ground beef, lettuce, and then turned to get soap, furniture polish, and other cleaning supplies. She still hadn't purchased something to prepare quickly for the evening's meal. Finally, she decided she could buy a couple of frozen pizzas and add browned ground beef, fresh bits of green pepper, onion, and more cheese to each one before she baked them.

She was going back to the produce section for a green bell pepper when she saw Mrs. Lockwood limping along the aisle with another woman who was a little younger. She didn't want Mrs. Lockwood to mention the bank to her, so she quickly asked about the woman's sister, who was bedridden with cancer.

"How's your sister?"

"She's wonderful," Mrs. Lockwood said. "She went to heaven this morning."

Serena could only stare at the bank customer. Suddenly tears filled her eyes.

"Oh, don't cry, honey. I'm okay. This is my niece, Mildred, and we're getting some things to make sandwiches. I know people from the church will bring a lot of food to the house later, but right now we don't have a thing to eat. My sister does not have to hurt anymore. I'll miss her, but I don't want her back the way she was."

Serena stood in the aisle with her grocery cart and watched the two women move away. Mrs. Lockwood had lost a member of her family, but she looked the way she always looked, wearing a simple, gray cotton house dress with a small, red hat on her head.

Slowly, Serena wiped the tears off her face and moved toward the cash register.

What's wrong with me, she thought to herself as she placed groceries on the counter for the cashier to ring up. *I'm thirty-six years old, and I'm acting as if I never heard of anyone dying.*

She also had no problem with the idea of someone going to heaven.

Occasionally Serena had argued with Phil, who always asked her a lot of questions about her beliefs in God and heaven. He was the friend that she had mentioned to Trey because he claimed to be an atheist. Serena had said to him more than once, "There has to be a higher being who knows how we came to be here and why."

Now she thought of her conversation with Bowman and the words of Chief Red Jacket and Grandma Twylah. Chief Red Jacket had resented his people being told that their faith in the Great Spirit was wrong and that they needed to adopt the religious practices of European missionaries. *Maybe the Great Spirit is waiting until all professing Christians here on Earth learn what we're supposed to learn. Maybe we must learn to respect other people, other races, and other peaceful cultures, and then he will return and totally reveal his plan,* she thought.

Tonight, Serena didn't want to think about religion. She also didn't want to think about Mrs. Lockwood and the death of her sister because, somehow, the parameters of her own life had disappeared. Her decisions had always centered on her family, and now her thinking centered on Trey Bowman. Sometimes, for a few hours, she seemed to be floating with no anchor. At these times, she felt vulnerable and exposed. Doing something for her family usually put her back on track.

Trey Bowman had been visiting Cameron now and then for almost a year, and no arrests had been made. He would soon be leaving the area and might never return. However she tried to avoid it, she knew that, when he left, he would be taking part of her inner spirit with him.

Her life was no longer on a firm path because she spent each day waiting to see him again. When she was in his presence, she was no longer a simple bank teller in the north Georgia mountains. She was the friend of an FBI agent who knew a lot about other lifestyles, a man who listened to her, who liked to explore Indian cultures, and a man who knew what it was like to grow up and live your adult life without knowing your biological parents.

She wanted to tell Bowman how much he meant to her. She wanted to spend the rest of her life in his presence, but she knew it was impossible. He couldn't stay in north Georgia, and she couldn't leave her daughters. She also could not take them away with her. And what would her departure do to Fred? He had not changed. He was still the same man she had married, doing the same things he had always done.

I'm the only one who has changed, she thought. *If I left with Trey, Fred and the girls would be almost destroyed, not because of something they did, but because the bank was robbed, and an FBI agent came into my life.*

She felt as if she was living two lives. In one life, she gloried in the presence of one man and with him she had no obligations, no promises to keep. Her other life was filled with duties, obligations, and promises that she must always keep. In one life she felt as if the world was hers. In the other life, she sometimes felt as if the housework, her job, her duties as a wife, a mother, and a granddaughter had placed the world on her shoulders.

She didn't know when it had happened, but her attitude about the bank swindle had changed. She no longer felt lonely and threatened by the investigation, but she still worried about who would be arrested. She would probably be questioned again, but she would be okay.

At home, she turned on the oven as soon as she was in the kitchen. She browned the hamburger meat, cut the peppers and onions, and sprinkled each ingredient on the pizzas. Extra grated cheese went on each one before she put them in the oven.

Fred and the girls had been eating cookies because supper was late, and they were hungry. All three were seated at the table when she took the pizzas out of the oven. She cut slices, put them on plates, and gave them each a cold Coca-Cola.

Penny hadn't yet made a decision about the college she wanted to attend. She wanted to continue playing basketball and eventually become a basketball coach. Nicole wanted to play basketball in college, but, more than that, she wanted to get married and begin a family.

The girls talked about their future plans, and Fred commented now and then, while Serena was finding it hard to participate in the conversation.

After supper, Serena began gathering the dishes and putting them in the sink. The kitchen this evening could be cleaned in five minutes, and neither girl had homework. "Just go on out into the living room and watch television," she said. "I'll join you as soon as I put some clothes in the washer."

Serena loaded the old washing machine with Fred's work clothes and turned the water on hot. She pulled the button to let the washer begin filling before beginning its agitating action, then began to separate the other clothes and towels into stacks of white and colored.

Her eyes were focused on the pieces of clothing she wanted to wash, but her mind was filled with Trey Bowman's face. She almost felt like a teenager as she performed the duties she had been doing for more than eighteen years. She felt excited and full of energy.

Chapter 35

Three days later, back at the FBI office in Philadelphia, Bowman prepared papers for the arrest of Sandy McMahon and his bodyguard, Jan Godlewski. He knew where both men lived, and they would probably be taken into custody the next day, or as soon as he could get approval signatures on his papers.

All efforts to find Jarvis Salisbury had failed. Telephone calls from the Philadelphia and New York areas that came into the Cameron bank during the previous September were assumed to come from Salisbury. All the calls had been traced to pay phones in different locations, sometimes in Philadelphia, sometimes in New York.

A wiretap on McMahon's phone line had produced nothing except conversations between the man and the different females he was trying to impress, but Bowman had other evidence against him.

The Merrill bookkeeper, James Maxwell, had been behind bars since the theft was discovered, and a thorough background investigation on Maxwell had turned up no criminal history, not even an unpaid traffic ticket.

After telling Maxwell he was facing a thirty-year prison sentence, they offered to drop the charges of theft and bank fraud if he would talk. A signed contract on the plea deal was presented to Maxwell, and, after reading it, he added his signature and began complete cooperation.

Throughout the following days of questioning, Maxwell persisted in saying that the only thing he had done was provide McMahon the Merrill checks with facsimile signatures. He didn't know any other people who were involved, but Godlewski had always been with McMahon when they had talked. He also didn't know what bank had been used. More than once, Maxwell referred to what he considered shabby treatment from the Merrill management, as if he thought the robbery was justified.

Bowman looked forward to getting McMahon behind bars and seeing that he talked.

As for Sandy McMahon, his life had changed since the time he met the Merrill bookkeeper each evening and planned the bank heist with the Merrill checks. In filing for divorce, his wife, Rebecca, had not asked for support for either her or their two boys, ages eight and nine, but McMahon liked being married to a respected pediatrician. He had hired an expensive lawyer to fight the divorce petition.

The costly divorce was now final. Rebecca had been granted custody of their two children, and McMahon had weekend visiting rights. He was still living with the airline attendant, but he also was finding much pleasure in the company of a red-headed real estate agent.

Meanwhile, he was trying to keep informed on his ex-wife's activities. On the same day that Bowman filled out the papers for his arrest, McMahon drove past his ex-wife's home on the way to the red-head's apartment for dinner. Cars were parked in the driveway and beside the road, and he slowed down to get a better look. Suddenly he saw the car of a man he knew, a truck driver.

McMahon had pursued many trades in the past, including driving a truck. Brad Stephens, another truck driver, had always made comments about McMahon's good-looking wife. It was Stephens's car that he saw in Rebecca's driveway.

McMahon's blood ran hot as he pulled off the road and stopped his car. He leaped out and walked rapidly toward the house, but, before he got around the last car, he saw one of his children step out the front door. He wheeled around before he could be seen and headed back up the street to his car.

Stephens obviously was making a play for Rebecca, but McMahon vowed that Stephens would never get to first base. She might no longer be his wife, but she was still a part of his life. She was the mother of his children, and a respected pediatrician with a good practice.

He drove on to visit the real estate agent, but he couldn't get his mind off the idea that Brad Stephens was courting Rebecca. He said little, then left early for home and again drove past Rebecca's house.

Stephens's car, a late-model black Ford Thunderbird, was now the only other car in the driveway. McMahon pulled his vehicle in beside Stephens's car, and this time his mind was icy cold as he walked toward the house and into the front door.

Inside the foyer he could see Stephens and Rebecca standing in front of the living room fireplace. He did not speak but methodically walked over to Stephens, grabbed him by his shirt, put his face next to his, and said, "You're dead meat!"

Stephens was too surprised to move. Neither he nor Rebecca spoke.

McMahon turned around and walked back out the front door with the same purposeful stride. Rebecca stared after him with her mouth open, as Brad smoothed his shirt and tie.

"That man is a maniac," Rebecca finally sputtered. "I'm afraid he is an evil, dangerous man. I didn't know that when I married him, and I tried to believe in him for the sake of our children. I'm sorry and ashamed that this has happened to you, Brad."

"I know your ex-husband, and you're right. He's an evil, dangerous man," Brad answered.

Brad Stephens was a handsome man with curly blond hair. His formal education had ended after one year of college. At that time, he had purchased his own eighteen-wheeler and began his trucking career.

He liked being his own boss, and he liked traveling. He was a proud man, at ease with himself and with other people. He was comfortable in either khaki work clothes or a black tuxedo. He read constantly and could talk easily with people on almost any subject.

He had known Rebecca McMahon about five years and had always been attracted to her beauty. Since he had begun regularly seeing her, he had fallen in love with her warm-hearted attitude and her unwavering respect for the diverse talents of other people.

He had known her ex-husband, Sandy, about the same length of time. He had liked Sandy's aggressive attitude when he first met him, but soon he began to distrust him.

It became obvious that Sandy McMahon would do anything to get what he wanted.

Later that evening, at his own home, Brad Stephens still felt injured by Sandy McMahon's words. He believed that his life was in danger, but there was no point in going to the police to report a verbal threat.

Before he went to bed, Stephens pulled his .38 revolver out of a bottom drawer, loaded it, and placed it on the nightstand. It was a long time before he went to sleep, and at 3:00 AM he was suddenly wide awake. Someone was in his bedroom. He could see more than one shadowy figure hulking between his bed and the faint glow from a streetlight outside.

Stephens eased his hand over to the revolver, picked it up, and began firing just as gunshots came toward the bed. The loud sound of gunfire was followed by thuds on the carpet. It sounded like more than one body had hit the floor. There were no more shadows between Stephens and the window, and total quiet was heavy in the room. Cautiously, Stephens reached up to turn on his bedside lamp.

In the light, he could see both McMahon and his ever-present bodyguard lying on the floor. Red stains were spreading slowly from both bodies over the white carpet. A sawed-off shotgun was on the floor beside Godlewski. Stephens stared at them with his gun ready, but they did not move. He tried to get out of bed, but his legs did not respond. Looking down, he saw blood on the sheets.

He picked up the telephone beside his bed, dialed the operator, and asked for the police.

Chapter 36

Christmas and New Year's Day passed again, and in northeast Georgia people were still whispering about Cameron National Bank and Paul Norris.

More than a year had passed; no one had been arrested, and the missing money had not been found. The bonding companies representing Merrill Construction Company and the bank were still fighting it out in court as to which one would pay for the loss. The bonding companies had each spent $300,000 in attorney and investigator fees, but no arrest had been made. Bonding officers rated both the bank and the construction company as high-risk operations.

Paul Norris and Carolyn had moved to a house in the mountains. The Norrises' son continued to run the feed store in Cameron. He believed his father was totally innocent, and he also wanted to leave town, but he didn't know what else he could do to make a living.

Serena did not see Trey Bowman after he told her about the Miami drug bust and they rode past Mama T's house. She wished she could see him again, just for a few minutes. She wanted to tell him what knowing him had meant to her.

Tiny buds of new leaves were visible on bare limbs of the deciduous trees when he called her again. "I regret to tell you that no arrests have been made on the Cameron National Bank case. We know the two main players, and one of them has been shot and killed. His ex-wife's boyfriend killed both him and his bodyguard in self-defense.

"We know how they selected the Cameron bank, but we still haven't found the man who claimed to be Jarvis Salisbury.

"I'm in town for the last time and would like to see you again if you have time after you get off work."

Serena performed her work routine methodically as she tried to control her racing heart. She met Bowman at the depot at 4:00 PM, and, after he seated her in his rented car, she watched him as he walked around to the driver's seat.

"Where can we go?" he asked as he began to back out of the parking space.

"Just drive toward Clarkesville," Serena said.

"I hardly know where to begin with the details. This is the strangest case I've ever worked. I've never heard of another case that even compares. I must tell you first that it was caused by a woman who decided to quit her job and get married." Bowman smiled at Serena as he said this.

"Her name was Evelyn; she had been with Merrill Construction for a long time, and she operated the bookkeeping department. After she gave her resignation, her boss did everything he could to keep her there, but Mr. Merrill didn't know how important she was. I think if Mr. Merrill had tried to prevent her departure, she would have left anyway, but her boss was mad at the company for not keeping her there.

"That in itself is strange, but the man who planned the whole thing was shot and killed last month just before we arrested him. His name was Sandy McMahon, and he became acquainted with Evelyn's boss, James Maxwell, at a bar. We know exactly what they did. McMahon got Maxwell, who was Merrill's head bookkeeper, to supply him with company checks containing the facsimile signature. McMahon arranged with the man we know as Salisbury to come here, deposit the checks, then cash checks made out to himself and share the money.

"The bookkeeper squealed on McMahon and told us everything he knew so he could go free. Unfortunately, Maxwell never knew the man who came to the bank here in Cameron," Bowman said.

"Just tell me why they used Cameron National Bank," Serena said.

Bowman continued talking as he drove down the road.

"Sandy McMahon's plans with the Merrill checks meant that a bank was needed that wouldn't ask too many questions. He first planned to use a bank in Chicago, but the president of that bank was arrested the same day that the Merrill bookkeeper delivered the checks with the facsimile signatures."

Serena suddenly felt afraid again. "Is it Mr. Norris?" Serena wanted to put her hand over her mouth, but the words already were out.

"No. He allowed himself to be tricked, that's all," Bowman said. "We haven't found criminal involvement by anyone connected with your bank. The Cameron National Bank was recommended to the people who had the bogus checks because Norris had a big heart and headed a loose banking operation," Bowman said. "The bank was recommended by a man here in Georgia, a man who lives in Jasper."

Serena could not believe her ears. She felt great relief and great curiosity at the same time. How could someone in the distant mountain town of Jasper recommend Cameron National Bank for a robbery?

Slowly, Bowman began to tell her what had led to selection of the Cameron bank.

After his banker friend was arrested, McMahon didn't know of another bank, so he called a former jail mate, Glenn Irving. Irving didn't know of a bank, either, but he called another man he had met in jail two years earlier. That man was from Jasper, and his name was Cliff Brogden.

"After I learned of Brogden's involvement, I talked with him and his wife at length, and also to others in Jasper," Bowman said.

Cliff Brogden was trying to lead a straight life. He had served time in prison for growing marijuana plants in the Chattahoochee National Forest, then selling the cured product in Atlanta. Brogden knew that the local sheriff's deputies watched him constantly, and suspected him of continuing the marijuana activity, but, after he was freed from prison, he obeyed the law and installed carpet to make a living.

Shortly after release from prison, Brogden married Ruth Westmoreland, a classmate from his high school years. Ruth had known Brogden all her life and corresponded with him while he was in prison. She knew he had dropped out of school and become a member of the wrong crowd in his youthful years, but he seemed sincerely remorseful for crossing the law. She believed him when he said he wanted to go straight.

As a cashier at a local family-owned grocery store, Ruth made enough money to buy a few groceries and pay their utility bills. Brogden made regular trips to Dalton, where he picked up carpet and installed it in homes and businesses all over north Georgia. He used his earnings to pay the rent on their mobile home and keep the dented, rusting old van in good traveling condition. Sometimes he would leave home at dawn to pick up the carpet and not return home until late at night, but Ruth didn't doubt him when he said he was working hard.

Cliff and Ruth were both in their late twenties, and, more than anything, they wanted to buy their own home and start a family. They found five acres with a four-room house that was about twelve years old and in good condition. All they needed was $2,000 for a down payment, and then monthly payments on the little house wouldn't be as much as the rent they were paying. A spot near the house had rich ground that was perfect for a vegetable garden, and if they could get the down payment, they would make it.

Brogden was installing carpet in a home in Cameron when he asked the home's owner, a lawyer named Tom Smith, if he knew a place where he could borrow $2,000. Smith was on the board of directors of Cameron National Bank. He knew Brogden's background, but his hard work and efforts to lead a straight life were impressive. Smith wanted to help him and said, "Go see Paul Norris, president of Cameron National Bank, and tell him I sent you."

The next morning a paranoid, nervous Brogden went to the red brick building with the white columns and glass front on Cameron's Washington Street. He tried to hide his tremors as he walked in and asked to see the president of the bank. A secretary motioned him toward Norris's office, and Brogden could see a man at a desk reading the morning newspaper.

He went slowly into the office, approached the desk, and said, "Mr. Norris, I'm installing carpet in Tom Smith's house, and I need $2,000 for the down payment on a little house in Jasper. Mr. Smith told me to come see you."

Paul Norris did not speak and did not look up from what he was reading. Brogden waited almost a full minute before he repeated his words exactly.

Again, there was no response.

A request for a routine loan usually went to the loan officer, and

Norris was irritated because he had been interrupted while reading the morning paper. This man was sent to him by a member of his board and, to Norris, this meant he was a good risk. He finally reached across his desk, picked up a piece of paper, scribbled a few words on it, and handed it to Brogden without ever looking up or asking his name.

"Here, give this to the teller," Norris said.

Brogden found reading difficult, but he stared at the paper as he walked toward the teller. The teller took the paper, looked at Brogden, asked his name and mailing address, then scribbled words on a form and asked Brogden to sign it. Brogden wrote his name very slowly, and the teller went to a walk-in vault, returned, and rapidly counted out $2,000 in one-hundred-dollar bills. She handed it to him, along with a copy of the paper he had signed.

"Thank you," Brogden said before he self-consciously walked out the front door of the bank. He expected someone to stop him at any minute and take the money back.

Outside, he stuffed the money in his wallet, threw both arms straight up and turned his face toward the sky for a minute of thanks. He was astounded at what had happened. He had never dreamed borrowing money could be so easy.

He thought about how the banker had never looked at him, had not asked for a credit reference, and had not even asked his name or occupation. He was almost sure this was an unusual happening, but he was too excited to worry about it. He could hardly wait to get home and tell Ruth.

They were actually going to buy that house. He, Cliff Brogden, really had a chance now of making it!

More than a year passed before Brogden got the call from Glenn Irving, his old prison mate. Irving said a friend of his was looking for a bank where he could deposit some hot checks. Could Brogden help them out?

Brogden was not about to take part in any easy money scheme. His life was going too well. He had a wife who loved him; they were buying their own home; and business had been so good he already had been able to pay back the down payment. The only debt they owed was the one for their house, and they were never late on their monthly payments.

"I know of a bank that's easy to do business with. It's Cameron National Bank in Cameron, Georgia, if that helps you any. That's all I can do," Brogden had said before he hung up.

Chapter 37

Bowman and Serena were going through Clarkesville when he finished the story about Cliff Brogden, and both were silent for a few minutes.

Serena was finding it hard to grasp the story of how the Cameron bank had been chosen for the giant swindle.

Bowman looked toward her and said, "It's difficult for me to know that I'll probably never see you again."

"I feel the same way," Serena said.

"I know we haven't spent much time together, and we really don't know each other very well, but when I'm here in Cameron with you, my problems seem to melt away. If anyone in Philadelphia had told me I would lose my heart in Georgia, I would have laughed at them," Bowman said with a small laugh.

"I don't want you to go away," Serena said.

"We see things the same way, and we have so much in common," Bowman said. "When I'm with you, I begin to think that I can do anything. I guess I begin to think I'm invincible. Can we go somewhere to be alone for a while before we say good-bye? I want to look at you, not have to always look at the road and drive a car during our last time together."

"If we are alone in a private location, it probably will only make it harder for me to say good-bye," Serena said.

"I wish you could go with me and meet my grandparents. I wish they could meet you."

"Maybe you can bring them back to this area."

"No. After I leave, I won't come back. I have to get you out of my mind and move on. I was dating a girl in Philly before I met you, but I haven't even called her in months. Every time I start to call her I think of you and wish you were with me."

Serena could not respond immediately, and silence filled the car.

Finally, she said, "You have made me feel special and given me new confidence. I don't want to think about never seeing you again."

Silence filled the car once more.

Suddenly, Serena asked him to turn toward her grandmother's house and said, "My grandmother has gone on a trip with some members of her church. We can go there."

No words were spoken as Bowman drove to the Nacoochee Valley. He parked the car in front of the big, silent house. Rufus was not there to greet them because he had been boarded with a neighbor.

Bowman put his arm around Serena's waist as they walked up the steps of the porch. Before she could sit down in one of the rocking chairs he pulled her hard to him and kissed her. He moved his mouth away only to ask if they could go inside the house.

Serena knew an extra house key was hidden above the front door. She reached up to get it, and he took it to unlock the door.

Together they stepped inside, and Bowman shut the door. "This is the house where I grew up," she said.

Serena felt that the two of them were the only people on Earth. "I wish there was some way that you could remain a part of my life. I have spent so little time with you, but sometime after I met you, your mind began to blend with mine. Whatever it is, I feel like you and I are one," she said.

She showed him through the house and into her old bedroom, where her high school senior picture was still on the wall. He looked at the photo, then looked at her. "You're far more beautiful now than you were when this picture was made."

He pulled her to him once again and kissed her gently this time. "I want to make love to you," he said.

Serena pulled his head to hers and began to kiss his ear and neck. Only one man had made love to her before and that was after they were married. But she didn't think about any other person now. She only wanted to truly become one with Trey.

He pulled her to the bed. They were two people hungry for each other, and they held one another and kissed as they undressed.

As each tried to absorb the mind and spirit of the other, it seemed as if light and dark swirled together without mixing. Joy and sadness stood side by side, neither dulled by the other.

Fingers teased, and ripples ran through their bodies as the nooks and crannies tried to guess where the next caress would be. Each mind enjoyed the warm ecstasy of the other's full attention, and an electrical current seemed to pulsate between them. Each fed off the other, circling, winding, rushing.

Then all became calm and still again. Each pair of eyes looked deeply into the other's eyes, trying to read the other mind.

"It seems like I have always wanted to make love to you and only you," he said. "I have seen how you work, and I know you're strong and courageous. You understand and respect human nature and are always willing to listen to the problems of others. I've been looking for you all my life and now …"

He did not finish the sentence and kissed her again. Then he rose up on his elbow and began to trace her facial features with his fingertip. "When I am old, I want to still be able to recall every inch of your face," he said.

"You have made me feel complete and whole," Serena said, slowly and softly. "Now I'm the one who feels invincible. I feel that I can handle whatever comes my way."

"I want to take you home with me, but I know without asking that you cannot leave. Do you remember when you were in the hospital, and you told me that you wanted to do whatever was necessary to make sure your daughters always had their mother and their father at home with them? That is one of the things that caused you to lodge in my heart," Bowman said.

"No. I cannot go with you," Serena said, tears welling in her eyes. "When you leave, you will take part of me with you, but if I left my children, I would leave part of myself behind. I would not be the person that I am today. I cannot take my daughters with me. I cannot ask them to leave their father and friends."

She widened her eyes and then closed them, trying to keep the tears from overflowing as she rose slowly from the bed and reached for her bra. Bowman pulled her back down and said, "I know I have to let you go, but not yet."

He pulled her nude body to him and held her tightly before he raised his head and began kissing her again.

He ran his tongue down her neck, kissed her breasts and then her stomach before pulling his head back up to her breasts again. "I cannot stop after having you only once. I have waited too long," he whispered.

This time, he was in her much longer. When he finished, he collapsed beside her on the bed and closed his eyes. Serena rested her head on his chest.

There was no sound in the house and no sound outside. Both Serena and Trey were deep in sleep when the sounds of a catfight began to float up to the bedroom. Pffft and rrrrraw were sounded loudly over and over again. Obviously, two visiting tomcats were fighting for their own mating privileges.

Serena opened her eyes and, after a few seconds, jumped from the bed and started to dress. "I don't want to leave you, but I have to go home to my family."

Bowman also began to dress. He helped her straighten and smooth the bed, making it the same as before. They held on to each other as they approached the front door of the house. On leaving the house, he pulled her to him, put his hands on each side of her head, kissed her slowly, then held her close again.

Finally, they parted, and he made sure the door was locked as before. He kept his arm around her as they walked to the car, and he opened the door for her. Back in the car, neither spoke again until he drove up beside her car at the depot.

"I will not contact you again until we find Salisbury. I will see that you know who he is," Bowman said, looking toward her, then turning his face straight ahead, taking his eyes off Serena.

Serena wanted him to look at her again, but he didn't. The tears escaped from her eyes and flowed down her cheeks.

"You will always be a part of me," she said, trying to control the sob in her voice. Neither of them had spoken the words "I love you." Maybe it was because such words would have deepened the heartbreak.

Maybe it was because the words seemed too small for what was in their hearts.

"I hope you always find happiness in whatever life offers you," Bowman said.

Serena opened the car door and stepped out as he said the last words. He did not move and still did not look toward her. Neither said good-bye. As she drove away, she looked in her rearview mirror, and his car had still not moved from the parking place.

It was much later than usual when Serena got home, and she felt that she was totally different from the person who had left the house that morning.

Fred still was watching television. "I don't know where you've been so long, but you've missed *All in the Family,*" he said.

Maybe he cannot see that I'm not the same person he married, Serena thought.

Penny and Nicole were in bed together but not asleep. "Mom, we were worried about you. We were afraid you had had another accident," Penny said.

"No, my darlings. I did not have an accident," Serena said. "I'm sorry I caused you to worry."

Chapter 38

Serena continued to take care of her family and go to work every day, but she no longer enjoyed the different yards or looked to see what the cement duck was wearing. It had been dressed in somber black, forecasting disaster, before she crashed under the logs. It had worn shiny rhinestones, forecasting a shimmering new adventure, before Trey kissed her the first time. But she still didn't think about the duck.

Months earlier she had been afraid that a careless action on her part had caused the bank to lose more than a million dollars. Now she could have felt guilty about her desire for another man, but she only felt terribly alone and emotionally empty. One evening Fred became angry and accused her of being cold toward him.

"Why are you mad at me? What did I do? You don't talk to me, and I don't ever see you smiling or laughing anymore," he said.

A minute passed, and he said, "Tell me what's wrong."

"I'm worried sick about the missing money at the bank. No one has been arrested yet," she said.

"No one is blaming you," Fred said.

"I'm not mad at you. I just want the bank robbery to be solved. The other day some people were talking about an armed robbery that happened in Gainesville, and they looked at me as if I would know who did it," she said.

"I want it solved, too. But, more than that, I want you to be happy again."

Serena was surprised at Fred's words. She could not remember him showing concern for her happiness before.

She stared at him, but saw only worry in his eyes. "I'll be happy. Just give me some time," she said.

Deep down, Serena felt like she could never feel deep emotions or happiness again.

The previous evening she had visited a neighbor whose child had been diagnosed with leukemia, a disease that always left mothers frozen with fear and dread for their own children. She had taken a baked chicken with a package of rolls from the grocery store. She talked to the mother, but she felt no sadness, no fear for her own children, nothing.

Two more weeks passed before she decided she would visit Mama T. It was a rainy Saturday morning, and she told the girls she would be back in a couple of hours. She had to talk to someone and tell them a little about how she felt. Maybe Mama T would make her able to feel again.

Rufus was not in the front yard to greet her when she arrived. Walking in the front door, Serena called her grandmother's name, but there was no answer. In the kitchen, she saw Mama T's breakfast plate and coffee cup in the sink. Then she heard Rufus bark. The sound came from the back of the house.

Hurrying out the back door, she saw Rufus standing in the rain at the foot of the back steps. He looked toward her and barked again, then turned to run toward the barn.

Something is wrong, Serena thought, as she hurried after the dog.

Inside the barn, she saw Mama T lying on her back in the hallway. Her eyes were open, but they weren't seeing.

Kneeling beside her, Serena grabbed her hand and called her name, with no response. She closed each eyelid and held her left hand over both eyes as she tried to remember what she had learned years ago about administering cardiopulmonary resuscitation. She put her right hand on Mama T's chest but could feel no heartbeat.

She must call the emergency ambulance service. She ran back to the house and grabbed the telephone directory. The number had been printed prominently on the directory's cover. Serena dialed and, after getting an answer, asked for an ambulance and twice gave directions to her grandmother's house.

Running back to the barn, Serena folded her sweater and placed it under Mama T's head. Then, she blew into Mama T's mouth, attempting to expand her lungs. Next, she pushed hard on her chest fifteen times. *Blow into the mouth two times and pump the chest fifteen times.* Serena repeated the old instructions to herself as she worked. Deep down, she knew her effort was in vain, but she had to try.

"I'm so glad you weren't out in the pasture this morning. You've got to talk to me. I love you. I need you. Please talk to me," Serena said as she pumped Mama T's chest.

Mama T's cows had long ago stopped coming into the barn, and it was home to only three felines that the veterinarian had neutered. The cats had the specific responsibility of catching and killing rats. Mama T probably had come to the barn to see if all was well with the cats.

* * *

Three nights later, Serena, her brother Steve, Steve's wife and children, and other relatives of Mama T's received friends at the funeral home. Dressed in their best attire, Serena and Steve, as well as their spouses and children, were almost strangers to each other. For years, Steve had brought his wife and children from North Carolina for annual family reunion picnics. During those times, they all were attired in their most comfortable leisure clothes. Serena saw other people she hadn't seen since she was a child, and seeing them kept her mind off Mama T's death.

Mama T's casket was open, and sooner or later everyone had walked up and looked down at her body wearing a navy blue dress. Her face, which had always been so alive and welcoming, was serious and still. It was not the face they had always known.

Almost every person wanted to tell Serena and Steve about their own memories of Mama T. One elderly man told about growing up with her, using her first name, Lucille, and her nickname, Lucy.

"Lucille loved every living thing," he said. "I remember one time when she killed a snake and then grieved after she found out it was a harmless king snake."

He laughed as he told about her catching a baby skunk when she was about ten years old. "Lucy found this little skunk in the hen lot. It was probably dining on eggs, and the dogs were barking something fierce and looking at the lot, but staying far away. Lucy went in and started to come back out holding this beautiful silky black kitten with white stripes down its back. She was carrying it by the skin on the back of its neck like a mother cat carries her babies. She knew it was a skunk, but she had never actually smelled a skunk's defensive odor. She also thought it was too little and too beautiful to spray her.

"She was wrong, and that little skunk had plenty of power. I was just thankful that she was still inside the lot when it zapped her, and none of that stuff hit me. She had to drop it, and it sauntered off like nothing had happened. The smell was so bad that the dogs didn't even follow it. Rotten eggs don't smell that bad. She soaked herself in tomato juice because it was supposed to take the odor away, and she poured the juice around in the hen lot. I think she used her mother's entire store of canned tomato juice, but it didn't erase the odor. We teased her about that for years."

More than one hundred people attended Mama T's funeral, and the front of the church was filled with flowers from family members and friends. Two different preachers read portions of scripture and talked about Mama T's continuous involvement in the church and in the community.

Serena, Fred, Penny, and Nicole sat at the front of the family section, with Steve and his family. Serena felt as if she were in a bad dream. She had not yet shed a tear about Mama T's death, but this time she couldn't remove her thoughts from what had happened and wait for a new day, as she had done after the traumatic family accidents.

Despite her disbelief, she had tried to find her second cousin, Charlie, to tell him about Mama T's death. She also wanted to tell him about the drug-smuggling arrests in Miami and Martin County. But he had left without a trace, and she hoped that he and his wife were enjoying new peace wherever they were.

A preacher was talking, but Serena didn't hear the words because she couldn't stop wondering what she would do without her grandmother. Mama T had been her shield against life's problems, her anchor, and the friend that she could always trust. Serena had been planning to talk to Mama T about Trey Bowman. She had wanted to tell her about the way Trey made her feel different about herself. Trey was gone, and there was no way she could join him because her family must always come first. She had only wanted to hear what Mama T had to say, but Mama T's heart had stopped, and she, too, was gone.

Suddenly she began to hear the preacher's words. He said that Mama T was the anchor for a big family—her grandchildren and her nieces and nephews. He talked about her love for her family and said that First Corinthians 13 described Mama T. "They are the beautiful words of the Apostle Paul telling Christians how they should love one another," he said, before reading, "Love is patient; love is kind; love is not envious or boastful or arrogant or rude. It does not insist on its own way; it is not irritable or resentful; it does not rejoice in wrongdoing, but rejoices in the truth. It bears all things, believes all things, hopes all things, endures all things. Love never ends."

The funeral service concluded with everyone turning to page forty-two in the hymn books and singing the first and last stanza of Mama T's favorite old hymn, "Amazing Grace." The family and guests then got into their cars for a funeral procession to the grave site. Serena, Fred, and the girls were in the first car behind the long, black Cadillac hearse. In front of the hearse, a deputy drove one of the sheriff's cars with its blue lights flashing.

About thirty cars were following with their lights on to show they were part of the funeral procession, and the approaching vehicles in the other lane pulled off the road and stopped until all the funeral cars had passed. Something about the cars respectfully stopped on the side of the road while Mama T's casket passed brought tears to Serena's eyes. *If only the drivers of the cars could have known Mama T,* she thought. She hadn't cried about Mama T, and now she fought for control. She didn't want to cry in front of all these people.

At the graveside, the family sat in chairs underneath the canopy over the grave while others stood around them. One of the preachers talked about Lucille Tatum, Mama T, now being in heaven before the casket was lowered into the grave. He concluded with prayer for the grieving family, and everyone began moving out from underneath the canopy. Serena did not leave her chair, and two men began shoveling dirt into the grave.

Clods of red dirt began bursting on the coffin, and Serena surprised herself and the few people still standing near her by bursting into sobs. The two men stopped shoveling, and Fred stepped forward to put his arms around her. Neither Penny nor Nicole had ever seen their mother sob aloud. They put their arms around both their parents, and the four stood in a huddle beside the open grave. Serena could not say the words even in her thoughts, but she was crying because she had completely lost her path in life.

After a couple of minutes, they began walking toward their car, still holding to each other. Serena had not planned to stay by the graveside until the blanket of red roses, the colorful wreaths, sprays, and green peace lilies were placed over the raw red dirt. They would come back later to look at the fresh flowers before they wilted.

Serena was feeling again, but the only thing she felt was desolation.

*   *   *

It was five days before she was able to go back to work.

Mama T had left all her belongings, with the land being the most valuable portion, to Steve and Serena. The will had named Serena executor of the estate, and, after Serena promised him she could handle everything, Steve and his family had gone back to their home. She would notify the Gainesville auction barn that Mama T's cattle were for sale. Whoever bought them could come and get them.

She planned to list the property with a real estate agent to be sold, but first she had to remove Mama T's personal belongings. Serena had not been able to go back into the house. How was she going to be able to sort through Mama T's favorite dishes and her favorite clothes?

The last year had totally changed her life. All the employees of Cameron National Bank still were considered suspect because no person had been arrested for the missing $1.1 million. With Trey Bowman, she had experienced personal ecstasy and lost rational thought and self-control for the first time in her life. Now she had lost Mama T, her safe haven, her refuge.

If she could paint pictures of her life, she would make all her previous years a pale blue. She would splash the last year with every color in the rainbow, and the current period would be black.

Chapter 39

After mechanically going through her daily responsibilities for three weeks, Serena went back to Mama T's home on a Saturday. She wanted to get the sad tasks behind her before Penny graduated from high school.

As she drove up, she noticed the complete quiet. There was no joyful welcome by Rufus. The dog had been given to the neighbors who had always kept him when Mama T was away. The three neutered cats had been almost wild, and they were probably still roaming in or around the barn. The cattle had been purchased and had already been taken away.

She took the key from the top of the door frame as she had done when Bowman was there with her. She could hardly make herself go into the house. It had always been a friendly, welcoming structure. Now it was an empty shell where memories roamed like ghosts.

After she began her tasks, she felt more comfortable in being alone, but the sadness did not lessen. First she spent two hours getting clothes packed for Good Will. She could not do it quickly because each dress, each sweater, and even the shoes stirred her heart with memories. She kept one blue dress and one white sweater because they were Mama T herself. They were reminders of her warm spirit and continuous helping hand.

Finally, she turned to go through papers on the desk. There were bills she had to pay and utilities she needed to disconnect.

Sorting through the desk drawer, she found old black-and-white pictures she had never seen before. First, she found photos of herself and brother as children. She also found pictures of Sarah, the young woman who was their mother. One picture showed young Serena and Steve with the two people who were their parents. The young, smiling mother had long, blonde hair that curled around her shoulders and bangs across her brow. The young father had coal-black hair combed straight back from his forehead. Both were sitting on a porch swing, and Serena, a toddler, was standing on the seat beside her mother while Steve, an infant, was held by his father. She looked at the picture a long time before she placed it in the stack that she wanted to keep.

Picking up the last picture, she saw an old loose-leaf notebook. Opening it, she found yellowed pages with dates and Mama T's handwriting.

It was a diary with sporadic brief entries about life. On one date was a sentence about Serena's parents: "Sarah and Thomas were married today."

Three weeks later was another entry of a few sentences. "Sarah is so happy. I wish all newlyweds could know that their marriage will hit rough roads. I wish they could know that a lasting marriage takes constant work. Happiness is not given to us by someone else but develops slowly within us when we stay true to our beliefs."

Serena could hear Mama T's voice speaking the words.

There was not another entry before Serena read about her birth months later and, still later, about the birth of her brother Steve, complete with descriptions of the new babies. Steve had a head full of dark hair, and Serena was described as "a quiet baby who came into the world with a peaceful expression on her face. She was serene, and that's what we named her."

She read brief sentences about Sarah, Thomas, and the children moving in with Mama T. Months later, a sentence announced that they had moved out again. She was nearing the end of the writing and noticed another entry about her mother.

"Sarah is learning that being a mother is life's most difficult and most important job. The responsibility sometimes can be overwhelming, and there is no vacation. Nothing else provides the joy or the heartbreak."

Mama T might have been worried about Sarah and Thomas, but she had written nothing more about them. The remaining entries only mentioned a new pastor at church, getting a good report from her doctor, receiving a good price for twenty head of cattle, and planting a new pink camellia beside the front porch. The entries ended almost six months before the date when Serena's father shot her mother and then himself. *Mama T must have been too heartbroken and too busy with two small children to write in a notebook.* There was also nothing written about the accident that caused the death of Serena's grandfather six years later.

Serena placed the notebook with the pictures she wanted to keep. She cleaned the desk thoroughly but found no other diary writing. She worked all day with Mama T's belongings and prepared to leave the house when everything was almost finished. She would arrange a public estate sale and sell the furniture and appliances before the house was put on the market.

She taped a paper with the handwritten words, "Do not sell," on two pieces of furniture. One was the old desk that had been made by her grandfather. It was probably made of oak wood that had been painted black, and the paint had worn off its single drawer where various hands had pulled it open through the years. The top of the desk was built on a slant that was intended to make handwriting easy, and two small, partitioned shelves at the back provided places for bills and letters. The other piece of furniture that she was keeping was her grandmother's rocker.

Serena left the house with deep sadness, and, as she drove home, she could hear Mama T's voice speaking the written words about her mother and father and about marriage. "Happiness is not given to us by someone else but develops slowly within us when we stay true to our beliefs."

Mama T had always talked about her own experiences when she gave advice. *I wonder if Mama T ever fell in love with another man but stayed true to her beliefs,* Serena thought. *I wanted to run away, but I didn't. I am still here, but I won't ever be happy again.* Trey had given her life new meaning. Being with him had made her feel safe when her world seemed to be falling apart. His words had made her feel special when she had begun to feel that her life was no longer important. He had made her feel confident.

In her marriage vows, she had promised to love and cherish Fred "till death do us part." When her daughters were born, she had looked into each of the infant faces and vowed always to love them and be there for them. Now, if she wanted to stay true to her beliefs and always be there for Penny and Nicole, she had to find a way to put her broken heart back together again.

She reminded herself that she had been married to Fred for almost twenty years, and they were the parents of two children. He helped pay the monthly bills. He was always available. He picked up their children every afternoon after school. Their children adored him.

Trey was gone. Mama T was gone. Mama T's death had left her as the female head of her family. Could she become the family's respected matriarch the way Mama T had been? When she had grandchildren, would they want to come to her for encouragement and advice? Could she love all members of her family the way love was described in Corinthians—a continuous love that was patient and endured all things?

Dear God in Heaven, Dear Mama T, please help me become the person you want me to be, Serena prayed.

She parked in her driveway and began to walk toward her house. Before she reached the porch steps, she heard the screeches of a nearby bird. She noticed a large redbreasted robin jumping around in the trees and stopped to look. Her presence failed to scare it away, and it continued to shriek. Then a fluttering noise made her look down. There, almost at her feet, a smaller robin was flapping one wing and tumbling around on the ground.

It was completely entangled in fishing line. It had probably tried to free itself, resulting in the clear plastic string becoming tightly wrapped around its feet, one wing, and even its beak.

Serena went into the house to get scissors. She came back, picked up the tangled bird, and began to cut the line while the bird's mate continued its screeching from the trees. When the bird was completely untangled, Serena kept her hand wrapped around its body. Its breast was not nearly as bright as the bird in the tree, confirming that the shrieking bird was a male, and the bird in her hand was a female. She looked at its eyes while it stared back at her. Then she opened her hand, and the smaller bird flew toward its mate.

It wasn't until she watched the two birds lift together toward the sky that Serena realized she had actually held a small, feathered creature in her hand without feeling fear. She had not once thought of bantam roosters or Alfred Hitchcock's birds.

How could a robin have ended up in her yard entangled in fishing line when Fred didn't fish?

As Serena asked herself this question, she realized that the answers did not matter. For her, the robin was a gift from Mama T. In releasing the robin from the fishing line, she released herself from her foolish fear. Maybe the reunion of the two robins and their flight toward the sky was Mama T telling her that her own life with her chosen mate would someday soar again.

Chapter 40

Serena kept waiting and watching for the news to be broadcast or published about the bank robbery culprits, but two months passed, and it didn't happen. All participants had been located except Salisbury. No arrests had been made, and the news media didn't report that the Cameron bank heist was going into the FBI's cold case files.

Serena was no longer the woman she had been before the bank heist. She never looked at the yards she passed each morning on her way to work, and she constantly wanted to be alone.

Weeks passed before she finally decided she could wait no longer to tell her coworkers how the Cameron bank was selected. She told Joyce and Phil she wanted to talk with them as soon as their workday ended. Joyce took them to her house, and Serena told them about the Jasper connection and everything Bowman had shared with her.

"I'm so glad that it wasn't Paul Norris," she said. "Maybe he was foolish in his manner of making a loan to the Jasper man, but I always knew his name would be cleared of wrongdoing."

"If he had been charged with this robbery, it would have been a reflection on all of us because we were his employees," Joyce said. Serena and Phil both nodded.

"I talked with Mr. Norris a couple of weeks ago. I know a little bit about what happened when Salisbury opened those accounts," Phil said.

Serena and Joyce both asked questions at once. "Is he okay? What did he say?"

Phil said, "You remember when the Interstate 85 connector was built to Gainesville, and we were promised that it would come by Cameron? We thought it would bring in new business. Well, Salisbury told Mr. Norris that his company was going to build a big shopping mall at the edge of Cameron. Mr. Norris thought Salisbury needed that cash to buy land. He must have followed the usual banking procedures in allowing him to open those accounts and cash those checks. Now we know that Salisbury simply used that story to get cash from our bank."

"I'd just like to know that Mr. Norris is okay," Serena said.

"He looked well. He said that he worried about us and our jobs at the bank, and I told him we were fine," Phil said.

Then he added, "You know how I've told you two that I'm an atheist? Well, Mr. Norris made me reexamine my thinking. He said he had been trying to find a good life in all the wrong places, and he found it in the Bible."

"I know the Bible can bring comfort when you're down," Joyce said.

"Mr. Norris said he now knows what Jesus meant when he said he would give 'abundant life' to all who believe," Phil said. "I'm still thinking about what he said and the peaceful expression on his face."

"The only major crimes that haven't been solved are the real identity of the man who said he was Jarvis Salisbury and the explosion of that house you used to live in," Serena said, looking at Phil.

Phil stared at her silently before saying, "The explosion has been solved. Two arrests have been made here in town, but they are two teenagers. I feel so bad about them, I didn't want to talk about it."

Serena and Joyce both looked at Phil, waiting for him to give them more explanation.

"Now that the FBI investigation is closed, I can give my resignation here at the bank and move to Atlanta," Phil said. "I'm getting married, and that's the reason the house was blown up. I had rented the house, and these two young men knew I had moved out. They believed no person would be hurt. They were only trying to send me a strong message."

"What kind of message? We don't understand," Serena said.

"I haven't told you, but I'm going to marry Marie Ivy," Phil said.

"The only Marie Ivy we know is the black girl who was a member of the homecoming court last year," Joyce said.

"She's going to marry me," Phil said.

Serena and Joyce couldn't believe his words.

Phil, a red-headed white man, was going to marry a black woman. White men in Georgia and throughout the South had been known to secretly make love to black women, and were called "honkies" by black people because they frequently drove up to the black woman's door and honked their horn to summon her. Black women often had the children of white men, but interracial marriage had been forbidden by state law in Georgia and about thirty other states.

Georgia's law had called such marriages "unnatural," and a Virginia judge had once blocked an interracial marriage by ruling that God had created each race on a different continent because he did not want them to mix. Only five years earlier, the United States Supreme Court had invalidated all such state laws that were still in effect by ruling them unconstitutional.

Both Joyce and Serena had read about white and black marriages between Hollywood stars, but they had never known such a person. They were finding it difficult to find the right words.

"You will face a lot of criticism, and you may face violence, both you and Marie," Joyce said.

"I'm sure there will be a lot of criticism behind my back and some to my face," Phil said.

"How did you get to know her?" Serena finally said.

"Her mother came to help my mother with housework every Saturday, and Marie always came with her," Phil said. "I would talk with her, and the more I knew about her, the more I wanted to talk with her. Marie is not only beautiful; she's wise. You would enjoy knowing her."

"I met her at your uncle's fishing camp when the agriculture commissioner was there for dinner. I wish I could really know her," Serena said.

"Me, too," said Joyce.

"I know that society may frown on our marriage, but this year has been stressful. I kept thinking there was a possibility that one of us had unknowingly caused the swindle. It's more accurate to say that this year has been nerve-racking. Marie helped me find peace, and I asked her to marry me. I want to keep her with me forever," Phil said.

"I noticed you talking to her father or giving him notes when he came in the bank," Serena said.

"I was just sending word to Marie about a book I was reading and wanted to discuss with her. Sometimes she would select the book for us. She loves literature, and we could never go anywhere together. After we read the same book, we would stay at the house and discuss it or read articles about it on Saturday," Phil said.

"I hope both of you will be safe," Serena said.

"Marie never doubted my innocence where the missing money is concerned. She always encourages me to be positive about life. We have talked about everything, even religion," Phil said.

"What does Marie say about religion?"

"She has a deep faith in God. One day I asked her if God was a white person or a black person. She looked at me a full minute, and then she said, 'God is the color of water.' She had read about God's color in a book, and I couldn't argue with her. She knew I couldn't say anything to weaken her faith."

"Will your wedding be here?" Joyce asked.

"No. Her parents and friends are worried sick about her marrying me. We'll say our vows before a justice of the peace in Atlanta," he answered. "We plan to make our home there, and Marie plans to attend Spelman College and major in political science."

"Will you please bring Marie to the bank and let us wish her well before you leave?" Serena asked.

"Yes, I'll bring her by," he answered.

"Wait. You haven't told us who has been arrested for blowing up your house."

"It was two boys who went to school with Marie. They were very upset that she plans to marry a white man," Phil said. "I know there were rumors of a plane flying over and setting off the explosion, but they simply crawled under the house with two sticks of dynamite, and they set them off from an adjoining field."

"I guess that when a black woman marries a white man, the black men who admire her feel betrayed, even more when she is beautiful," Serena said.

"You said it exactly," Phil said. "They both had spent a lot of time with Marie when they all were younger. Marie thought she could tell them her plans, but they were hurt and very angry."

"Will they be tried by a local jury?"

"They've already confessed and will be sentenced by a judge. I just worry that they will have to go to prison. But they both have strong families with both a mother and a father. I hope their families will be able to help them."

Later, when Joyce had left the room for a moment, Phil said to Serena, "I was afraid you were becoming involved with Bowman, the FBI agent. I know he always wanted to see you, and I saw how you looked at each other when we were on Lake Burton. I was afraid you were going to leave your family."

"He's gone back north and won't be back again," Serena answered. She didn't want to say another word, but the expression on her face must have caused Phil's next question.

"Are you going to be okay?"

"Yes. I'll be fine," she said without emotion as Joyce came back into the room.

As Serena and Phil took separate paths, leaving Joyce's home, Serena thought of Phil's plans. He and Marie would have larger hurdles to cross than any other newly married couple. They were challenging a long-established social order in both the white and black populations. The white people were not the only ones judging people by skin color. Some black people viewed the darker-skinned members of their own race as inferior, and no black person wanted one of their race to marry outside the color line.

Serena would miss Phil, but she was glad he and Marie were going to move to Atlanta where their chances for a successful union would be a little better. She would not tell anyone his plans, not even Fred, and she wished she had asked Joyce to do the same. She was also relieved to know how Phil's former home had exploded. All the unusual crimes she had known about had been solved, except that she still didn't know who Jarvis Salisbury was. Until he was found and tried, the cloud of suspicion would remain over all people connected with the bank.

As she drove up the road, she noticed the cement duck again. It had been moved close to the house and was not wearing a hat, scarf, or wrap. Today it was nothing more than a lawn ornament. Suddenly she turned into the driveway of the house. She wanted to know who had been costuming the duck. A large, covered truck had been backed up to the front of the house, and two men were carrying a couch out the front door.

"Do you live in this house?" Serena asked one of the men.

"No. The owner is inside," he said.

Serena stepped over to the open door and knocked. An elderly man came from inside the house and looked at her.

"Do you live here?" she asked him.

"I do at this moment, but I'm moving," he said.

"Someone at this house has been putting hats and other props on that duck that was sitting beside the road."

"That was my wife," the man said.

"May I see her? I want to tell her what that duck has meant for me," Serena said.

"She's gone. She died about two weeks ago, and today I'm getting ready to go live with one of our sons," he said.

"Oh, I'm sorry," Serena said, pausing before she said, "I wanted to tell her what her duck and its attire meant to me. I looked every day to see what it was wearing."

"Other people told her they enjoyed seeing the duck. She was so sick during the last months of her life that dressing that duck was about all she could do. She kept it up because she didn't want to disappoint any of the passersby who looked at it. At the last, I had to bring it into the house for her and take it back outside when she had finished," he said.

"I wish I had stopped to thank her for adding pleasure to my trips. I can at least thank you, sir, for helping her."

"Dressing that duck seemed to help her live a little longer. I wanted to keep her with me as long as I could. We had been married forty-nine years," the man said.

"It's a pleasure to meet you. I'm sorry I never stopped to meet your wife, and I wish you a pleasant and rewarding life with your son," Serena said as she shook hands with him.

She walked back to her car, and he came behind her. "I'll make sure no cars are coming so you can back out into the highway," he said. He motioned when the road was clear, and she was soon back on Highway 197 headed toward Cameron.

She had tried to poke fun at her own fear by pretending the duck's attire was predicting the kind of day she would have. It had worn exaggerated, star-shaped sunglasses, almost like explosions, on the day she arrived at work and found the bank filled with bank examiners and FBI agents. She had told herself that morning that the exaggerated sunglasses meant she was going to have an unusual day, and it truly had been bizarre. Of course, the cement duck's attire could not predict anything, but it had been entertaining, and thinking about her fear so often as she passed the duck had helped to eliminate it.

A woman she did not know had used a lawn ornament to entertain passersby, an action that changed Serena's fearful attitude. Another woman she did not know had accepted a marriage proposal and resigned her job in Philadelphia, leading to a giant swindle at Cameron National Bank. Mr. Norris, the bank president, had been forced out of the bank because of the swindle, but now he was enjoying the Bible's promise of abundant life. The swindle had guided her and her friends to see beyond skin pigmentation and begin recognizing the value and uniqueness of all humanity. An FBI agent investigating the swindle had caused her to passionately examine and recognize her own purpose in life.

I talked to Trey Bowman about how the living beings in Mother Nature are intertwined, but our lives are intertwined with people we don't even know. We live inside a strong invisible network. We can be deeply affected by simple random actions of someone we never knew existed. The action of one woman was disastrous for my friends and me, but we gained new knowledge. Maybe that came from the positive thinking that happens if someone seeks guidance from a higher power, Serena thought.

She remembered Dr. Norman Vincent Peale's book, *The Power of Positive Thinking,* which she had read in high school. She frequently repeated to herself the first words in Peale's book, "Believe in yourself." Serena had never told herself to think positively where feathered creatures were concerned, but she had believed in herself, believed that she could overcome her fear, and it had worked.

Now I must believe that I can stay true to my beliefs. I must remember that I am doing what I have always said was important, making sure that my children have both their mother and father.

Chapter 41

On a Saturday evening in early June, the girls were in Gainesville to see the movie *Deliverance*. They had gone with friends to a late-afternoon matinee. The movie was about three men from Atlanta who planned to demonstrate their machismo personalities by tackling white-water rapids in north Georgia, but who suffered fear and sexual violation at the hands of wicked fictional mountain men. The movie had been filmed in Clayton and at the Tallulah Gorge, a deep and beautiful gash in the earth's crust just north of Cameron.

Serena had sat down in the living room and was attempting to watch *Hee Haw* on television. The show featured Junior Samples, a man from Cumming.

Cumming, Clayton, and the Tallulah Gorge were all less than an hour's drive from Cameron, and Serena was wondering how north Georgia people and places had suddenly become known in the national entertainment world. *And the swindle at Cameron National Bank indicates that we've become a target in the world of big crime.*

She heard Fred's truck come into the driveway. He had said earlier that he was going to town and didn't explain the reason. Junior Samples was attempting to be amusing on the television show when she heard an unexpected noise. She got up and went to the kitchen to determine the problem and found Fred standing at the open refrigerator door. A plastic storage container full of spaghetti had fallen from a shelf onto the floor, and he was staring at it. Serena waited for Fred to pick up the container, but he didn't move, and she picked it up and placed it back in the refrigerator.

"What's wrong with you?" she said.

Fred said, "I'm sick."

When he spoke, Serena could smell liquor on his breath. At first she didn't believe what her olfactory sense was telling her. She had never known Fred to drink any kind of alcoholic beverage.

"Are you drunk?" she said with a strong emphasis on *you*.

"I'm going to bed," Fred said, finally closing the refrigerator door. He staggered as he began to walk toward their bedroom, and she followed him.

"Fred, I can't believe you've been drinking. I'm glad our girls are not here."

He did not answer her, but sat down on their bed and began to take off his shoes.

"Fred, what's wrong? Why have you done this?" Serena said, sitting beside him.

"Why would you care?" he answered.

Neither said anything as he fumbled with his shoelaces.

Finally, he said, "I know you don't care about my problems. I'm going to bed." But he didn't move from his seat on the side of the bed.

"What is your problem?" Serena said.

After a long pause, Fred said, finally looking at her, "If you really want to know, I'm worried about you and our family. You don't care about us anymore."

"Fred, I care deeply about our family. I care deeply about you. I may not be perfect, but neither are you. I have wondered many times what marriage means to you," Serena said.

"I can't explain what marriage means to me," he said.

"Please try. I'd like to know why you married me," Serena said.

After a full minute or more, Fred said, "I can explain what it means to build a good cabinet. Sometimes I think that building a good family works the same way."

"Then tell me what it means to build a good cabinet."

Fred spoke slowly: "I have to have clean, stout wood to build a good cabinet, but it doesn't work if I don't cut the wood the way it's supposed to be. Sometimes, to make it fit, I have to use sandpaper and a planer. If the wood is good and the tools are used wisely, a good cabinet is created. I think marriages must have two clean, stout people, and they must work with marriage tools wisely to create a good union."

Serena did not speak immediately, and both were quiet. Finally she said, "Fred, I am trying my best to use marriage tools wisely. I am trying to be the best possible fit. You can help me by showing concern now and then for the load I am trying to carry."

"I guess you mean you want me to wash the dishes sometimes," he said with a touch of irony.

"Yes, Fred. It would mean a lot to me to have you wash dishes now and then, but it's more than that. I'll try to be a better fit in our marriage if you'll try."

Serena started to tell him again that their family was still the most important thing in her life when she heard the front door open again. Several voices let her know that the girls had brought their friends home with them.

"Fred, go to bed, and I'll go see about the girls," she said before leaving the room.

In the living room, all the young people seemed to be talking at once. Some of them liked the movie, and others thought it portrayed mountain people poorly. They all said they wanted a recording of the music, "Dueling Banjos."

"I could hardly stay in my seat while that music was playing. It made me want to learn to buck dance," said Vern, Penny's friend, and others said they had tapped their feet to the music.

Serena listened to them while she thought about Fred. Two hours later, she went to the bedroom, and he was asleep and snoring. The next morning, she cooked bacon, eggs, and grits while he remained asleep. He was sitting on his bed and holding his head when she went back into the room to get dressed for church.

"Fred, I'm sorry you've been worried about me and our family. You and our girls are the most important things in my life."

He didn't respond or raise his head, and she went to the kitchen to get him a cup of coffee. "Here, drink this. You'll feel better," she said.

"I know better than to drink store-bought whiskey. I always heard that White Lightning won't give you a hangover," Fred said, still speaking his words slowly.

The day passed with little action from Fred. He read the morning paper and drank coffee, then spent the day either sleeping or watching television. He made no further comment on the future of their family, and Monday morning he was up and ready to go as if nothing had happened. When he got up from the breakfast table, he washed his plate and coffee cup and put them in the dish drain. Neither he nor Serena mentioned the incident again.

In late June, Phil had resigned from the bank as he had said he would, and now it was Friday, his last day. Marie was expected to come by later in the day, probably at the time they were serving cookies and punch and offering Phil their best wishes.

At 10:00 AM, a regular customer who always amused Serena came in. His thick, dark gray hair was combed straight back, making his large, snow-white mustache seem out of place. He always wore denim overalls and drove a pickup truck with a shotgun in the back window. He sold red earthworms at four cents each to the area's fish bait stores. He also allowed "pickers" to come to his farm and dig up their own earthworms for three cents each. Serena knew that two of his brothers had been arrested and served time for making liquor, and he probably had his own still, but he had never been caught.

He talked about his "worm farm" as if it provided his only income. He especially liked to talk about his "stud worm" named Sam. "Sam's been with the ladies for about a week, so I'll have plenty of bait for fishin'," he said, smiling with pleasure at his own words. Serena knew that each earthworm had both male and female organs, but she had no idea how they copulated and reproduced. She smiled at his comments about Sam, the "stud worm."

Later, Violet Jones came in and deposited one hundred dollars in her savings account. She told Serena that she had lost her billfold the day before in the grocery store parking lot. "It also had my driver's license an' the man who found it knew where ta return it. I didn't even know I lost it till he knocked on my door," she said. "I was so glad. I tried to give him ten dollars, but he refused it. He said he cudden take money for just bein' honest."

The next person coming to Serena's window was her lifelong friend, Miller, who had been traveling for several months. He was widely known for his unusual ability to play the piano. Serena had visited his house when they both were children, and she had asked him to play "Doll Dance" over and over again. She had sat on the floor and leaned backward against the bottom of the old upright piano. His feet worked the pedals beside her while his hands flew across the keys, and Serena's heart had danced. Now, he had been on a concert tour across several states, and Serena was glad to see him after his lengthy absence.

"Has anyone been arrested for stealing all that money?" Miller asked.

"The FBI learned that it was someone in Jasper who suggested this bank for the robbery, but he refused to be involved otherwise. That's hard for me to believe, but it's true. The man who orchestrated the whole thing lived in Philadelphia, and he was killed by his ex-wife's boyfriend," Serena answered. "We still hope that the man who opened the account here will be arrested, but the FBI has stopped working on the case. I'm afraid it's in the cold case files."

"A person with that much money probably could live the rest of his life without working. I'd like to know what was done with it," Miller said.

"I wish we could know, but I don't think we ever will," Serena said.

At the noon meal, Serena and Joyce ate sandwiches together in the back room and made last-minute arrangements for Phil's farewell party, which would be held after closing time.

A last person hurried in the door just at closing, and Serena went to her window to help him. He said he had to take money from his account to send to his brother in New Jersey. "My brother's pickup was stolen, and he needs a bus ticket to get home."

"Gee, I'm sorry. Do the police have any leads on the thief?" she said.

The customer laughed. "No, not yet, but whoever got that truck is gonna get the surprise of his life. It's got a dead body in the back"

"A dog? A deer? A bear?"

"No, my uncle."

"You're kidding. You mean, your dead uncle was in the back of the truck?"

"Right. My uncle always was a loner, an' he was homeless a lot o' the time. In fact, he died in a homeless shelter, an' someone there sent word to us to come get tha body. My brother bought a big wooden box an' put 'im in it surrounded with bags o' crushed ice. He was gonna keep 'im preserved just long enough to get 'im here and bury 'im."

"What can you do?" Serena asked as the man began to move away.

"I don't know. The police know about the theft, and we'll just wait and see if the body turns up somewhere," he said.

"Good luck," Serena said as he walked away.

Marie Ivy came in just as the doors were locked for the day. She was dressed to meet her fiancé's coworkers at the small reception in their honor. Her pale yellow dress dropped to midcalf length, and her black patent sandals were high-heeled. Three gold-colored bangle bracelets jangled around one wrist, and gold metal hoops fell from her earlobes. She looked extremely shy, and Serena wanted to say something to make her feel at ease.

"I hope you and Phil have a good life in Atlanta."

"We have a lot of plans. Phil already has applied to three different banks for a job. I know we'll have an uphill battle, but I think we'll be okay," Marie said.

While Serena was talking to her, Phil walked up to them, put his arm around Marie's waist, and said, "This is the woman who has said she will be my bride."

With his words, Marie's glowing smile appeared. Phil's face was serious, but the glow on his face matched hers. Their happiness was contagious, and Serena felt her own heart lifting.

As she went home that evening she noticed that pink, red, and white crepe myrtles were blooming in yards here and there. Lantana was blooming in golden mounds in several yards, while white, pink, blue, and purple hydrangeas were making their own colorful splashes.

Serena thought about the hydrangea she had planted about eight years earlier in her own yard. Its puffball blooms were pink when she bought it, but now they were blue. She learned that she should have sprinkled cups of lime around its base to retain its pink color. The flower might have changed color through the years, but its blooms today were as beautiful as ever.

People are like hydrangeas. All can be beautiful, no matter the color. Marie and Phil are so happy, and I hope they can always love each other.

Suddenly she decided she must begin to make future plans for her family. Penny had received a small scholarship and had applied for a student loan that would allow her to go to the University of Georgia. Nicole probably would follow in her footsteps.

Soon they would be gone, and Serena had not yet taken them to Washington, DC. She thought about cooking sirloin steaks for supper because it was Fred's favorite food. *Maybe, just maybe, Fred will go with us to Washington*, she thought.

Chapter 42

Six years passed—312 weeks, 2,190 days—without leads on Jarvis Salisbury. Cameron residents stopped making hurtful remarks to bank employees, but if a new person moved into town, military personnel or retirees returned home, they soon heard that no one had been arrested for the huge amount of money that was taken from the bank and still missing.

Only one small story had appeared in the news media since the theft, and it told about the death of Sandy McMahon, the swindle's mastermind. No information was released to the public describing how the bank was selected for the bogus checks, and bank employees knew that rumors continued, as local people searched for answers.

Interstate 985, the I-85 connector, still ended at Gainesville, but a divided four-lane with crossroads and two traffic lights now extended the road from Gainesville past Cameron.

Evelyn Farrell, the woman in Philadelphia who had fallen in love and resigned her job to marry, leading to the Cameron bank heist, was now living in Florida with her husband and two young children.

Evelyn's boss, who had escaped prison by squealing on McMahon, was now operating a pornography store in San Francisco.

But the man who identified himself as Jarvis Salisbury was the kingpin of the swindle. He had walked into the Cameron bank in the fall of 1971 and eventually taken out briefcases and brown paper bags full of money. He still had not been found.

It was 1978, and, on a cold January morning, an inmate in the Atlanta federal prison named Jerry Battle contacted the US Attorney's office. Battle was serving life without parole, and he had adult grandchildren that he had never seen, had never talked with. Battle said he had terminal cancer and wanted to die a free man. He would give information about the "Merrill Mess" if the officers would let him go free.

After verifying Battle's medical diagnosis, an agent went to the Atlanta prison where he was incarcerated, and the ailing prisoner began to spill his tale. Battle earlier had been a cellmate of Ralph Shocker in the Missouri Federal Penitentiary. Shocker had related the story to Battle with great amusement.

Battle said a man named McMahon had been the architect of the Merrill scheme. Battle didn't know the names of others, but he could describe them enough to identify each one.

The inside man at Merrill had been in the accounting department. He had pilfered the checks and signed them with the company's facsimile signature machine.

McMahon had called a former prison cellmate, an old man in Florida, to get advice on a good bank. The old man had told him about a bank in Indiana, but, before the scheme could be pulled, the president of the Indiana bank was arrested.

The old man then called his former cellmate in Jasper, Georgia.

The Georgia man had served time for growing marijuana in the Chattahoochee National Forest, and he was laying carpet at a lawyer's home in another Georgia town when he discovered a bank with a very unusual way of doing business. "That Georgia bank loaned the convicted felon a couple thousand dollars to make a down payment on his home. They didn't even ask 'im to fill out an application. They didn't ask for references or collateral," Battle said.

"McMahon knew then that this was the bank where they could do business. McMahon and Merrill's accountant pulled off the slickest swindle I ever heard of. They netted well over one million dollars. The accountant got $300,000 of the money, and McMahon got $300,000. They sent the old man in Florida $25,000, and he said they gave one of their banker friends $50,000 because he had given them expense money in the beginning. Shocker was the only one who was put into peril by the project, and the only one who could pull it off. He got $425,000."

Battle said Shocker laughed about being able to pull everything off. He also laughed because McMahon's death had been caused by his jealousy of an ex-wife. Shocker told Battle the ex-wife had married the truck driver, and they were living in California, where he was driving his truck, and she was still practicing pediatric medicine.

The FBI immediately began investigating Ralph Shocker, and found him in a New York jail charged with another check scam of $500,000. Shocker was soon transferred to Georgia and jailed in McDonough.

Each individual at Cameron National Bank who had seen the man claiming to be Jarvis Salisbury was notified that a suspect had been captured. Serena and Joyce were elated and wanted to call both Phil and Mr. Norris, but they didn't know how to get in touch with either of them.

The few bank employees who had seen him were brought to McDonough and asked to identify Shocker. Paul Norris was there, and it was the first time most of his employees had seen him since the swindle. He greeted each person individually and asked about their health and families. Some hesitated to talk with him, but Serena Sheppard and Joyce Williams were among those who were glad to see him looking well.

Phil Anderson was there, and it was a small reunion for him, Serena, and Joyce. "How is Marie?" both asked him.

"She'll soon graduate from Spelman College. It's taken her a long time because she's been working full-time while going to school. You'll be interested to know that she's been working as a bank teller."

"We're both still working at the bank," Joyce said, laughing. "We've talked about leaving, but we feel like we would be deserting people who depend on us."

"My daughter, Penny, is getting married next month. She's finished college and is marrying a young man she met in high school. They're planning a big church wedding and have bought a small house in Helen. That's where his family owns a business," Serena said. They quickly told each other about their lives as they waited to view a lineup of suspects.

Each Cameron National Bank person had a strong desire to see Shocker get a long prison sentence, an action that, at long last, would conclude investigation of a criminal act that still left them wondering.

Questions finally would be answered about who had taken all that money from the bank and what had been done with it.

An FBI agent that no bank employee had ever seen before wrote their names on a tablet along with other information such as ways to contact them. When it was possible to talk privately, Serena went back to the agent. "Can you tell me about Trey Bowman?" she said.

She had tried to tell herself that she did not want to see Bowman and did not want to know anything about him. But all vows of unconcern departed when she was on the scene with someone who might give her information.

"Trey Bowman left the FBI," the agent said.

"We became friends when he was investigating this case. Is he okay? Do you know where he is?" Serena said.

"He wanted to learn something about his father who was a Seneca Indian. He went to live on the Seneca reservation in New York State, and I haven't talked with him for years, but I heard that he married a Seneca widow with two daughters, and they live near the Lake of Two Mountains in Quebec, Canada," the agent said.

"Thank you," said Serena, and she went back to her seat. Trey apparently had done what he wanted to do. He had immersed himself in the Seneca tribe to investigate his heritage. If he had married a widow with two children, he now was a father himself. She remembered his last words to her years earlier, and now she whispered them to him. *I hope you find happiness in all that you do.* Then she added, *My own life is peaceful and full.*

One by one, the bank employees were ushered into the room to view the lineup. Each person looked long and hard at each face, but too much time had passed. Not a single one could identify Shocker as Jarvis Salisbury. They left knowing that they had failed horribly. They had this one chance to remove the shadow of guilt that still was hanging over their heads, but their efforts were futile.

Serena later wished she could have heard his voice. Maybe the sound of his voice would have helped her identify him.

When Shocker was arrested in New York, he was carrying a kit with makeup, plastic molds, mustaches, and wigs. A search of his apartment found more than a dozen photos of Shocker in different disguises, each one totally different.

The FBI agents weren't ready to give up. They asked Shocker to give them a sample of his handwriting because they intended to compare it with the handwriting on bank documents. He refused to write anything.

After several weeks in the McDonough jail, Shocker wrote to the local judge complaining that the jail's sleeping conditions and food were destroying his health. Also, his letter said that the guards were "unnecessarily abusive."

A McDonough jailer contacted one of the FBI agents to tell him that he thought an example of Shocker's writing was available at the judge's office. After being contacted by the agent, the judge released the letter. And the handwriting in the letter matched the handwriting on the backs of the checks made payable to Salisbury and Salisbury Construction Company. Finally, there was solid evidence that Shocker had acted as Jarvis Salisbury.

An agent began preparing paperwork to charge Shocker with major theft of Merrill Construction Company. Meanwhile, the judge began to worry about having intervened in the case. Maybe to ease his worries or maybe because he believed Shocker's complaints, the judge ordered that Shocker be transferred out of the McDonough jail.

Shocker was moved to the Clayton County Jail in Jonesboro at the same time the FBI again contacted the bank employees to tell them that official charges were being made against the man they knew as Salisbury, and they would be expected to testify at his trial. Serena and Joyce were happy about the news, but both had become doubtful that an explanation of the swindle would ever be announced.

Was the man who claimed to be Jarvis Salisbury finally going to be tried in court? Was the public finally going to learn how the money was taken and what happened to it? Was it actually going to happen this time?

When Shocker was officially tried for the theft, the complete story would finally come out for the public. Everyone would learn that no bank employee was involved in the swindle. No bank employee received a penny of the money. Maybe the questions about what happened to the million dollars would finally stop.

On the morning of March 16, 1978, Shocker was scheduled to be arraigned. He intended to plead innocent, after being told about the charges against him. He had been dealing with law enforcement almost all his life and was amused that they finally were about to charge him with the Cameron bank swindle. He knew that no bank employee could identify him and believed that a conviction would be difficult on a crime that happened that long ago.

He was expected to be dressed in street clothes for his appearance in the courtroom so he was escorted upstairs and asked to take a shower and change from his Jonesboro jail uniform.

Shocker bathed for fifteen minutes. He left the shower, brushed his teeth, combed his hair, and changed to his gray suit, complete with a white shirt and tie. He no longer looked like a jail inmate but had the appearance of a distinguished businessman.

Ready for his arraignment, Shocker looked for a deputy to escort him to the courtroom. But he could find no one in the jail. Evidently, all the sheriff's personnel had gone to lunch.

Shocker went to the jail's back door, straightened his back, and marched with purposeful strides into the chilly March air.

Chapter 43

On May 8, 1980, Serena was looking through a stack of the bank's business mail and found a plain white envelope with handwriting addressed to her. A ballpoint pen had been used to address the envelope and mark it "personal." It had no return address.

She opened it casually, expecting to find something about a bank transaction. Inside was a single page, and, when she saw the name at the bottom, she closed it quickly and placed it in her purse. It had been nine years since the bank lost a million dollars. It had been more than seven years since she had seen Trey Bowman. She didn't want to read his words until she was alone.

She continued to perform her duties as vice president and told her secretary that she had personal errands she must run during her lunch hour. She usually ordered a sandwich delivered from Joe Ward's grill, but she wanted to get out of the office to read her letter.

When lunchtime came, she didn't get anything to eat. She didn't even think of eating, but went to the post office to buy stamps and stopped at the drugstore to refill a blood pressure prescription for Fred. Although she was alone, she changed her mind about opening the letter and decided she would do it after work.

Finally, when the day ended and she was in her car again, she took the letter out of its envelope and began reading.

"Dear Serena,

"I don't work for the FBI now, but yesterday I talked with an old friend in the Philadelphia office. He looked up the Cameron National

Bank file and told me that no one was ever charged with the missing money. He said they had gathered evidence to convict a man named Ralph Shocker who masqueraded as Jarvis Salisbury, but he escaped from a Georgia jail and has never been caught.

"I can't think of another swindle that compares with the Merrill Mess. I know how embarrassing and painful it was for you and the other bank employees because no one was arrested after it happened. I hope the old cliché, time heals all wounds, applies to you in this case.

"I called the bank and learned that you still work there. Despite the failure of the investigation, I'm glad I was sent to Cameron."

The letter closed with only one word: *Trey.*

Serena read the words over and over. She felt like Trey was sitting beside her. Once again, she had the strong surge of confidence that she once had felt in his presence.

She wanted to answer his letter. She wanted to say:

"I distinctly remember each time we were together, the words and wishes that we shared. I have heard more than once that each person we know becomes a part of our identity, our character. My experience with you is a big part of who I am today."

She held the page in her hand a few minutes before she put it back into her purse, turned the ignition, backed out of her parking place, and began traveling toward home.

Bibliography

Church, Mary L. *The Hills of Habersham*. Clarkesville, GA: Mary L. Church, 1962.

King, Duane H., Ed. *The Cherokee Indian Nation*. Knoxville: University of Tennessee, 1989.

Patton, Darryl. *America's Goat Man*. Gadsden, AL: Little River Press, 1994.

LaVergne, TN USA
29 August 2009
156388LV00002B/3/P